MANHATTAN AFFAIR

JACK SUSSEK

ISBN:
 978-0-615-58007-4 (trade paperback)
 978-0-9851055-0-1 (Kindle)
 978-0-9851055-1-8 (ePub)

Cover design by Rickhardt Capidamonte

Park Ave. Photo by midweekpost (Eric E. Yang) on Flickr

Print design by eBooks by Barb for booknook.biz

This book is for
Lydia and Johnny Quattro

And in memory of Lou Willet Stanek

To Nestor & Beth,
Former members of '55!
Enjoy!

Dick Smith

ONE

THERE ARE SOME THINGS IN life a person never forgets. The scent of your father's after shave perhaps; or the flavor of bubble gum when you were a child. The flash of fractured sunlight shooting through Grand Central Station early on a summer morning, or what Rockefeller Center looked like at Christmas. There are other things, of course: like when your mother first warned you never to accept rides from strangers or where you were when one of the Kennedys was shot. These thoughts and more had raced chaotically through my mind while I anxiously sat in my lawyer's office that afternoon. The weird thing was that the erratic rushing of those thoughts suddenly stopped when I recalled an old professor's favorite quote about the *Iliad:* "Violent force is as pitiless to the one who possesses it as it is to its victims – the first it intoxicates, the second it crushes."

As I sat in my lawyer's office it had all lucidly come back to me. Those college lectures on Greek mythology and Shakespearean tragedy had suddenly seemed foreboding and I found myself cynically amazed at how those fabulous tales illustrating the forces of fate and the broad strokes of hubris had lasted through the centuries. Clearly I did not learn much from those lectures. For if I had I wouldn't have been sitting where I was that afternoon.

I recall how my lawyer sat comfortably behind his large, nicely polished desk patiently waiting to hear my story. I also recall the cold chill running up my spine and the hollow pit forming in my stomach as I realized when I finished he would accompany me to the 19th precinct to turn myself in as a 'person of interest' in a grizzly double murder. How I had come to be in such an awful spot that afternoon seems embarrassingly simple now. But as recently as the day before my lawyer's office in midtown Manhattan was the last place I believed I would be.

Morris Bergman wasn't actually *my* lawyer. He was an old college friend who just happened to be a lawyer, the only lawyer I knew to call in my time of need. We met when we attended school at a small, somewhat prestigious college in New England. After rooming together our senior year Morris moved on to law school in Boston and I took a job in advertising for the *Times*. That was fifteen years ago.

Since then I worked my way up the ladder in ad sales while Morris worked his way through the Manhattan District Attorney's office. Eventually he left to start a private practice defending the kinds of people he used to prosecute. He's done quite well for himself. I, on the other hand, remained with the *Times* where I am now Vice President of Advertising Sales.

My name is Jared Chase. I am known as Jed and I suppose I should tell you about my parents and the rest of my family but, frankly, it's not truly necessary and I'm certain they'd prefer to be left out of this sordid tale. Suffice it to say I descend from a long line of blue-blooded Yankees who had landed in Boston not too long after the first ones did in the early 1600's.

One interesting bit though is the one about my great-grandfather, a man whose name was Ezekiel Isaiah Chase. The story is he ran away from home while a teenager after having gotten into some sort of scrape. A women's honor and an act of revenge are mentioned but no one seems to remember exactly what it was and after a period at sea my great-grandfather landed in New York City. A disavowal and disinheritance by the family in Boston quickly followed as punishment for his disappearance and splash of dishonor upon the family. That episode of Yankee stubbornness caused us to become known as the 'poor' Chases. But my grandfather, and my father after him, stiffly stuck their Yankee chins out, both having gained seats on the New York Stock Exchange. Now we are not as poor as some would have us. Nevertheless, there are two distinct Chase families, the New England Chases and the New York Chases. I am a New York Chase.

***

The sun fell behind a building, darkening the room a shade, and I watched Morris slowly twist a fat cigar between his fingers. Suddenly I found myself envious in a melancholic way. Not of his career or office or anything like that. No, I found myself envious of Morris because when this day ends he will return to his home, enter his living room with shoes off and a martini in hand, and watch the evening news. I, on the other hand, stood a very strong chance of being fingerprinted, strip-searched, and locked up in the Manhattan House of Detention. No doubt one of the news stories Morris would be watching as he sipped his martini. I could tell Morris sensed my anxiety as he continued to roll his cigar back and forth between his thumb and index finger.

"Well," I said. "Are you going to light that thing, or what?" I reached into my pocket for my cigarettes. Morris slowly shook his head.

"You can't smoke in here," he said, laying the cigar carefully on top of the ink blotter, his sorrowful eyes gazing at it with open disappointment.

"Why not?" I asked. "This is your office, isn't it?"

"Well, according to a recently passed New York City law this office is now a 'smoke-free' environment. We can go outside if you wish." Morris' eyes drooped like a basset hound's.

"That's okay," I said. "I'm trying to quit anyway."

"Well then, Jed, old buddy," Morris said as he picked up the cigar again, licking it and running it under his nostrils slowly. "Tell me everything from the beginning. Wherever you think that is."

The beginning, I thought. He wants the beginning. Where was the beginning? Was it yesterday when Katherine met me at the coffee shop on Third Avenue? Was it three weeks ago when she pulled me into her plan? Was it ten years ago when I first met her? No. Morris meant the beginning of the nasty business that brought me to his office. The reason I am sitting here. He wants only to know the story of why I have become embroiled in a case of murder. Nothing else.

TWO

I SUPPOSE YOU COULD SAY this whole affair started three weeks ago over lunch at the Carlyle Hotel.

"Oh, Jed, you mustn't tell anyone," she said over coffee. "Let's keep it our little secret. Shall we?"

"Sure," I calmly replied, flattered she would confide in me this way. Katherine's secret was a bond that tied us together. Something, until this lunch, I'd only dreamed about. My chest trembled and I felt butterflies in my stomach.

I'd known Katherine for years. She was beautiful. Gorgeous would not be an exaggeration. I was secretly in love with her and had been since I first laid eyes on her. But that was my secret, not hers. I had other secrets about her too. I was jealous when she dated my college friend Steve Cahill, terribly envious when they married, and ecstatic when she told me she wanted a divorce. However, by that time I hadn't any doubts about my feelings for Katherine. I was hopelessly possessed, even haunted by her. I'd given up fighting these feelings long ago: it was a losing battle. She had me, whether she knew it or not. I lit a cigarette and signaled the waiter for more coffee.

"How long have you known about this?" I asked. I was anxious to return to our secret. She reached over for my hand and took my cigarette, our fingers touching ever so slightly, and

I felt a charge, a zing, as I let it go. She inhaled deeply and let the smoke slip slowly out of her nostrils as she exhaled. Then she delicately placed the cigarette, the filter now covered with smudges of her red lipstick, in the ashtray between us. Blue smoke curled upwards from the table and as her green eyes leaned toward me I watched her silky blonde hair fall over her shoulders.

"I just found out," she said. "Completely by accident. I never knew a thing about it. We never talked about it." She reached for my cigarette again.

"Do you want one of your own?" I asked as she drew in a lungful of smoke.

"No." She exhaled and placed the cigarette back in the ashtray. Her eyes continued to gaze at mine, as though waiting for me to do or say something. I reached for my pack and lit another cigarette.

"When does he come back?" I asked, although I already knew the answer.

Her eyes flickered as though she recognized someone and she smiled.

"End of the month," she said. She reached for the cigarette again.

The 'he' was her husband Steve. He was in London on business. He always went to London for the month of August and usually returned on Labor Day. In years past Katherine would join him after a week of shopping in Paris. They would then spend the remainder of the month entertaining business associates and clients and attend a string of corporate functions. But this year, instead of joining Steve in London, they got divorced and Katherine was moving her belongings out of the Park Avenue apartment. In the divorce settlement she chose to leave claiming the apartment was way too big for her. It was in packing up her things when she discovered Steve's will in his desk. Their divorce had come through earlier than expected, a week after Steve left for London, but he had not, as Katherine discovered, changed his will. In his will he left everything to Katherine. And since they had no children that translated into something north of fifteen million dollars.

"You can imagine my surprise when I found it," she said. "I had no idea." She took a last drag of her cigarette and stabbed it into the ashtray. In one smooth elegant motion she reached for her coffee cup as she exhaled. While the last wisps of smoke left her lips she gently held the cup to her mouth and sipped. Her green eyes darkened and she looked directly at me over the rim of her cup through tiny curls of light steam.

"I mean," she said rather pensively, "the divorce just became final. Even though he's in London you'd think he would have changed all that before he left."

"I'm surprised his lawyer didn't insist on it."

"I thought that too."

"Maybe he forgot."

"Maybe he doesn't know we're divorced yet. He's been in London nearly two weeks and the papers just came through."

The divorce was amicable, although one would not have thought so at the outset. Steve resisted at first claiming he truly loved her. But Katherine was adamant and unyielding. Just before their war was to begin Steve pulled an about-face and suddenly relented. I know all this because Katherine's lawyer was my friend (and now, suddenly, *my* lawyer) Morris Bergman. Morris doesn't do divorce but his firm does. They're all heavy hitters over there and I recommended Morris's firm thinking Steve would hire some highpowered legal gun to rake her over the coals. But I was wrong. Morris's colleagues are a bunch of pit bulls, however in this case they weren't required to unleash their viciousness. Katherine said she and Steve had finally worked things out, had agreed on the separation agreement which, barring any unforeseen developments, would become the divorce agreement. Katherine desperately wanted a divorce and she agreed to almost everything. "Bad decision," Morris had said. But Katherine didn't seem to care; she simply wanted out. Anyway, at the end her divorce seemed to be amiable enough, or rather I should say, there didn't seem to be any lingering animosity or vile hatred or anything like that.

From the outside they appeared to be the perfect couple. It was disgusting. Two young, good looking, successful people seemingly made for each other. When the divorce became public among those who knew them or thought they did – and I exclude myself from this group – there was much surprise, disappointment even. It was as if their splitting up invalidated something thought to be sacred, further proof of the dictum that if it could happen to them, it could happen to anybody. To everyone else it simply appeared to be typical of the culture; yet another boring Upper East Side, Wall Street wealthy, glamorous magazine-cover marriage gone bad.

When word of the separation spread through the soirees and social events it was assumed Steve was the one who initiated the action. Why, it was thought, would a woman without employment or substantial means of her own choose to leave? Surely she could ignore the common flaws in her husband and endure the marriage. Why, *everyone* did that. No, it was generally assumed in the blocks between Park and Fifth Avenues that Steve wanted out. Another woman perhaps, an actress or a fashion designer, they were 'in' these days.

Morris and I, on the other hand, knew it was Katherine who sought the divorce. Katherine told me Steve was manic, almost violent, in opposing a divorce, and it had taken quite a feat to bring him around. Even still, it took almost two years and, she told me today, now that it was official it seemed almost anti-climatic.

"So," I said, "assuming Steve doesn't die in a plane crash or something before he changes his will, what are you doing for money?"

"I've put some away," she said, glancing down at the ashtray. Her cigarette was crushed in the center and mine lay on the edge, burned right down to the filter, leaving a skeleton of gray ash. "He's giving me a lump sum settlement and buying an apartment for me. He offered our place but I didn't want it."

"That's not so bad."

"No, it's not actually," she said, letting her voice trail off slowly. For a moment she seemed to be thinking of something else, her eyes betrayed a distance but then, instantly, she was back and smiling at me and I felt warm and giddy she was confiding in me such things, that we now shared secrets. *Her* secrets.

"Frankly," she continued, "I thought the divorce was worth more than anything he could give me. That's why I agreed to everything, I really didn't want to fight, but," she paused a moment, glancing down at the table, scratching her red fingernail against the white linen tablecloth, "it's funny, since I found the will I've had second thoughts."

"What?"

"No – not about the divorce," she said. "About the money."

THREE

OUR LUNCH THAT AFTERNOON WAS one that lingered. I could have stayed with Katherine all day. I would have been perfectly content to sit and talk and look at her and have people look at us until dinner. Then, I imagined, we would tear ourselves away from a deep conversation and order dinner. I'd have the filet mignon with béarnaise sauce, scalloped potatoes, and spinach and Katherine the poached salmon with rice pilaf and peas. We'd have a nice Burgundy and then, after a pair of cappuccinos, slip into the Café Carlyle, order a bottle of their best champagne and listen to Bobby Short sing and play piano. At the end of the first set we'd stroll out to the street, her arm in mine, and head toward her apartment where she would ask me up for a night cap. I would, as the gentleman I am, politely hesitate. She'd insist, gently. The moment her apartment door shut we'd abandon all pretenses and swiftly embrace, powerfully kissing while fumbling with our clothes. Passionately we'd engage ourselves on the foyer floor, our hearts racing, our breathing heavy, and then somehow make it into the living room where we'd fall onto the thick plush throw rug and ravenously devour each other. Later we'd go into the bedroom for another round and in the morning she'd make coffee and we'd watch the sun rise over the city from her living room, sitting comfortably on the couch in thick white cotton bathrobes.

"Excuse me," Katherine suddenly said as she stood up. "I'll just be a minute." She glanced at her watch as she walked away. The waiter appeared and gingerly slid the check onto the table. I watched Katherine walk toward the lobby. Her fine blonde hair bounced off her back as she threaded her way through tables, heads subtly turning as she did. She had a fine body. One of the finest of any woman I've known (and I say this strictly as an observation and not from first-hand knowledge). She was of average height, not too thin, and her breasts were full and well proportioned in relation to the rest of her body. Her hips were rather slender and her buttocks firm when she walked. She had good posture and stood straight, with her chin angled forward, but was not stiff. She was not a fragile or delicate woman and beneath her appearance I always felt there was a hidden hard streak in her.

I picked up the check and remembered thinking I had never spent more than a hundred dollars on lunch before. At least not out of my own pocket. And although I hate to admit it I also remember thinking it was a cheap price to pay for Katherine's confidence. What surprised me even more as I watched Katherine return to the table was that I decided without the slightest hesitation to charge it to my expense account. I normally don't do those kinds of things and as a rule of thumb I have always been legitimate with my expenses. The auditors at the *Times* are notorious and my fear of getting caught padding my expense account has always plagued me.

Anyway, in a moment of deceit I abandoned my fears and signed the charge slip and wrote down the name of one of our biggest advertisers on the back of the receipt and stuffed it into my pocket. I stood up as Katherine approached.

"I should get back to the office," I said. "What about you?"

"Let's go," she said. "I've got some things to do."

Out on the street the sweltering air hit me hard. There was a slight breeze but it felt like a blast furnace. My shirt stuck to my skin and sweat began to bead on my forehead.

"Thanks so much for listening to me," Katherine said, her fine hair sweeping across her face. A few thin strands blew across her mouth and stuck to her lips as she spoke. "And don't forget, you're sworn to secrecy."

"My lips are sealed," I said. Then she did something I'll never forget for the rest of my life. She gently brushed the hair away from her face and leaned in toward me. With one hand on my shoulder she pulled me to her and kissed me on my lips. I felt as if I was going to die. I smelled her perfume, tasted her sweet mouth and then, very quickly, felt her tongue dart into my mine. I felt my stomach tremble and before I knew it she stepped back and smiled.

"Call me," she said.

As I stood on the hot sidewalk I felt as if everything were in slow motion. The doorman whistled for a taxi. Katherine stepped out onto Madison Avenue. A cab pulled up and I watched her slip into it. As it drove away I saw her bright blonde hair catch the sun through the rear window as the taxi raced up the avenue. I remember how blue the sky looked, how white the clouds were, and how shiny the yellow taxi was.

FOUR

"ALL RIGHT, JED. SOUNDS WONDERFUL," Morris said. "But what does it have to do with murder?" He impatiently tapped his cigar against his phone. I couldn't stand it any longer.

"Come on," I said. "Let's go outside. I need a smoke."

We went downstairs and stepped out onto the sidewalk. The September air was warm. We found a bench, lit our smokes and quietly sat. I stared at the tall steel and glass building where Morris' office was. The noise on the street seemed muted and the late summer sky with its soft filtered light suddenly made me feel nostalgic, even melancholy. I was born and raised here and now I suddenly realized how familiar the seasons were to me. It depressed me to think this might be the last time I would sit on a bench in the middle of Manhattan on a beautiful summer day. That I was spending my last day of freedom with Morris Bergman depressed me even further.

"All right, Jed," Morris said, puffing his cigar with relish. "Let's get to the meat of the matter."

"You were never one to beat around the bush, Morris." I leaned over and placed my elbows on my knees. The sleeves of my sport jacket bunched up at the elbows and pulled my shoulders in tight. I turned and faced Morris. "Were you?"

"I'm a former prosecutor."

17

"Right," I said. "Precisely my point."

***

I was not surprised when Katherine called my office the day after our lunch. The memory and sensation of her lingering kiss and warm tongue stayed with me all that afternoon and right on into the evening. I was still drunk with thoughts of her when I woke the next day and when my secretary Marie told me there was a Katherine Cahill on line two I reached for the phone as if I knew at precisely that moment she would call me.

"Jed," she said, not too softly but seductively breathless. "I want to thank you for lunch yesterday, it really helped. You know, clear my head a little. These last few weeks have been awful. You're a good friend."

"Oh come on, Katherine. What are friends for?"

"I've done some thinking. I must see you again."

"Oh? When?"

"As soon as possible."

"Is anything wrong?"

"No. Nothing. Nothing is wrong. I need to talk with you about something. It's important." She paused and I heard her take a breath.

"Okay," I said. "How about tonight? We can meet for a drink, dinner if you like."

"That would be fine," she said. "Where?"

"The Royalton?" I knew she liked that place.

"Nah."

I heard her light a cigarette and I waited a moment. When I heard her exhale I said, "What about one of those places on Third Avenue you like, McMullen's or J.G. Melon's?" Now I could hear her walking across her kitchen. I could tell by the way the taps on her shoes sounded against the tiles. All apartment kitchens on the Upper East Side sound the same.

"Nah," she said again. I heard her open the refrigerator, the jars on the door banged against one another. "I'm tired of the same old places up here. Take me somewhere I've never been."

"Sure," I said.

Katherine Cahill would never have described herself as a feminist or a vocal defender of women's rights. She believed there was a need for that but the needs they served were for women unlike her. Women who, for a variety of reasons, felt an institutional conspiracy against them, or felt abused by the culture perhaps, a culture consisting of a class mentality rooted in a long history of male dominance. But Katherine never felt oppressed by men and always seemed comfortable in the defined role she had been raised in. She was, one might say, comfortable in her skin. Therefore it was perfectly natural for her to say "take me" rather than "meet me." It's a minor distinction but an important one.

"Nice or lowdown?" I asked.

"Take me where you hang out."

"All right," I said. "Let's meet at a place called the Lion's Head. It's on Christopher Street, just off Seventh Avenue. We'll have a drink and decide from there."

"What time?"

"7.00," I told her.

***

My job isn't bad. I've grown into it, or perhaps it's grown into me. The pay is decent, the expense account and benefits are good, and the hours are terrific. I'm at my desk by 10.00 and I generally leave around 6.00. Advertisers are big on lunches but there are dinners too and the job isn't overly demanding. Basically, anyone who has the means wants to advertise in the *Times* so to some extent there is a captive market. My secretary Marie is as loyal as they come and my boss, the President and

General Manager, Joe Lieberman, has made sure I've risen up the ranks along with him.

Like many fortunate things in life Joe and I met by accident. I had recently graduated from college; it was summer still, and I was supposed to be looking for a job. I didn't want to do what others in my class did; work in the family business or on Wall Street or for any of the big corporations. I had no desire to go to law school or graduate school of any kind; I'd had it with the classroom. I wanted to head out into the world, travel, see stuff. I wanted to be a writer. I'd written some short stories in school and had some published in small, obscure literary magazines. What I wanted to do now was write a novel. None of this, though, was making me any money. I was living at home and my father was beginning to give me the evil eye in the morning before he left for work. I got into the habit of staying out late at night so I wouldn't have to talk to him about the non-existent job interviews I was supposed to be doing all day downtown.

On one of those late evenings I was in P.J. Clarke's on Third Avenue drinking with some college buddies who had just landed jobs on Wall Street. I was, I thought, 'gathering' material for my novel. It would be a story with New York City and Wall Street as the setting, the conventional wisdom being that this was the center of the world in the last decades of the 20th century, the so-called American Century, and it would have some sex and maybe a little violence and corruption and these guys I was drinking with in P.J. Clarke's were getting in on the ground level. Great material, I thought, and I listened very carefully to everything that was said.

Anyway, after a couple of burgers and some beers my friends looked at the clock and said, "Meeting some chicks, Jed, you remember Sue and Wendy and those guys? You know, China Club, Shark Bar, do some Jell-O shots, maybe we'll get lucky. Why don't you come along?" I begged off and watched them leave and I remember thinking Wall Street was just like college for these guys. They haven't really graduated; they've just gone on into another year. And I remember asking the barman for a scrap of paper and a pencil. I wanted to jot this thought down. This was going into my novel.

I had another beer and was watching the Yankee game on the television above the bar when the couple sitting next to me began an argument. It got heated. Their voices raised and people began to look. The bartender moved closer when suddenly the woman, an attractive, well built brunette, slapped the guy across the face. Hard. One of her nails caught his cheek and a thin line of blood trickled down his chin. She abruptly turned on her stool, stood up and left, the sound of her high heels loud in the suddenly quiet bar. I watched her hips swing defiantly as she strode over the sawdust to the door.

The guy sat there, calmly took a napkin to his face, and finished his drink. The bar got noisy again and customers went back to their drinks and to the Yankee game. He turned and asked me what the score was. We talked. He bought me beers and I bought him drinks. Two hours later we were stinking drunk and two hours after that he asked me to take him home. The last time he was like this, he said, he had gotten mugged. The mugger had taken his keys, along with everything else, and he fell asleep in his lobby until the super showed up in the morning.

That's how I met Joe Lieberman. Today he is one of my best friends. And my boss. Oh, and he eventually married the brunette, too. Lisa. I went to the wedding.

***

Anyway, in order for me to meet Katherine at 7.00 I could easily leave my office by 6.30 and probably beat her to the Lion's Head. But by 6.00 I was anxious and I couldn't concentrate on anything anymore. I left some things for Marie to do in the morning, cleaned off my desk, and left. I put on my sport jacket, felt for my cigarettes, and grabbed the sports section off my colleague Charlie Jackson's desk on the way to the elevators.

FIVE

MIKE, SOMETIME BARTENDER AND OWNER of the Lion's Head, is a gray haired, leathery faced, cranky man who, when he's not tending bar sits at the end of it with a newspaper and a cup of coffee. There is always a burning cigarette resting in the black Bakelite ashtray by his elbow. Like a lot of former alcoholics Mike drinks more black coffee than he ever did booze and I've never seen him without that cigarette close by. He's very tall and wears thick black rimmed glasses, worn jeans and a flannel shirt, and from his seat at the end of the bar he has a perfect view of all who enter and leave. If anyone enters he does not know he gives a good evil eye which is magnified at least five times through those thick eyeglasses.

I've known Mike nearly as long as I've lived in Greenwich Village and the Lion's Head has been around a lot longer than that. It's a New York bar in the classic sense. You step off the sidewalk down into it, like a cellar, and everything is made of dark wood and is dusty and smoky and smells like stale beer and cigarettes. It has one of the two best jukeboxes in New York City (the Whitehorse Tavern over on Hudson Street has the other good one) and Mike is always taking quarters out of the register to play some of his favorites. A lot of newspaper men and magazine writers and novelists hang out in the Lion's Head and on the walls all around the bar are framed dust-jackets of all the books the regulars have written. Mike often throws parties for an author whose book has just been published or a journalist who has received some award. I started hanging out there because of Joe Lieberman; a lot of guys from the *Times* frequented the place, and for me living around the corner made it easy.

Anyway, Mike nodded at me when I walked through the door and Paul, the other bartender, had my vodka martini up before I could open my paper.

"Glass of seltzer, too, Paul," I said. I was early and wanted to nurse my drink until Katherine arrived. I unfolded Charlie Jackson's paper and looked for the box scores.

"Early for a Tuesday," Paul said.

"Meeting someone."

"Right."

Paul was a man of few words. To be a good bartender in a place full of writers you had to be and that was why everyone liked him. He was a retired sea captain who had sailed freight-ers around the world and had gotten himself into the Merchant Marine during World War Two by lying about his age. Late at night, just before closing, when you'd had way too much to drink and the words stopped spilling out of your mouth, Paul, quiet and unassuming, would tell you one of the most fantastic sea stories you ever heard and by the time you woke up the next morning, head throbbing and tongue so dry it felt like sandpaper on the roof of your mouth, you'd remember the story and it would somehow justify your staying out so late, smoking too many cigarettes and drinking way too many martinis. Paul was one of the best kept secrets of the Lion's Head.

I sipped my drink and sucked down half my seltzer while reading about the Yankees and I wondered what it was Katherine wanted to see me about. Seeing her twice in two days was unusual for me now although before she married Steve we saw each other quite a bit. That was before I realized my love for her would be unrequited. But now it felt like old patterns were re-emerging and for some reason, in the back of my mind, something in me was resisting.

When you were with Katherine she made you feel as if you were the most important person in her life. She was open and honest, telling you everything, what she felt, what she knew, all her secrets. But when apart she always seemed to be surrounded by mystery, not openness. You heard things, at parties, among friends, at social events. Things like, "...you'll never guess who I saw with Donald Resnick, the real estate guy, the other night." "Who?" "Katherine Cahill." "Without Steve?" "Yeah, and they didn't behave as if they were simply friends..." or, perhaps the wildest thing I ever heard, and I have no way of knowing whether it is true or not, she was spotted on a nude beach in the Caribbean with the billionaire Harry Crump, a man three times her age. Nevertheless, she was one of those people who never seemed real unless you were actually with her.

"Hey, Jed."

I turned and saw Katherine behind me.

"Sorry I'm late," she said. She placed her purse on the stool next to mine. A light musky perfume wafted around me.

"Let's sit over there." I nodded toward the wall of dust-jackets across from us where there were a few stools and a little counter. I signaled Paul.

"Katherine?" I asked.

"I'll have what you're having."

I took our drinks over to the narrow counter. Someone plugged the juke box and some bluesy jazz began. We each took a stool and Katherine moved a little closer to me. Her knee touched mine.

"So," I said. "What's got you out and downtown to see me?"

Katherine reached over and touched my arm. "Our lunch yesterday was so good for me, you know. Get out of the house, away from all the divorce stuff and everything. God, if I talk to another lawyer I think I'll scream. Please, Jed, if anything happens to us, no lawyers. Promise me."

"What are you talking about, Katherine? Why would we have lawyers between us?"

"They seem to be everywhere, don't they?"

I watched Katherine take a long sip from her martini and I tried to imagine living with her and watching her grow old. I couldn't. I didn't even want to think about it. I wanted her to stay whatever age she was, twenty eight or thirty, and only remember her that way. No gray hair, no wrinkles or sagging breasts, no protruding blue veins in her calves. No, I could never imagine Katherine getting old. The concept was inconceivable.

"When I got home yesterday I did a lot of thinking. I think I've made a decision," she said. For a moment her eyes seemed to flash from behind, like a cats eyes in the dark, and I suddenly realized she had been waiting to see me all day. She slowly reached for the pack of cigarettes in my shirt pocket, her fingers lingering a second longer than necessary, and took one. She slipped it into her mouth and looked right at me as she struck a match and put it to the tip of her cigarette. She inhaled slowly causing the orange tip to burn red and she sucked the smoke deep into her lungs. Then she casually let the smoke stream out of her nose and mouth before she sipped her drink again. "I need your help," she said.

"How?"

"The money. Steve's money. The will, the Swiss accounts, all of it. I want it. It's mine. It belongs to me. And I need you to help me get it."

SIX

KATHERINE'S EYES WERE STEADY AND wide and stared blankly into mine. Her face was frozen like a statue and showed no emotion whatsoever. Then it broke, the ice cracked, and she suddenly looked innocent, like she might have looked as a girl after she kissed a boy for the first time. I turned away. I saw Mike push another round of quarters into the juke box and I heard the old Ventures classic, "Walk, Don't Run."

I sipped my drink and saw Paul talking to a guy named Eddie Turner who was a crime reporter for the *News* and a juicehead and suddenly I knew that my life with Katherine was about to change. But I also realized her life was about to change too, and moreover, that she was picking me to change it with. "I want the money," she had said. By saying it she had opened a door, a secret door, through which only she and I entered. By saying it she reached out, took my hand, and pulled me along without giving me a chance to hesitate. The strange thing was even though I'd been waiting for this moment for years I did not truly enjoy it. The moment felt anti-climactic, a let-down of sorts. Moreover, the fact that this moment happened in the Lion's Head further dampened the spirit of the affair. Almost made it seem seedy, in an odd sort of way. That said, it did little to suppress my desire for her. She had me and there was no way around it. Willingly or unwillingly I was surrendering myself. Right then and there I decided I would let her take me where she wanted and I smiled at the thought, remembering what she had said earlier in the day. *"Take me where you hang out."* Suddenly I realized it wasn't I who was taking her, it was she taking me. And I decided, right there as I sat in the Lion's Head, I would go with her. There had to be limits, this I was sure of. For she was the kind of woman where there had to be. What those limits were I didn't exactly know yet but I hoped I would recognize them when I needed to.

"What do you mean the money is yours, it belongs to you?" I turned back to face her and knocked back the rest of my martini, pushing the lemon twist back into the glass with my tongue.

The look of innocence that only a moment ago had melted my heart was now replaced by a hard mask forming across her face. But it didn't stay. She quickly returned to the Katherine I knew, the Katherine I had lunch with yesterday, the Katherine I met just over ten years ago.

"It's complicated," Katherine said.

"These things are."

"I know."

"But Steve was on Wall Street long before you married, no? He made big bucks before you tied the knot, right? Doesn't New York law state that anything prior to the marriage is off limits?"

"Yes and no. Well, some. He made a lot before we married but he made a lot more after. I helped him."

"You're losing me. You're not a stockbroker."

"Steve isn't either."

"All right, investment banker."

I was a little confused about where Katherine was going with this and I decided the Lion's Head was not the place to continue this conversation. We needed to go someplace else, someplace with a little better atmosphere, more intimate, a nice place where we could sink into anonymity and talk.

"Let's get out of here," I said. She stabbed her cigarette into the ashtray and grabbed her purse.

"Sure," she said. "Where?"

"Do you want to eat something?"

"I could eat."

"Italian?"

"Sure, I like Italian."

"I know a good place. We'll have to get a cab."

"Fine," she said. "Let's go." She smiled as she stood up and I saw Mike standing at the bar behind her looking over at me. He winked and gave me the thumbs up.

SEVEN

"LONG TIME, JED."

"Hi Sally, yeah, I know. How's Vin?"

"Vinnie's doin' good."

Salvatore Campo and his brother Vincent owned Bocce, an old well established Italian restaurant situated in a cavernous turn of the century building on Chambers Street, in Tribeca. Lunch was a business and government crowd and dinner was a hip downtown crowd. I discovered the place several years ago when a big shot buyer at one of the agencies took over a bunch of accounts that were heavy advertisers with the *Times*. This buyer was originally from the Midwest and when he came to New York Bocce was the first Italian restaurant he ate in. He loved it and in the way some people are about first impressions, Bocce became his Italian haunt of choice. He ate the same dish every time; *Capellini Primavera,* Angel hair pasta with vegetables. This is how I was introduced to Bocce and later, when Sarah and I were hot and heavy, I'd take her to Bocce for dinner all the time. She loved it. It became "our place." I got to know the owners Sally and Vin but I hadn't been here since Sarah and I stopped seeing each other last year.

It felt strange to walk in here with Katherine. It was like going back to a school reunion with a girl other than the one you dated while you were there as a student. Like some kind of betrayal of the past or of a memory or something. By taking Katherine to Bocce it officially ceased to be Sarah's and my place. The death of one thing and the birth of another, perhaps. I guess that's one way to look at it. I watched Sally take Katherine's hand and kiss it.

"Welcome to Bocce, *signorina*." Sally bowed and I saw the sconce light shine off his slick black hair.

"This is Sally, Katherine. He owns the place."

"Hi, Sally," Katherine said, somewhat amused at Sally's theatrics.

"How's a table for two look?" I asked.

"No res, right?"

"No."

"Give me a few minutes."

"Sure."

"Let me buy you two a drink."

"Great."

We edged to the bar which was packed. It always was. A lot of guys in suits, a few women in office clothes, a few film types dressed in black. Chambers Street was sort of a demarcation line between Tribeca and the Financial District to the south. This is one of the things I love about New York. You could walk into a place like Bocce in the late afternoon, stand at the bar, and find an arbitrager who had made a killing that day standing next to a painter who had just sold a canvas for an ungodly amount of money standing next to a writer who was trying to sell a screenplay to one of Robert DeNiro's assistants who was busy making time with a gorgeous secretary who needed to be sure to catch the last express bus back to Staten Island.

7 pm was as meaningful a time atmospherically as Chambers Street was geographically. At 7 pm the guys in suits and the women in office clothes would make their way uptown. Those under thirty would head to the Upper West Side to places

like the Shark Bar or the China Club and those over thirty would head to the Upper East Side to places like Campagnola's or Jim McMullen's. At 7 pm those dressed only in black would begin to trickle in – after all it was *their* neighborhood – and more people dressed in black would arrive so that by 10.00 Bocce would look like an ecumenical gathering of New York hipness.

Sally made room at the bar for Katherine and me and signaled the bartender. "Give them whatever they want," Sally said. The bartender glanced at us and I could tell he was trying to place us. Film? Art world? Restaurant owners? Sally moved away and said, "Hiya Joey," to some guy at the door. He turned and put his hand on my shoulder and squeezed it. "Good to see you back," he said. Then his restaurant swallowed him up and he disappeared.

The bartender stood behind the mahogany bar wiping his hands with a white bar towel and asked us what we wanted. I ordered two vodka martinis each with a lemon twist. Katherine stood by the wall.

"I like this place," she said. "I've never been here before. I like the places you hang out in."

"This is an old timer," I said as I passed Katherine her drink. "Sarah and I came here a lot. I guess you could say we were regulars."

"Is that how you know Sally?"

"Well, yes, I guess so. I used to come here a lot with a buyer. He liked this place too."

"Oh." Katherine sipped her drink, spilling some. She stood back holding the drink out in front of her, trying not to spill any on herself. "I didn't think you were the kind to mix business and pleasure."

"I try not to," I said after taking a long pull on my drink. "You're right though and I shouldn't. Look what happened to Sarah and me." I laughed. "Hell, even the buyer stopped taking me here. He assigned my accounts to his assistant. And since the assistant liked another place more that was the end of lunch for me at Bocce."

Katherine looked like she was going to say something but I wanted to change the subject. "Anyway," I said. "Tell me more about Steve's money."

Katherine looked over the rim of her glass and her eyes seemed to say she had another secret she wanted to share but wasn't sure just when or how.

"Katherine Cahill!"

I heard the shout come from behind me. I turned and saw a tall man in his mid-fifties. He was fit and good looking in the way local television newscasters are.

"Hi, Arthur," Katherine said, clearly startled. "What are you doing here?"

"What am I doing here? The question is what are you doing here? You are strictly an uptown girl. Long time, no see." He had the distinctly deep, gravelly voice that men who do voice-overs for radio or television have. He leaned over to kiss Katherine and she turned her cheek to him and closed her eyes. Then she stepped back next to me.

"Arthur, this is Jed Chase. Jed, Arthur Barrett." We shook hands. "Jed's an old friend. He lives in the Village."

I immediately detected a reserve in Katherine. A shield came over her. Nothing abrupt, very subtle. As though she were trying to distort the level of friendship between them.

"Where in the Village?"

"West Tenth Street."

He looked at me the way other men look at me when I say I live in the Village. *Are you gay?* That's always the unasked question and there are two distinct looks you get. One kind of look comes from straight men and another kind of look comes from gay men. I was certain Barrett gave me the second kind of look. Katherine, I sensed, picked up on this and suddenly she said, "Jed recently broke up with his girlfriend." But the way she said it sounded like she was trying to kill two birds with one stone.

"Katherine, it's been so long, you look terrific, as always. How's Steve?"

"We got unmarried."

"I heard. Too bad. A shame really. You two were terrific together. I hope it wasn't nasty."

"No, no, nothing like that. You know Steve. It just came through."

"Well, should I congratulate you?" Barrett put his empty glass on the bar and waved at the bartender for another. He turned to us. "Can I buy you two another?"

"Sure," I said. Katherine gave me a look.

"How about you, Arthur? Still happily married?"

"Sure, sure, of course."

Barrett took our empty glasses and passed over two new ones.

"Oldest in college, second on her way. Mary is still big with the Republican Women's Committee and Mother's Against Drunk Driving. She stays busy."

"Still living in Jersey?"

"Yeah, still got the old homestead. Mary won't leave. Maybe after the kids get out of college. Florida or Arizona or something."

For a moment I saw the hardness I had seen at the Lion's Head. And, again, it was just a split second but in that moment I realized she and Barrett knew each other much better than either was willing to let on. And I had the distinct feeling this coincidence was a terrible mistake, one meant to be avoided at all costs.

"Well," Barrett said, holding up his glass. His smile widened revealing bright fluorescent teeth. "Here's to old times."

"Yes," Katherine said. "To old times." She turned to me. "How about you, Jed? To old times?"

"Nah," I said. "I'd rather drink to new times."

"Jed works for the *Times,* Arthur," Katherine said.

"Oh? That's sounds interesting," Barrett said. "Reporter?"

"No," I said. "Advertising."

Suddenly Sally appeared. "Hiya, Arthur," he said. "Didn't see you come in. Staying for dinner?"

"No, Sally, not tonight. Just having a drink before I head out."

"Well, hope to see you next time." Sally turned to me. "Jed, you're all set. I'll send your drinks over. Follow me." Sally took our drinks and handed them to the bartender.

"Nice seeing you again, Katherine," Barrett said. "Maybe we can get together and catch up." He said nothing to me. As I followed Sally I turned back and saw Katherine say something to Barrett but I could not hear it. Then she rapidly shook her head and shot him an ice cold stare before she walked away.

EIGHT

WE SETTLED INTO A NICE booth in the back. The ceilings in Bocce are very high, more than twenty feet, so conversations tend to rise and evaporate rather than get tossed over to the next table. The waiter brought our drinks from the bar. Katherine faced the back wall. I faced forward, toward the front of the restaurant, where I could see Barrett slapping the back of a guy who had an uncanny resemblance to Richard Nixon.

"I don't think I care much for your friend Arthur Barrett. Nothing personal."

Katherine was fumbling with her lipstick, a bright red that stood out against her sleeveless yellow and white summer dress. A delicate string of pearls hung from her neck and I saw tiny, almost imperceptible, pearl earrings I hadn't noticed before. She smiled as she ran the tube over her lips.

"He's a sleazebag," she said.

"How do you know him?"

"Oh God," she sighed. "How do I know any of those guys?"

She dropped her lipstick back into her purse and looked around the room.

"Can we smoke?" she asked.

"I don't know. I don't know if we're in the smoking section. Go ahead. We'll soon find out."

She reached across the table for my cigarettes. Her bare arm hung before me, her lovely skin smooth with some faint hairs, like fine golden threads, barely visible on her forearm. There were a couple of tiny freckles near her elbow and I suddenly found myself aroused. It was a gorgeous arm that I now found unexpectedly erotic. I began to imagine her arm around my neck, or waist, or between my legs and I suddenly wanted to have sex with her in the worst way. I reached for my drink.

"So," I said, shifting in my seat, watching her light her cigarette. "How do you know 'those' guys? And why don't you ever have any cigarettes?"

"I know 'those' guys because of Steve," she said, looking away as she inhaled. "And yes, I do buy cigarettes. I keep them at home."

"What good are they at home?"

"Keeps me from smoking too much."

She puffed away and turned sideways to face the room offering me a wonderful profile of her face. She had a fine face with a pert nose that was slightly pushed up and thin lips that curled in when she said certain words and classic cheekbones that weren't too high but rather in good proportion to her jaw. When she smiled her eyes crinkled in the corners and her skin was the color of milk with a little coffee stirred in.

"Arthur Barrett..." She let his name drift up and away. I had the feeling she was waiting for me to ask about him and she began to speak slowly, measuring her words. As she did I saw Barrett wave to the bartender, turn, shake someone's hand and leave.

"I met him through Steve, of course. He's somewhere near the top of Goldstone, Meyer."

"The investment bankers?"

"Yes. He met Steve at business school."

"He's looks a lot older than Steve."

"Oh no, he is. He didn't go to school with Steve, he recruited him there. After Steve got his MBA Barrett brought Steve into Goldstone, Meyer. Brought him in under his wing. That's how Steve got his start in the business. When Steve eventually left to start his own company, Cahill and Company, he wanted Barrett to come with him but Barrett didn't. He stayed at Goldstone. Steve was disappointed at first but it didn't stop them from doing deals. But in the beginning Cahill and Company was just Steve."

"Really?" I was surprised. "I always thought Cahill and Company was his father's firm. That it had been around forever, like since the forties or fifties or something."

"That's Cahill, White, and Company. Steve wanted everyone to think that too but no, Cahill and Company was his own, nothing to do with his father. His father retired from Cahill, White, he's now chairman emeritus or something, but back then he tried to keep Steve from using the name. They haven't spoken to each other since. It's terrible. His father never approved of the way Steve did business, and vice a versa. Steve's mom died broken hearted over the whole thing. She dreamed of the day her husband and son would work together. Not many people knew or realized the extent of it, the rift between them, which is amazing for Wall Street, where it's your business to know about other people's business. Most people simply figured Steve wanted to go out on his own, and assumed he and his father did deals together. Barrett promoted the idea, and after a while, with Steve's success, his father didn't discourage those ideas. Talk about irony."

"I never knew," I said. "Steve never let on about his father. But now that you mention it he never spoke about him much. Actually, I can't remember him saying anything about him at all, even in college."

Katherine finished her drink. She tucked her hair in behind her ears and I felt she wasn't entirely comfortable talking about Steve. I knew him as well as anyone, I guess, I'd known them both for quite some time. Perhaps that was why, I thought. Because we weren't strangers. Because maybe I knew more than she thought.

"So, getting back to Barrett."

"Like I said, I met him through Steve. Before we got married, around the time Steve was getting ready to leave Goldstone. They were inseparable, very close. Did a lot of deals together, a team. Still do as far as I know. Arthur taught him the business, everything, took him under his wing like a son. It was strange for me; the age difference, the closeness. They were like their own little private club. In a weird way I always felt Arthur became the father Steve didn't have. The kind of relationship he'd always wanted from him, you know? But it got weird too, they fed off each other, and Steve could behave in ways, do things, one would never do with one's father. They were like fraternity brothers, the stuff they did."

The waiter came and we ordered. I asked for the wine list.

"Why do I get the feeling this has something to do with Steve's money?"

"Because you have good instincts."

The waiter slid the wine list onto the table.

NINE

ALTHOUGH I WORK FOR A newspaper I am a salesman. I sell advertising space. It's my job to make people like me, to make them feel good about me spending their money, to make them feel satisfied with the way the *Times* treats them. However the past two days with Katherine seemed to me to create the opposite scenario. The roles had somehow been reversed. It seemed as if Katherine were the salesperson selling something to me. It was a soft sell, of course, but effective nonetheless. Perhaps even more so. Any salesman worth his salt will tell you the first thing you sell is yourself, then the product. Katherine had me sold already, and I'm sure she knew it, but the product she was selling as yet remained unknown. But boy, did I want it.

She had me sold in ways she couldn't possibly fathom. I wanted to spend all of my money on her. I wanted her to keep making me feel good. And I wanted to keep doing this business, whatever it was, with her. But I wanted more than that. I wanted to come home to her at night, I wanted to spend week-ends with her in the country, at the beach; I wanted to make love to her, to kiss her neck, her breasts, her stomach, to stroke the inside of her leg, to fuck her good and wake up in the morning next to her and watch the sun stream through the windows and across our naked bodies. And I wanted to make her feel about me the way I felt about her. I wanted everything from her and for some reason, wishful or not, I thought by listening to her, helping her with anything she asked, would lead me to precisely that.

"All right," I said. "Why do you say Steve's money belongs to you, that it's yours? First of all he's not your husband anymore and second of all you could have gotten it a lot easier before you signed the divorce agreement."

"Well, aside from the fact that I was his wife, I helped him get it. But I had no idea. I had no idea it was so much until I saw his will. I thought the lump sum and an apartment was fair based on what I knew. I simply never knew he had so much." Katherine put out her half smoked cigarette.

"Explain to me how you helped him get his money."

Katherine took in a breath and unconsciously reached toward the ashtray. When she realized she had already put out her cigarette she drew her hands together, folded them, and leaned toward me over the table. Her hair fell forward and her arms pushed her breasts together exposing a deeper than usual cleavage. Her clear, cool green eyes looked right into mine.

"I did things. For him. For Steve. For the business. Arthur Barrett was involved too, and others. Arthur cooled off after a while, sort of quit while he was ahead kind of thing, but Steve kept on going. They did risky things. But Arthur was instrumental at first, you see it was his and Steve's plan. You have no idea what a shock it was to see him tonight. I haven't seen him in ages it seems. At least a year, year and a half. All that seems so long ago now."

"Sounds like you and Barrett knew each other fairly well."

"I guess we did."

"So tell me. What things did you do to help Steve get his millions?"

"Well..." she paused. She was clearly hesitating. She reached for the pack of cigarettes again. I was growing impatient with her now. I felt like she was playing with me, purposely tantalizing me. Maybe she was having second thoughts about the whole thing. But I also felt if I didn't at least try and pull it out of her, get her to tell me what she did, what she knew, if I didn't engage her and get her to trust me, I'd lose her. And I did not want that.

"Well what?" I said. "Come on, Katherine. You can't shock me. This is the nineties. Nothing is shocking anymore. O.J. Simpson murdered his wife and got away with it, remember? What could you have done that could possibly top that?"

"Oh, my." Katherine abruptly sat back. "No, nothing like that. Jesus, Jed."

"Well, all right," I said. "But, I mean, you know, you're being awfully coy and mysterious and everything. Why don't you just spit it out? It's me. I'm your friend, remember? You said you wanted me to help you, well fine. I want to. But I can't help you if I don't know what it is exactly you need help with, can I?"

Katherine looked hurt, as if scolded. I reached across the table and took her hand. She let me and squeezed mine back, keeping her eyes cast downward.

"I'm sorry," I said. "I didn't mean... look, let's forget it for now. We'll talk later, okay?" I reached for the wine list.

"No," she said. "It's all right. It's just complicated, that's all. I'm not sure I even understand the whole thing myself..."

The waiter appeared with Katherine's salad. He said, "Do you need two plates?"

"No," I said.

"Did you select a wine?"

"Yes. The Amarone, please."

"Very good."

"And a bottle of water," Katherine said. "With gas."

"Pellegrino?"

"Fine."

When the waiter left Katherine looked at me, gave a quick

smile, and said, "Anyway, basically Steve operated with inside information, had a kind of system, a program going on to produce it. But after all the stuff in the eighties, you know, Giuliani and everything, Milken, Boesky, Drexel, Burnham, all those guys, it got more complicated, riskier."

The waiter appeared with the wine. He swiftly opened it and poured some in my glass. I sipped it.

"Fine," I said to the waiter, throwing my hand up. He poured our glasses while the busboy arrived with the bottle of Pellegrino and two water glasses. We now had two martini glasses, two wine glasses, four water glasses, and two bottles on the table. That's a lot of glass. I thought of how the French and the Italians love glasses and bottles. They have one for everything, extras even, just in case. But the Americans? Well, we invented Styrofoam cups and paper plates. That's our contribution to fine dining. Make it to go.

I lifted my wine glass. "Cheers," I said. We clinked glasses. "To the future."

"Yes," Katherine said, "To the future. To *our* future."

We drank and put our glasses down. I like that toast, I thought.

"So," I said. "How did Steve produce all this inside information?"

"Sex," Katherine said.

TEΠ

BY THE TIME WE LEFT Bocce Katherine told me the story of how Steve Cahill and Arthur Barrett had set up shop in an apartment on East Eighty-Second Street. It was pretty simple when you looked at it, pretty basic. It combined the two things most men desire: money and sex. And for one there was always the other.

Steve had had a lot of friends in school. I knew as much being that Steve and I were both classmates and fraternity brothers. Steve was your typical BMOC. He had been a fraternity brother, a member of some secret society, held office in school government, a varsity football player, and President of the economics club. I was the opposite. Although I had been a fraternity brother of Steve's the only club I belonged to was the book club. Aside from the book club, playing intramural sports and writing for the school literary magazine, that was it for me. I didn't have the desire for much else. After all, I was in college, I didn't feel the need to overextend myself. But I knew Steve, and he knew me. We lived in the same frat house, but we lived different lives. In my senior year I moved out of the fraternity house and lived off campus with my friend Morris Bergman, who was also a member of the book club.

After graduation Steve went on to get his MBA and afterward began his business career at Goldstone, Meyer. Under Barrett's tutelage Steve began to provide 'dates' for certain clients of Barrett's. College girls, acquaintances of Steve's, friends of friends. After lunch or dinner they would end up in the Eighty-second Street apartment. The girls, young women fresh out of college, in the big city, working as editorial assistants, secretaries, waitresses, assistant museum curators, all of them barely making the rent let alone a life, found that dinner in a restaurant they could never afford with a wealthy middle-aged man and a few hours of sex afterward in exchange for a couple thousand dollars was not a bad way to spend an evening.

Some of the women, Katherine told me, asked Steve to keep calling them, they liked the money, and oh, by the way, they had a friend or two who might be interested. Some said no after the first date. Some said no right from the start. But all in all, the presidents and CEO's of privately held companies who came to Wall Street shopping for an investment bank to take them public, men who came from places like Omaha and Portland and Lubbock who were looking to raise millions of dollars through a stock offering, who saw that when you were talking that kind of money there wasn't much difference between Merrill Lynch or Morgan Stanley, would, after a night of the best sex they'd had in years with a twenty-four-year-old, smart, attractive, clean woman provided by Arthur Barrett, senior partner of Goldstone, Meyer, give Goldstone the last look at any deal they were about to make. They would, after all, be coming back to New York once their companies went public. This, Katherine told me, was what Steve Cahill and Arthur Barrett did the two years Steve worked at Goldstone, Meyer. By then they had made a small fortune. Simple enough. Yet for some reason, as we left Bocce, I had a strong suspicion this was only half the story.

We sat in the back of a taxi heading uptown. Dinner was good, mine at least, Katherine had barely touched hers, although we did finish the bottle of Amarone. By the time I asked for the check Katherine still had not told me what she had done to deserve Steve's money and I was wondering where this was going. Hence my suspicions about hearing only half the story.

"Do you want to get a coffee or something?" I asked as we sped up Church Street. Outside the cab bright neon streaks of red, yellow, green, and purple flew by. Korean grocers were rearranging fresh flowers under sharp fluorescent light in their outdoor stands; the ubiquitous green trucks of waste management companies whined and hissed as they began to make their rounds, and as we moved further uptown people began to emerge onto the street looking for taxis. It was a black night with umbrellas of orange light from overhead street lamps dimly illuminating the avenue. I rolled my window all the way down and felt the thick August air wash over me. It was almost 11.00 as we drove into Soho and the streets were suddenly crowded.

"You have to work tomorrow," Katherine said. "I wouldn't want to keep you out late."

"I could think of worse reasons to stay out late."

"I bet you could."

"Do you want to go to Raoul's?"

"Sure, Jed. You know I love being with you."

At Prince Street I told the driver to stop. We strolled along the narrow sidewalk and I saw the restaurant Provence on the corner of MacDougal Street.

"Do you go there anymore, Jed?"

"No, not really. That's where Sarah and I broke it off."

"Oh," she said. "I didn't know that. You used to like that place, too. I remember you always threatened to take me there. I don't think of you as sentimental, Jed. Does it make you sad to think about it?"

"No. I don't think so. Just a place in my past that went bad, that's all."

I remembered how Sarah and I had argued. We had been fighting, sniping at each other for weeks, months. Sarah had wanted to move in together. I was hesitant. We talked about it endlessly; I resisted, and tried to hold it off. But the more I resisted Sarah only pushed harder. "We'll save money," she said. "On rent, on food, on utilities." I knew she saw it as step toward marriage, something she wanted but never directly stated. But I was uncertain about living with her and certainly about anything approaching marriage. I liked my privacy. I liked being alone when I wanted and I wasn't sure I'd like Sarah the same way I did if we lived together. The truth is I wasn't sure I even loved her. The sex was good. She was funny, smart, and easy to see movies with and have dinner with but I was not convinced it would carry over to living together, about seeing her every single morning when she got out of bed. One night at dinner, in the restaurant Provence about a year ago, she threw down the gauntlet. It was a bad mistake. "If you loved me," she had said, "you'd want me to move in with you. Why don't you want me to move in with you?" I mumbled something about liking things the way they were and didn't quite give her a straight answer and we ate the rest of our dinner in silence. I drank nearly all the wine, a nice Cote du Rhone as I recall, and afterwards we set a date for Sarah to come by my place when I wouldn't be there so she could remove the few things she kept there.

"That's too bad," Katherine said. "I always liked her, you know."

"Yes, I know. Everybody did."

"But you didn't love her."

"No. I didn't love her. How did you know?"

"I knew, Jed. I know you." Katherine paused and said, "Where is she now?"

"She went back to Minnesota; married her college sweetheart."

"Wow," Katherine said, turning toward me. "She really did want to get married."

"Yes. She did."

We crossed MacDougal Street, walked down Prince, and stepped into Raoul's, another nice French place I liked. They have a large velvet curtain hanging inside the door to keep the cold out in the winter and the cold inside in the summer and you push it aside and walk into a cozy, semi-private little place. I saw two empty seats at the far end of the bar. We sat and ordered cappuccinos and brandies and a bottle of water. Katherine drank a lot of water. She said it was good for her skin.

"Do you miss her, Jed?" Katherine asked.

"A little," I said. "But not that much. At night sometimes."

ELEVEN

THE FIRST TIME I MET Katherine Cahill she was Katherine Hall. Steve Cahill had recently begun to date her and he anxiously called me one day to invite me for a drink. He wanted me to meet someone, he said, someone special. And I knew Steve was making the rounds, showing whoever it was off, as if she were a new car. But the truth is, when I met her, I thought she *was* special. I had never met anyone like her and was instantly jealous of Steve. Once Katherine and I started talking to each other that was it, I was blinded, numb. It was then that the first seeds of our connection were planted. Seeds which led to a coolness in the friendship between Steve and I but I didn't realize it, or admit it, until much later.

When I met Katherine she was a beautiful woman of eighteen and the minute she opened her mouth and said hello to me I fell completely in love with her. The sound of her voice, the way she looked. It was like a death grip of sorts, a force much more powerful than me. A poet might say I had surrendered myself to her at that moment, to the power of this emotion, of what I thought was love, I don't know. What I do know is since then I have never felt I loved a woman more, or as much, as I did Katherine. It was, I had decided long ago, just one of those things. Hopeless or otherwise. And I knew then that I would never love any other woman as much.

Ours became a relationship based on friendship, though. Not love. An admiring but flirtatious, yet altogether safe relationship. There were no boundaries violated, no borders crossed. We were careful about that. We had Steve between us. But we also had, it soon became obvious, at least to Katherine and me, a rock and a flint between us and when we were together, with or without Steve, there were sparks. I often dreamed of what the fire might have been like if it had ever ignited. What it might have felt like to be immolated by those flames.

One night several years after she started dating Steve, Katherine suggested Sarah and I have dinner with them. We did that often in those days. Especially before they were married. Usually Katherine or I suggested it. And Katherine and I often showed up early. Purposely. We'd stand at the bar and talk, hoping Steve and Sarah would arrive late. One particular night was no different than the others and Katherine and I met at the bar half an hour before the others. She appeared bored and she seemed preoccupied. She told me she and Steve had been fighting lately, a lot. We stood silent as I ordered drinks. By then I knew Katherine's drink: Johnny Walker Black, on the rocks. She turned to me, a light sadness in her eyes.

"Wouldn't it be nice if it was just us, Jed? I mean in a perfect world? Just us without all the bullshit, the past, the whole rest of it? Huh? Let's run off to New Mexico or something, get one of those big ranches, start all over again. You know, live happily ever after. All that stuff. Huh? What do you say?"

I looked at her and tried to judge her seriousness. The sadness had left and I could see the beginnings of an excitement in her eyes. It was a far off excitement but still, an excitement. Her eyes became bright, hopeful.

"Sure," I said, not too seriously. "Let's go. Why not right

now?" I said it as a challenge although I wasn't sure I had meant it that way. Katherine cracked a devilish smile and her eyes crinkled up. I watched as she glanced toward the door then quickly back at me. I could see she was focused and her face deepened as the blood rushed there.

"You want to?" Her voice had changed. She was serious. My heart jumped.

"Come on," I said. Now I was serious. I grabbed her drink and put it on the bar. She looked at me as I slapped down a twenty.

"Come on," I said again. "Let's go."

I took her arm and walked her to the door. She stopped and pulled at me, putting her lips to my ear. "Where?" she whispered. I felt her warm, moist breath on my face. "Where should we go?"

"Anywhere," I said. "I don't care."

Then I felt her tongue touch my ear. "Let's go to your place," she said. "Just for a while. We'll come back and say we went to the wrong restaurant or something." Katherine smiled. "We won't run away *yet*." I felt Katherine's arm tremble as she held on to mine. She was excited and suddenly I smelled her. A deep, rich, musky odor that seemed to be triggered by our sudden action. It penetrated me. In that instant I came as close to having an orgasm as I ever have without having physical sex. I was tingling. It was like a wet dream but I was awake. I glanced over and saw her eyes glazed over, like she was in some kind of trance or something.

"Okay," I said, my voice thick, a little throaty. "Let's go."

We stepped out onto the street. I wanted a taxi. Quick. I wanted to get back to my apartment as fast as humanly possible and rip Katherine's clothes off and fuck her on the floor right inside my doorway. I wanted to fuck her in the taxi. I wanted to fuck her right there on the sidewalk in front of the restaurant.

The world could end at that point for all I cared. Nothing else existed for me at that moment.

Thank Christ, a taxi pulled up to the curb. We'll take this one I thought. Just in time. I saw someone pass a few bills over the seat and then slide over to the door. I stepped up and reached for the door handle and swung it open.

"Hey," Steve said. "You guys just getting here?"

I stood on the curb frozen.

"Well, yes," Katherine said, her voice still deep and husky. "We were just wondering if this was the right place."

"Where's Sarah?" Steve asked.

"I don't know," I said. "She must be running late."

"Well," Steve said. "Let's go inside and get a drink."

That was the closest I had ever come to having Katherine. I can't begin to describe my disappointment, my envy, my jealousy, my resentment, my rage. It still haunts me. If I spoke ten words that night at dinner I don't remember them. I knew the opportunity was lost. And somehow I knew it was lost forever, never to present itself again. I remember Katherine's glances, her foot occasionally tapping mine under the table, as if to soothe me, to sympathize, to let me know she was sorry for what happened. I remember Steve's monotonous rambling about how great he was at investment banking and at Sarah's puzzlement over my dark, simmering mood. Later that night, back in my apartment, I made Sarah perform oral sex on me, in the foyer by my front door. I didn't even so much as say 'thanks.' I was too busy thinking about Katherine.

And I knew how right I was about the missed opportunity. The moment never returned, never presented itself again. We never mentioned that night afterward. As if it never existed, never happened. Like a bad dream. As if we had both been burned by a fleeting fantasy, somehow misplaced, never to be found again. But it did nothing to diminish my desire for her. In fact, it pumped my feelings for Katherine up to another level. No more was my longing for Katherine fueled by jet fuel. It had been switched to a super high grade of rocket fuel.

Katherine Hall came from upstate New York outside a small town called Windham. There is a ski area in Windham that my father would take me to when I was young so I kind of knew the area. Katherine grew up on a farm. There were a lot of them back then. My father and I may have passed hers on our way to Windham, I don't know. She told me her father was successful in the dairy business and was able to maintain a solid middle class lifestyle. Her father, she said, sent her to Miss Porter's in Connecticut and then two years of French and Art History at the Sorbonne in Paris. When I met her she had just taken a job as an assistant curator at the Morgan Library on Thirty-Sixth Street.

Steve Cahill dating Katherine caused me to become insanely jealous. When he married her four years later I hated him. But when Katherine filed for divorce last year, I started calling on her. We saw each other frequently. More than before. We were good friends but we did not have sex. We were comforting each other in a time of regret. For Katherine, regret over her marriage to Steve. For me, regret over not being able to make our relationship any more than just friendship. Occasionally, if I was little moody, Katherine would ask, "What's wrong?" and I would make her think it was over my recent breakup with Sarah. To Katherine we were two wounded souls. I felt the same way, only different from the way Katherine believed. I justified my restraint by convincing myself she wasn't interested in another relationship right now. She'd been married for nearly five years for chrissakes. I was being an understanding friend. What she needed was some peace and quiet. But, to be perfectly honest, there were times when I felt like the fox guarding the chicken coop. When she was ready for a deeper relationship I'd be there for her. I was waiting at the door, so to speak. One day it would open and my life with Katherine would begin. And since our lunch at the Carlyle the other day I felt that day imminent. I felt like she was opening the door.

Now, almost midnight in Raoul's, Katherine blew on her cappuccino, pushing the steamed milk up to one side of the white porcelain cup. She took a sip. She still managed to get some of the foamy milk on her upper lip.

"You have a moustache," I said as I watched her lick her lips.

"I'm glad we're still friends, Jed. You know that?"

"So am I," I said. "We have been now for over ten years. I don't have to tell you that."

"I know," she said, looking toward the velvet curtain and the window next to it. Still gazing there she said, "It's too bad about all those years I spent with Steve. I hope I don't become bitter and spend my days regretting them."

"No, Katherine, you won't. You're young, you've got some money, an apartment. You have a lot to look forward to. You're single again, think about that. You are far too young to start dwelling on your short past."

I sipped my brandy and watched her eyes as she turned toward me.

"I know," she said, smiling now. "I have you, don't I?"

"Yes," I said, slowly. "You have me."

TWELVE

THE FRONT ROOM IN RAOUL'S is dark with soft hues of yellow and burgundy and high ceilings. There are small white candles lit under French café posters hanging on the walls. Behind the bar is a large framed mirror with lots of bottles in front of it so that it looked like there were twice as many. It is a very intimate place. The kind of place that once inside you felt happy and young and carefree. It was a place where time and age stopped the minute you stepped behind the velvet curtain. And now, sitting here with Katherine, I thought if we could spend every night in Raoul's, sipping our brandy and drinking our cappuccinos as we gazed at each other in the soft filtered light we'd always be young. We'd always be happy.

Suddenly I felt foolish at such a thought. Ultimately, if we ever had a life together, we would have to look at each other when we got out of bed in the morning after a night at Raoul's. At some point we'd see each other out in the open, alone in the cruel garish light of dawn, and the true test of our devotion I knew would be then, at that moment, on a cold gray morning, naked, with no defenses, no armor, no masks, just our bare souls and our stale breath.

Katherine reached into my shirt pocket for my cigarettes and when her hand was inside I placed mine over it and held it to my heart. She looked at me, into my eyes, and I could see her smiling, a genuine smile, those familiar corners wrinkling, and then she leaned over and kissed me.

"That's for being my friend, Jared Chase. For being who you are. You are a good person and I have always taken comfort in that."

I was thrilled she had called me by my birth name, no one did that. She leaned over again and kissed me harder, pushing her tongue into my mouth, pushing it far in and rubbing it against my own tongue before pulling back. Then, smiling, she lit a cigarette and passed it to me and then lit another for herself.

"Okay," I said. I wanted to get back to Steve and the money and what role, what part, she wanted me to play. It was late and before we went home I wanted to know what she had in mind about all this.

"Okay, what?" she said, mocking me.

"If you want me to help you I need to ask some questions."

"Shoot," she said.

"With all due respect, why would you marry someone who was, in effect, a kind of pimp?"

Katherine's expression took a subtle turn. So subtle in fact that if it weren't me sitting there, someone so obsessed with her, who knew her, it would have passed unnoticed. But I noticed and in that subtle change I knew she was about to lie to me. She turned away from me toward the window.

"I don't know," she said, coolly putting the cigarette up to her red lips, sucking slowly, her nostrils flaring and then, just before she pulled the cigarette away from her mouth blue smoke streamed through her nose. She turned back to me, her green eyes boring into mine, her face, her mouth, her whole body talking to me but for some weird reason I felt like she was talking to someone else, not me. Herself perhaps.

"I didn't know, Jed," she said again. "I didn't know a bloody thing at first. I had no idea what he and Arthur were doing. When I found out I tried to deal with it, what did I know? We were going to get married, this was not *our* life, it was his *business* life. That's what he said, it was just business, not a big deal. Some people take customers to Vegas, the Caribbean, buy them gifts. He offered something different. On Wall Street, he said, people came to do business, it was a huge marketplace, and there were hundreds of firms like his fighting with each other to get those deals. He had to be ready, he said, to give potential clients what they wanted. He told me a lot of these guys, for all the money they had and the powerful companies they ran, were nothing more than bland, boring men who spent most evenings working late and eating late and getting up early and going back the next day to do it again. A daring thrill might be to watch a porn flick on cable television at an airport hotel during a business conference. Steve said to me that a twenty-four-year-old woman could get him more business than anything he learned at Wharton."

The other part of Raoul's, in the back behind the kitchen, was emptying and a few customers stopped at the bar for coffee or cognac. I saw John F. Kennedy, Jr. with the woman he dumped Darryl Hannah for emerge out of the back room and as they walked through you could feel the restraint being exercised by the staff and those of us at the bar. I glanced quickly out the window and saw a dark limo parked across the street and I knew it was for him even though he lived nearby. The woman he was with was pretty and demure and I could see why he'd dump a Hollywood actress for the understated charm and beauty this woman carried. Katherine looked at her in the way one beautiful woman looks at another. Competitively. As Kennedy walked by us I saw him throw Katherine a glance and a subtle smile and I could feel his charisma thicken the air. Katherine smiled back just as Kennedy's date pulled him toward the door. A moment later they were gone and I could hear the hushed whispers of the others. "Geez," Katherine said, turning back to me. "He's much better looking in real life."

Then she looked down at the bar and fiddled with her brandy glass, sliding it back and forth. "When I found out about the girls," she said slowly, "I think it was because Steve wanted me to. When I finally asked about what had become obvious he was relieved and anxiously explained everything to me. His business was growing, he was making a lot of money, we were living well. You know that, you witnessed it. Now he told me one of the reasons why. He traded sex for the inside track, the last look, specific information. He had a small hedge fund going, he was being talked about on Wall Street as a new up and coming wonder boy, he was becoming somebody down there. Listen, Arthur had a lot to do with it too, he steered a lot of those guys to Steve."

Katherine reached for my cigarettes again.

"You smoke too much," I said.

"That's why I leave them at home." She lit another, inhaled slowly and said, "One day Arthur says he's finished with the girls. He doesn't want to do it anymore. Goldstone was having some kind of audit done by the SEC or something, there were rumors, and he told Steve he was on his own. Steve came to me and asked if I'd help him. He couldn't trust anyone else, he said." Katherine held the cigarette in front of her as if thinking about it and then quickly put it out in the ashtray. "He said just think about it like I do. It's part of the business."

"What did you do?" I asked. Suddenly I remembered her comment once about wanting out of the marriage right from the start. Was this why?

"I helped him."

"How?"

"I basically became his appointments secretary for the girls, working from the apartment, calling the girls, making appointments, all that kind of stuff. Steve couldn't do it from the office.

Before me Arthur had someone doing it but he severed all his ties because of what was going on at Goldstone. It wasn't every day and it wasn't that complicated. Steve would tell me so and so is in town next week, call Jane or Kim. Sometimes Steve would tell me to call a certain girl because the guy had her last time and liked her. I handled all the arrangements and paid the girls. Anywhere from five hundred to two thousand dollars, depending. They were nice girls. They were smart; all of them good looking, had regular jobs or were in graduate school, medical school, or law school. You'd be surprised; I was. Anyway, this is what I did. We got married and after a few years it began to wear on me and I was convinced by then that Steve was fucking half of them."

The way she looked at me, they way she said it, I knew this had to be true.

"How did Steve decide what to pay the girls?"

Katherine let out a snide, cynical laugh.

"You'll like this," she said, her mouth turning down. "It's so Steve. Arthur used to tease him about it. Said he was trying to apply what he learned in B school to trading in sex." Katherine drank some water. The restaurant was emptying.

"It was a sliding scale. The older the guy, the uglier, the fatter, all those things, the more money. Sometimes up to five thousand for a weekend. If the guy was a young, good looking dot com start up from Silicon Valley, a guy who wanted to see the town, hip restaurants, hottest clubs, all that, maybe a thousand. Maybe even less. Steve had his own ratings system. The girls never complained about the money. One girl told me once she ought to pay Steve for the night."

"So when you found out Steve was having sex with them you decided to get a divorce?"

"Yeah, kind of. After a while it all became so overwhelming. It was beginning to affect me, you know, like was the girl I just spoke to having sex with my husband? I began to see things differently too. Then of course, ultimately I began questioning my life, our life, you know, all of it. I wanted out."

Now I saw again the Katherine I knew. Her speech, mannerisms. She wasn't lying about this part.

"Frankly, Katherine, I can't see how you put up with any of it."

"You know the old saying, 'Familiarity breeds contempt?' Well, this is what happened. I began to hate him."

There it is, I thought. The gate is opening a little wider. I reached for her hand and squeezed it. "I don't know how you did it, Katherine. Really. This is amazing to me."

"Anyway, it finally got to the point where I wanted out, right there and then. I was fed up with this business, with him, with Arthur, everything. But I didn't think he'd try and fight me. He didn't want to split up, he said. He'd do anything not to, he needed me, and he promised me all kinds of things, whatever I wanted. The only thing was he wouldn't stop the business with his clients and the girls. He said it was too important for the company; he was making too much money. Of course, I had no idea how much."

"Until you saw his will."

"Yes."

"And now you want me to help you get it. Or some of it."

"All of it. I want all of it."

Katherine seemed upset. I don't think she wanted to get into this kind of detail but I got her going a little and now she seemed relieved that I knew the story, the truth about her and Steve. But still, talking about it upset her some. There was a sense of shame and remorse and I couldn't blame her. When you think about it, it was downright disgusting, asking your wife to be a party to such things. As for the money, I could see her point. On the other hand, I could also see the benefits of simply washing your hands and walking away from the whole sordid mess. The truth is, since the divorce was already final, I couldn't see how she could get any more money. Especially since she agreed to the original settlement in the first place. Get a lawyer on a contingency basis to chip away at it? I didn't know about these things, I was certain of that, and Katherine, obviously, didn't either. In any case, I didn't know exactly what Katherine had in mind. She put her hand on my knee.

"The way I feel right now," she said. "I'd be willing to do almost anything to get that money." Katherine took my hand again and put it between hers. "You will help me, won't you, Jed? I don't know anyone else I can turn to."

"Of course. I told you I would. What should we do?"

"Meet me at the apartment. I'll show you the will. We can talk about it, maybe your friend Morris knows what to do, I don't know. How do you get money out of a will?"

"Well," I said. "The easy way is for the guy to die." It was a knee-jerk response and I regretted it the second I said it. It just sort of flew out of my mouth like a piece of food or a fleck of saliva. Katherine let go of my hands.

"I know," she said.

Suddenly I felt something unseen and unknown start to move, start to gather itself up and join us at the bar, hovering above our heads.

"Remember," Katherine said, taking my hand again. "This is our secret, like we said yesterday. Our little secret, just between us. No one knows about the girls except those involved and no one knows about the money, the will, except us. You and me. It's our secret."

"Don't worry about me," I said. "I'm good with secrets."

Katherine leaned over and kissed me.

THIRTEEN

THE DAY AFTER KATHERINE AND I had dinner at Bocce I went to work feeling somewhat perplexed over what Katherine had in mind regarding Steve's money. I knew she wanted it but exactly how did she think she would obtain it? She said there was millions. Tens of millions. The sound of it alone was staggering. People don't part with that kind of money easily. Unless, of course, they were dead. And even then it could be difficult. And what exactly did she think my role was supposed to be in this scheme of hers? I wasn't a lawyer, or a hit man for that matter. I was simply her friend. And her would-be lover.

But I didn't dwell on this too long because, as I had been doing all night, I kept replaying the way she kissed me at Raoul's and like the night after our lunch at the Carlyle, I became drunk with it. The sensation of Katherine's mouth on mine, her tongue flicking in and out and the way it aroused me, caused me to fantasize about having sex with her more than ever before. She was teasing me, I know, and I thought somehow I needed to keep that in some kind of perspective, but still, this feeling, this drunkenness, was overwhelming and made me feel things I had never truly felt before. Happiness, for one. Confidence and a healthy sense of self, for another. All good things.

But the thought of having sex with Katherine kept coming back to me and when I got on the train that morning to go to work I imagined her without clothes. I imagined lying in bed, in a hotel room somewhere, Europe I decided, Paris or Madrid. We would make love all morning and then do some sightseeing, Katherine would shop a little and I'd go to a museum or something. In the afternoon we'd meet at a café and take our time before going back to the hotel to make love some more. And afterward, lying in bed as a pink and orange dusk fell over the city, we'd watch the pastel light thin out as we kissed and stroked each other. Then, as darkness began to envelope us, we'd decide on dinner.

Twenty minutes later I was in my office. Marie, my secretary, brought me a fresh cup of coffee. She told me Joe Lieberman had called a meeting for 10.30.

"What's up?"

"Nothing," she said. "You know how slow August is. Rumor is he wants people to take vacations now." Marie laid a bundle of files on my desk. I recognized them from the night before. "These are all done," she said, scooping up others I had in the 'out' tray. "You remember last year," she continued, "when half the advertising department was asked to take a week off. All part of the new management philosophy on cutting costs."

"Yeah," I said. "I remember. He just wants everyone fresh and rested for the post Labor Day-Thanksgiving rush." I sipped my coffee and wondered whether I wanted to take a week or not. Maybe Katherine would go somewhere with me. Marie tucked the files under her arm and went to the door. Before she left she said, "Oh yeah, George Brown called this morning. He said the agency has another idea for the fall campaign and wanted to run the space requirements by you, see what's open."

"What did you tell him?"

"That you're probably flexible until the first week of September but to not let it wait, that you've already got a lot booked. He said he'd call you this afternoon with more specifics. He's got a lunch downtown or something."

Most secretaries today just type and answer the phone, take messages. For most of them it was a nine to five thing with an hour of shopping sandwiched in there somewhere. Not Marie. Marie liked to be involved. She's motivated. And loyal. She unabashedly hitched her wagon to mine with the intention of following me all the way to the top, which was fine with me except I wasn't sure I could live up to her expectations. She wanted to know what was going on at all times, not just inside my office, but outside it also. She knows all my contacts, clients, agencies, and the people above and below me and they know her. I trust her enough so that when I am not around, say at lunch or something, or a day off, she can field important calls, actually talk to them intelligently, and get something done. She's a schmoozer and gives, as they say, good phone. I can't tell you how many times she's saved my ass. Joe Lieberman has always threatened to steal her away from me but Marie says she wouldn't go anyway. She knows if she did she wouldn't get the freedom I give her.

"Oh," Marie called back to me as she sat at her desk. "I almost forgot. He said to tell you the Hudson Agency got the Banker Brothers account." She turned and smiled and I knew she had been waiting to tell me this. "That's where Jim Collins is, isn't it?"

"Right," I said, smiling back through the doorway. With my old pal Jimmy running the account I knew I could ease in some increases. Joe will be happy. I wondered if I should tell him at the meeting or wait until I have lunch with Collins.

At 10.30 I went to the meeting. Right off Joe asked if anyone wanted to take a week's vacation and only two guys volunteered. Joe looked annoyed.

"I'm telling all of you to take a week. I want only two in the office. This is coming from the top. The place is dead right now."

Joe rubbed his chin and ran his hand through his thinning hair. He knew there were complications. Like last year. Some guys put in for time last June and July and were just back, which meant they'd used their vacation time already. That meant a week off with no pay or use up their remaining sick days. Others had wives and kids and vacations planned for times other than now. There were moans and mumbling. I said I would take a week off. A few more reluctantly volunteered time and somehow schedules got worked out. Finally the meeting was over and Joe, a little disgruntled, called me over.

"I'm getting some bad vibes from upstairs," he said. "Shit's starting to roll downhill."

"What's up?"

"They want me to make evaluations, they're looking to reduce staff and consolidate. I'm a little worried." Joe looked serious.

"What are you saying?" I asked.

"I don't know what I'm saying yet. That's what I'm saying. I don't know what the fuck is going on. Eddie Carbone in Circulation has to do the same thing."

"Jesus, Joe."

"I know. Look, maybe I'm just being paranoid, I don't know. With all this new computer shit and new business models and all the shit I hear from upstairs I don't exactly know what it means." Joe turned to me. "Look, you're with me, Jed. Don't worry about that. What you gotta worry about is me."

"Jesus, Joe," I said again.

"Listen," Joe lowered his voice. "Keep this quiet, will ya?"

"Sure, Joe."

I went back to my office and did some work. I thought about what Joe said and I did what I usually do when bad stuff happens I can't control. I tried to ignore it. I checked my calendar to see which week would be best to take off and decided the last week of August, the one before Labor Day. I'd get an extra long weekend tacked onto the end. Maybe I'd go somewhere. Maybe I'd go somewhere with Katherine. Maybe Nantucket or Maine. Definitely not the Hamptons. I hated the Hamptons. Aside from all the pretentious posturing and the decidedly crass behavior of young newly rich New Yorkers the place simply leaves a bad taste in my mouth. It is *Long Island*, after all. And that is something you just can't ignore. No way. When I leave New York I want to leave it behind, *way* behind. Not transplant myself to a place where I will run into all the people I am trying to avoid. And just because it has a beach doesn't necessarily redeem it. After all, the world is full of beaches. Iran has beaches, so does Saudi Arabia and the Gaza Strip. Doesn't mean I'd go there on a week off from work.

At 1.00 Marie came back from lunch and I decided to run out and get a sandwich. Thinking about taking Katherine away for a week got me going again and I wondered if she really did have any options about the money. What would a lawyer say? Probably should run this by Morris before we pursued it any further, I thought. If she told her lawyer she changed her mind about the settlement, that she wanted more money, what would he say? Katherine said she wanted it all, whatever that meant, and in any kind of settlement, even one that favored you, you never got it all. At best, as far as I knew, you got half. Katherine seemed pretty adamant about *all.* Also, I imagined a lawyer's first response would be 'Sure, we can try.' Think of all the billable hours. It wasn't as if the money wasn't *there.* The question then became; how much would be left after a protracted legal fight? Katherine said there were tens of millions. What was wrong with just five? What was Cahill and Company worth? Was it worth what Steve indicated in the will? Owners of companies usually overstate their value. Was it even in the will? Were there any trusts? What about his father's company? Did he own any stock in that as well?

I walked out of my office and over to Forty-Second Street

toward Bryant Park. I realized there were a lot more questions that needed to be answered before Katherine could simply say she wanted it all, that she deserved it. What would she say? That she helped Steve run a ring of call girls in order to extract inside information on mergers and acquisitions, on IPO's, or upcoming patent and FDA approvals? And that because of Katherine's integral role she deserved all the money? Hell, a judge would forget about Katherine's miserable divorce and launch an investigation. SEC, New York District Attorney, U.S. Attorney, Christ, who knows what else? Those tens of millions would end up being spent on white shoe lawyers for chrissakes.

No. When you think about it this was much more complicated than simply saying you got gypped in the divorce. That you changed your mind, that you wanted more money than you originally asked for. I knew enough to know a judge in his right mind wouldn't reopen a closed case without a compelling reason. The sex for inside information angle, though, would certainly amount to a pretty compelling reason.

I got a sandwich and a coffee and sat on a bench in Bryant Park. The sun was warm but it wasn't humid which was unusual for August. It felt fine and pleasant sitting in the park. There were lots of pretty young women sitting on the grass eating and talking and young men in white shirts with their sleeves rolled up and their ties thrown over their shoulders like the ends of leashes tethered to their offices. Half of them were talking on cell phones and waving half eaten sandwiches around. You could tell the ones making deals and the ones losing them.

There was one pretty young woman near me sitting alone on the grass reading a magazine. She was stretched back with her legs straight out and then she pushed her knees up and as she did so a light puff of summer breeze caught her dress and lifted it for a second or two. I caught a quick glance of her black lace panties. She caught my eye and quickly smoothed out her skirt before deciding to turn around completely, leaving me only her back. The moment caused me not to think of her but to think of Katherine and her kisses of the night before. I had been in love with Katherine for years, or the image of her, like a movie star maybe, or a model, and my desire to have her had only increased since Monday. To be honest I was disturbed by the story she told of Steve and her involvement and a distinct impression was building in me that there was a lot more to this story than appeared. Once or twice I had sensed a lie, or a half truth, like she was holding back and not revealing everything. I needed more from her, more about Steve's business, more about his company. I needed to be able to ask the right questions. I thought of the famous bank robber Willie Sutton. When asked why he robbed banks he replied, "Because that's where the money is." Katherine wanted more money. I needed to know more about Steve's company. The money came from there, I reasoned, therefore it only made sense to start there.

I finished my sandwich and coffee and went back to my office. Marie was on the phone when I walked in but she waved a handful of pink message slips at me as I walked by her. I grabbed them and sat at my desk. There was one from Katherine. All it said was, "Call her."

FOURTEEN

"DO YOU WANT TO COME up after work and see the thing? See the will?"

Katherine's voice was unemotional. As if she was talking about a new toaster oven or something.

"Sure," I said.

"What time?"

"6.30 or 7.00."

"I'll have drinks ready."

"Terrific."

"We can go out and get a bite afterward."

"Great."

"See you then," she whispered. A breathy light puff like the gentle breeze that pushed up the young woman's skirt in Bryant Park. It teased me. It was the only sentence Katherine spoke which had any life to it. And I knew she meant it.

I quickly busied myself with some account files on my desk barely hearing the humming white noise buzzing around my floor. To get my mind off Katherine I thought about what Joe had said at the meeting. He asked me to keep it quiet, not to mention it to anyone. No one knew yet, he said, except him and Eddie Carbone in circulation. Joe said I didn't have to worry, I was with him. But whatever happened to Joe, I knew, would ultimately involve me.

Could this be true, I wondered? The *Times* downsizing? This is the 1990's, after all, the longest economic expansion in the nation's history. Times were good, not bad. But I had gleaned enough from the business pages over the last few years to know labor had taken a back seat to progress in the 1990's. The group that was the most important now was the shareholders. And not just our own. Everybody, it seemed, owned stock. If you didn't own any stock in the 1990's then you missed the biggest free ride that ever existed. Wall Street was in the business of printing money in the 1990's. It came in the form of IPO's, technology stocks, mergers and acquisitions, buy-outs, collateralized debt obligations, junk bonds, you name it. If it didn't exist some Wall Street whiz kid would invent it. Everybody owned stock in the in 1990's, even the blue collar wage earner. And if Coca-Cola had to lay off five thousand people in order to improve earnings no one said a thing just so long as their stock went up.

The *Times* had embarked on a big expansion program in the 1990's. They built a new state of the art printing plant in New Jersey. All digital. It eliminated about five hundred jobs, mostly pressman and typesetters. They went to color photographs. They could produce more pages in the same amount of time so they expanded sections and added some more which allowed for much more advertising space. Then, of course, the whole website thing. They had created an advertising office just for the website, separate from ours, and Joe hadn't liked that. The *Times* was preparing for the 21st Century and had spent a lot of money in the process. But to spend a lot of money you first had to make it. And if you weren't making enough of it you had to save it or make it somewhere else. Budget cuts. Lay-offs. Increases in the price of the paper and the advertising that goes in it. A big advertising campaign to increase circulation. The

Times had developed regional and national editions in the 1990's. You can buy today's *Times* in any city in the United States and some parts of Europe. If you want to survive you have no choice but to stay ahead in this new world. But let's face it. My department, along with some others, was still mired in the 20th Century. A remnant, a leftover. Like copy-boys and runners. If there were going to be any cuts or lay-offs they would look at us first. They had shareholders to answer to. Ever since lunch a question had begun to form in my mind: should I begin thinking about another line of work? Joe expected my confidence but in this case I wasn't sure I could afford to give him that. Friend or not, he was talking about my future.

"Marie," I called over. She didn't hear me. I picked up my phone and dialed her extension.

"Yes?"

"Get me Mickey Thompson's extension, would you?"

"You want me to connect you?"

"Sure."

Mickey Thompson is a financial reporter for the *Times* and a friend of mine. He came to the paper from one of the tabloids as a sportswriter. We are about the same age and as it turned out we went to the same private school in Manhattan although we were two grades apart and didn't know each other. When he first came to the paper we'd drink together after work, the Lion's Head in particular, but other places too. He was a good sports writer and knew a lot of people but when he came to the *Times* he wanted to be a financial reporter, not a sports repor-ter. This was in the late 1980's at the height of the takeover battle for RJR Nabisco. An event now looked upon as the one that ushered in the 'roaring nineties.' At least on Wall Street. Mickey had followed the takeover fight with the passion of a true aficionado. He told me then, "It's the new blood sport, Jed. It's where all the action is now. Forget heavyweight boxing or the NFL. Athletes make too much money nowadays; it's taken the edge off. Sports headlines aren't about great plays or a team's strategy anymore, they're about how much money Michael Jordan is going to get in his next contract. Magic Johnson is building movie theatres for chrissakes. Uh-uh, pal. You want to see real blood and guts? You want to see some real competitors beat the shit out of each other? Go to the boardroom. Go to Wall Street. That's where the action is. Forget Madison Square Garden."

And Mickey dived in with all the gusto and vigor of a dedicated enthusiast. He was like a kid who had discovered a new game and found he was good at it. He badgered the *Times* by day and took courses at night. Basic economics, marketing, statistics and analytical theory. By the early 1990's he was as well versed in corporate finance, mergers, acquisitions, and takeover battles as he had been in handicapping the Belmont Stakes, Major League batting averages, or the fine art of the three point shot in the NBA. Eventually the *Times* relented, Mickey was a good reporter, and moved him from the sports page to the business section.

"Mickey," I said, "Jed Chase."

"Jed, my friend, how's tricks in advertising?"

"Don't know, pal. Hearing weird stuff floating around upstairs."

"What kinda stuff?" I had Mickey's undivided attention. I could tell. He was a reporter. He had the ear.

"Don't know. Weird shit. Maybe bad shit. Thought you might have a handle."

"Uh-uh," he said. I could hear the gears clicking in his brain. "I'm wrapped up in that Crazyhorse dot com thing right now," he said, lowering his voice. "Haven't heard anything about us. What are you hearing?"

"Best to talk it over a drink."

"Roger that. How about tonight? After work?"

"Can't tonight. Tomorrow."

"Okay," Mickey said. He was disappointed. He wants to know *now*. Was it a story? "All right, tomorrow. How about the Lion's Head? I'm going to be downtown anyway. Say 6.00?"

"6.30," I said.

"See you then, Jed. Hey," he said.

"What?"

"You talking to anyone else about this?" He was in full reporter mode now.

"No. And I won't."

"Thanks, Jed. See you tomorrow."

FIFTEEN

I WAS AT KATHERINE'S AT 7.00. The doorman didn't know me so he politely asked who I was before he rang up Katherine's apartment. "Who shall I say is here?" he asked.

"Her cousin," I said.

He repeated it to Katherine twice before he said, "Go on up."

Katherine lived on Park Avenue between Seventy-Fourth and Seventy-Fifth Streets. It was Steve's apartment now. Major high rent district. Katherine had been looking for an apartment and was in the process of packing her things. She was going to put them in storage until she found one. She didn't seem to be in much of a hurry. Finding an apartment, that is. Given both their schedules they had been able to work out an amicable arrangement to share the space until Katherine was able to relocate. Steve was away a lot. So to was Katherine.

A lot of apartments in these buildings consist of entire floors and the residents themselves are like members of their own private clubs. It's a subtle, understated, almost incestuous world. These buildings are called co-operatives, which means you don't exactly own your apartment, you own shares in an organization that owns your apartment. They have been in existence in New York City since the late nineteenth century. In return for being a shareholder in the organization you receive an open ended lease to an apartment. You can live there as long as you want as long as you don't violate your lease which includes a monthly maintenance fee that is used to operate the building. There are general things of course, like behavior and noise and who your friends are, but the key is financial ability. Most of these buildings don't even allow a mortgage. You must pay for it in cash. In order to buy an apartment, or rather, buy shares in one of these organizations, one of these co-operatives, you must be approved by the board of directors of the co-operative. The board of directors, and only the board of directors, decides who is 'qualified' to buy shares in their co-op, who ultimately can live in their building. There is no law in the country that can change that. There is no such thing as equal opportunity on Park Avenue. Fair housing act? Not here. In effect, they are private, closely held corporations. They can decide to do whatever they want. Whether they conform to the traditional standards of society is not an issue. It is a legal way to determine who you want to live near, to choose who your neighbors are. To challenge them would be to challenge the essence of capitalism and the right to private property. In effect, you would be challenging the very concept that made America, well, America.

In New York, if you lived in one of these buildings on Park Avenue, or Fifth Avenue or any number of other blocks on the Upper East Side, you had, as Tom Wolfe might say, the 'right stuff.' You were at the top of the top. Steve Cahill had the right stuff. And the right stuff on this stretch of Park Avenue meant lots of money, the right friends, and deep connections to the world that operates behind closed doors.

It is a well-known fact that high publicity people - people like rock stars, movies stars, sports figures, certain politicians, anyone connected in anyway to the public world, the outside world, were *persona non grata* on this part of Park Avenue. Too much publicity. Too much attention. Too overtly nouveau.

"Those kinds of people," as Brooke Astor famously once said, "can live on Central Park West." Or Tribeca. Or Greenwich Village. Or anywhere else they wanted. Just not in her building. And she, like everyone else on Park Avenue, or Fifth Avenue, or almost anywhere within the blocks between Sixtieth and Ninetieth Streets and Park and Fifth Avenues, depended on their board of directors to make sure of that.

Former President Richard Nixon was turned down by a co-op board. So was Mariah Carey. Her broker told her to dress for the board interview like she was going to a funeral. She wore a thin halter top and a mini skirt (kind of obvious). The newly married son of one of the wealthiest families in America was turned down by a co-op board simply because he was Jewish. Every one blamed the real estate agent for that one. She should have known better. The building had never had a Jew, or any non-Christian, live in it since it was built. This is how serious living on Park Avenue is.

Katherine was right at home in this world and although she never seemed to me to be of it she moved around in it with the grace and charm of the best of them. But, at the same time, when it came to where she lived Katherine was aloof. Not Steve Cahill, though. He knew exactly where he lived and I knew Steve well enough to know if the board of directors had turned him down he would have been devastated, a little piece of him would have been destroyed. The rejection would have followed him around forever, like a shadow. The ghost of real estate past, as it were. No building would have been the same as the one he didn't get into. But Katherine, I knew, couldn't have cared less. To her every building on Park Avenue was the same and the people inside them were the same. I think that's part of why she liked me. I'm not like them but I know them. Like her, I can move around among the best and worst of them but I am not of that world, nor am I intimidated by it. One of my fears though, usually following one of my fantasies of Katherine, was that if she and I ever had some kind of life together would she be happy in Greenwich Village? Or somewhere else other than the Upper East Side? I was pretty sure she would be, but to be honest, I wasn't a hundred percent on it.

The elevator opened onto a plain white foyer facing a door. On one side was a black enameled umbrella stand and a black enameled coat rack. Opposite those stood a small black table with a simple black framed mirror hanging above it. The floor was made of white Italian marble and the walls covered in fine beige silk, and the apartment door, the only door in the foyer, was also shiny black.

I had been here before, a number of times, but the last time had been over a year ago with Sarah. It was just before we split up and I remembered how we used to enjoy coming to Steve and Katherine's parties. Afterwards we would always go back to my apartment and have great sex. For me, I know, it was because I was always aroused after being around a roomful of beautiful women in strapless gowns with their breasts pushed up and smashed together and the rest of their clothed bodies sleek and fine looking and I used to imagine what they looked like underneath. What did the inside of their thighs look like? What kind of underwear did they have on? Were some of these lovely ladies not wearing any perhaps? Some did that, I knew; Sarah had told me once. It would be unseemly, she said, to have underwear lines show through your dress.

Back in my bedroom on Tenth Street, with the lights out and deep into sex, Sarah would imagine we were in an apartment on Park Avenue like Steve and Katherine's. She told me that once. And Sarah always thought for some reason sex and life in general would always be better in apartments like Steve and Katherine's and one day we would be in one too. This was one of the fundamental differences between Sarah and me and was at the root of our breakup. If I had millions, tens of millions, if Katherine and I had tens of millions, Steve's tens of millions say,

I still would have no desire to live on Park Avenue. I like the village. The East Village or Tribeca, too. Even all the way down, in Lower Manhattan, where the city first began. There's real character in those neighborhoods. They're nitty-gritty, charming, and a little rough around the edges. These places I am comfortable in and I would be happier down there than on Park Avenue with my tens of millions. A bigger apartment, to be certain, but I'd stay right there. I can't stand the Upper West Side; you might as well live in New Jersey. And I don't like Murray Hill or Gramercy, either. For that matter, anything above Fourteenth Street.

SIXTEEN

KATHERINE OPENED THE DOOR. SHE was wearing a white terry cloth bathrobe with 'Villa d'Este' embroidered in gold on the breast pocket. Her hair was dry but smelled fresh and clean, as if it had just been washed. I detected the faint odor of lightly scented bath oil and her face and hands glowed with the warm softness that stepping out of a bath gives the skin.

"Hi," I said. "Am I early?"

Katherine leaned forward and kissed me on my cheek. I felt her hair brush my neck.

"No," she said, stepping back into the apartment, letting out a light laugh. "My cousin? Jed, I have no cousins."

"How did you know it was me?"

She laughed again and said, "Come on in, Jed."

She led me through the narrow entrance foyer into the large living room. There were some nice Degas pencil drawings hanging on both walls as well as two small Giacometti sculptures on opposite side tables.

"I'm sorry," she said. "I'm running late. I've been all over the city today and just got home, or rather, just got here."

"I guess that's right," I said. "You can't really call this home anymore. What are you doing about that, anyway?"

Katherine stood in the center of the living room. The sun

hung like a red fireball just above the building across the street, across Park Avenue, throwing a glow into the apartment tinting our skin and the walls and floor orange-red. I could see a uniformed maid pushing a vacuum cleaner in one of the apartments in the building opposite us.

"I just got back from renting an apartment on Seventy-Second Street. It's just until I find something to buy, you know, temporary digs. Most of my stuff still needs to be packed. I've been dreading it. Steve told me to take my time but I don't want to stay here any longer than I have to."

"I don't blame you."

Katherine walked over to the wet bar. I sat on the couch.

"I'm ready to move, though," she said wistfully. "Frankly, I'm tired of this place. I've been here five years. I don't think I'll miss it at all. It was always too stiff, too uppity for me. The snobs who live here are pathetic; the phony niceness, the icicle smiles, I mean, people don't yell in this building, they whisper. Even when they fight."

Katherine dropped ice cubes into two glasses.

"Vodka, right?"

"Please. With a twist of lemon if you have one."

I watched Katherine make our drinks and glanced down at her feet. I don't think I've ever seen her bare feet before. In sandals maybe, but never bare. Her toenails were painted red and I liked that. Then I saw her calves were smooth and I guessed she had shaved her legs while in the bath. I looked back up at her face and in just that moment she had the look that made me love her. She looked both serious and studied and a little naïve, as though right now the most important thing in the world was to make me the best drink she possibly could. My heart warmed with that look and as she half-turned, reaching for the vodka bottle, her robed opened slightly and I could plainly see her breast, full and supple, pale and creamy white and her dark nipple perfectly proportioned in its size and I saw, too, that it was hard and pointed.

I quickly looked away but it was too late. In an instant I had become fully aroused, tingling, my blood rushing madly. Even staring at the building across the street and watching the black maid in her white uniform push the vacuum cleaner back and forth did nothing to distract me or soften me up. I crossed my arms over my lap. Then I crossed my legs. I did not want the embarrassment of Katherine seeing me so aroused.

Katherine brought the two drinks over and placed them on the glass coffee table. There were a few magazines, *Avenue, Yachting World, U.S. News and World Report,* and the *Wall Street Journal.* I picked one up to help distract me but I put it back. I thought it might be rude. Katherine stepped around and sat in the hardbacked chair next to me. I had to turn to look at her. Her robe was loose now and I could see most of her breast when I looked at her. Part of her leg, above the knee, was exposed too and I felt my heart beating wildly. I could actually hear it in my ears thumping away.

"Cheers," she said, raising her glass.

"Cheers," I said, taking an extra long pull on my drink.

"What about the will?" I asked.

"Oh, I almost forgot."

Katherine put her drink down and stood up and said, "Let me get it." She walked out of the living room.

"How did you manage living here all last year?" I called after her. I wanted to get a conversation going and try and get some control back into this situation. "I mean going through the divorce and everything."

She walked back into the living room holding a plain manila envelope and said, "It wasn't that bad, really. He never wanted me to leave anyway and we did get along considering. He was away a lot. Business and stuff, you know Steve. I got away too. Visit my mother upstate, the Caribbean, St. Maarten, you know

Steve has a place down there. Sends clients once in a while. Business write-off."

"I never knew that. You never mentioned it."

"Yeah, well he does. It's nice. Good place to get away to. Right on the beach."

Katherine sat back in the chair as she dropped the large manila envelope on the table. She leaned over and reached for her drink and both her breasts practically fell out of her robe.

"Katherine," I said.

"Yes, Jed?"

Katherine, listen…"

"Yes?"

I looked right into her eyes.

"Look, Katherine darling, if you don't get dressed right now I'm going to have to rip that robe off of you and ravish the living hell out of your body."

I couldn't believe I said that. She didn't flinch. She smiled and slowly stood up. Then she leaned over and kissed me on my mouth. Her delicate breath was moist and her lips soft and warm and as easily as she opened her mouth I felt her tongue enter mine. She took my hand and pulled me up and placing her other hand on me she felt my hardness. Then she whispered, "I wish you would." She led me into the bedroom.

SEVENTEEN

THOSE HOURS IN HER BEDROOM were the most passionate, lustful, wonderful, fantasy fulfilling hours of my life. They were sublime. I had lived my whole life for those hours. I felt as if they were what I had been born for, that my life had been a series of events, causes and actions that ultimately left me there lying naked next to Katherine Cahill. Her arm was flung across my chest, her smooth leg bent at the knee and resting over mine, the hot wetness of her warmth on my thigh, and the once red and orange sky, long faded and gone, had leisurely washed the room through a rainbow of pastels before finally going black.

I knew she had been on this bed before, naked, without me, her legs moving back and forth, her hips rising and falling, with another man, a man I knew, inside her, on top of her, beneath her, between her legs, she doing the same, panting, whispering, gasping. But it did not bother me. It did not matter to me in the least. Perhaps because I knew Steve, knew his faults, his limitations. Perhaps because of something else. But no matter. That was now far past, gone really. It no longer existed for me in this entirely new world. Katherine had me, I knew that. But now I had finally had her. We had at last come together, joined ourselves intimately, and had come to know each other in what

I believed to be the truest sense. My hopes, my dreams, my aspirations about Katherine had finally been achieved.

We had exhausted ourselves and I listened to her breathe softly. The newness, the wonder of desire and discovery, the patience of learning, of wanting to please and to be pleased, to give and take equally, of pure pleasure and excitement, all that lay behind her breathing. Light, soft breaths, baby breaths, breaths at once peaceful, at ease, innocent. I imagine we all breathe this way at some dark hour of the night, whether alone or with someone. But now, in the early evening of this restless Manhattan night, in a darkened room, a silvery-orange wash of street light splashed across us, yellow squares and rectangles illuminated outside the window, a lone star faint in the ambient light, barely visible in the blue black sky above, I doubted there were many souls breathing as Katherine was. Not at this hour. Not in this city.

I studied the curve in her back where her hips joined her waist, the undulating lines smooth and seductive, the skin unblemished, flawless. Her naked bottom quite firm and I knew in years to come that would change but I didn't care. I remembered how her breasts stood above her flat stomach, proud and firm as she lay under me, then on top of me, and I devoured their shape, admired them, how they held their striking form, carried as well as any eighteen year old. She hadn't had children and she was still strong enough, firm enough, to fight gravity, unlike some women her age. In time that would change, she would have children maybe, age would intervene, and her breasts would start to sag as the rest of her but I could not think about that now. For me that was another world, different than this one, and here, deep in the heart of this Manhattan night it did not exist. It could not exist. It could *never* exist.

Now, in this moment, this first chance I'd had to carefully observe her nakedness, I loved her bottom and its firmness, how it had felt when my hands gripped it, how her spine sunk like a small canal snaking along her back, how her shoulders and delicate neck joined in absolute perfection, how her hair lay out like gold threads of silk across the white cotton pillow. As I observed her I realized I did not care that all this would change at some point in the future. I did not care because I would always have this moment, these few hours. And I knew my love for Katherine had become complete, that I loved her as truly as I could, that I accepted her past, no matter what it was, and her future, whatever it might be. Perhaps our future. Who knows? But no matter what, I would always have these hours with her in bed. They belonged to me and nobody, nothing, could take them away.

EIGHTEEN

I GENTLY LIFTED KATHERINE'S ARM and lay it alongside her. She was in a deep, peaceful sleep and I slid out from under her leg. I stood by the side of the bed and watched her stir slightly, then, slowly she turned over onto her back. Then she opened her eyes and saw me standing by the bed. She smiled.

"Ummm...," she said. "What are you doing?"

"I'm thirsty," I said. "That was a long workout."

She smiled again. "Me, too."

"What would you like? Water? Another vodka?"

"We didn't finish our first ones, did we?"

"No, we didn't."

"I'm an awful hostess, aren't I?"

"You're a wonderfully good awful hostess."

She reached over and turned on the light, then sat up and crossed her legs Indian style.

"I want champagne," she said. "Cold champagne. There should be a bottle of Moet in the fridge. There are some flutes by the wet bar."

I returned with the champagne and two crystal Cartier flutes. I opened the bottle, its sober 'pop' sounded sharp and fresh, and poured her a glass. I held mine and said, "A toast."

"Yes," she said. "A toast. A wonderful idea. To us?"

"Of course to us. Finally to us."

"And to the future."

"And to the future. Our future. What ever it is."

"What ever it is."

I slid onto the bed, careful not to spill my glass, and sat across from her, and I too crossed my legs Indian style. We drank our glasses and I refilled them again. The champagne was good. It cut the lingering taste of love in my mouth. In an odd way the wine sobered me up from the drunken hours I had just spent with Katherine. I felt my head clear. Suddenly I realized the two of us were sitting up on the bed naked in front of the bedroom window with the curtains wide open.

"Maybe we should close the curtains," I said.

"No," Katherine said. "Leave them. I like to be able to look out. See the sky. The tops of buildings. Closed curtains make me claustrophobic."

"But people can see in. What about the building across the street?"

"Jed," Katherine said, tilting her head at me. "The people in this neighborhood are so old they can't see each other, let alone anything outside their windows."

And I realized for Katherine there was a certain thrill, or maybe a better word is dare, to have the curtains open on Park Avenue. Let the world look in if they want to. Go ahead, she seemed to be saying, see what I care. In a strange way I felt a thrill too and I realized for all I thought I knew about Katherine there was still more. Much more.

"Okay," I said. "Let's talk about the will."

Katherine took a slow sip from her glass. Her clear green eyes looked right into mine as she reached for my hand. She squeezed it and then let it drop into my lap.

"Essentially it states that everything goes to me except his shares in his father's company. If he predeceases his father they revert back to him. If his father dies before Steve then they go to Steve and then to me."

I poured more champagne. I looked up and I could see in a window across the street a man in a tuxedo and a woman, much younger than him, in a flowing white gown. They stood there looking down at the street.

"Beside that," I said. "What else? What goes to you?"

"Okay. He values his company at twenty-two million. Steve owns sixty percent and Arthur Barrett the other forty. Of Steve's share of sixty percent I'm to get eighty percent of that and Arthur the other twenty. But Arthur controls the company. He has the voting stock. Strictly a business decision and that's fine with me. Then there is five million in cash in a Swiss account and eight million in stocks and bonds here in the U.S. He owns this place, valued at two point nine, and the property in St. Maarten, valued at just under a million. He also has a property in Ireland but I never knew about that, I don't know what it is. He values it at two hundred thousand. He has a car, some art, other stuff like that. All of it is to go to me."

I did a quick calculation and was very impressed with my friend Steve Cahill. Just shy of forty and he had made a small fortune of twenty, twenty-five million dollars.

"And what did you agree to in the divorce settlement?" I asked.

"Two million cash and an apartment."

"And now you want all of it?"

"Yes."

"At best, in a divorce agreement, all you'd get is half."

"I know." Katherine looked at me and then turned away. She downed the rest of her champagne and looked out the window. "Frankly, I don't care about the company and stuff. Just the cash and the stock accounts and the properties. I'd sell the properties. Arthur can do what he wants with the company."

Katherine was all business talking about this stuff. She knew what she was talking about, I could clearly see that. She had given it much thought. Steve's business was not as alien to her as she sometimes professed. Suddenly I felt strangely odd sitting in front of an uncovered window, naked, talking about taking someone else's money. Someone who owned the bed I was sitting on.

"Why do you think he hasn't changed his will?"

"Honestly?" Katherine held her glass up. I poured each of us another. I was beginning to feel lightheaded.

"I don't think he intended to. Not yet anyway. He knew I'd be here packing. He knew I'd find it. He left it in a place where he knew I'd see it. He wanted me to find it. He wants me to see what he's worth, wants me to see what I am leaving – wants me to see what his intentions were about me. He thinks it will change my mind about the divorce." Katherine looked at me. "I don't think he thought the divorce would come through until after he got back from London. The truth is, I thought that, too. Our lawyers both said after Labor Day."

"Does it? Does it change your mind?"

"No."

"Now that you know what he's worth, what his intentions were about you, you wouldn't change your mind, you wouldn't stay?"

Katherine's eyes turned cold as she looked at me. "No," she said. "You don't know him, Jed. You think you do, but you don't."

"Well," I said, downing the last of my champagne, my head swimming in it now. "Like I said before, the only way I know how you can get the money, all of it, is if he dies. Has an accident, gets killed." And just like a few hours ago, when I told Katherine I was going to rip her clothes off, I couldn't believe I had just said that. It must be the champagne, I thought. I was a little loose, my head high between fulfilling a ten-year-old fantasy and drinking on an empty stomach. And looking at

Katherine I could see I was more shocked at what I said than she was. She looked at me, holding my eyes with hers, a serious darkness in them, and as she placed her glass on the night table she said, "I know. I've thought about that, too."

But before I could follow that up she put her hand on me and pushed me onto my back and began to kiss me. I was immediately aroused again and as she put her mouth to mine my mind jerked back and forth between what Katherine was doing to me and what we had just talked about. The inference of what was just said was undeniable. How did we get to the point of suggesting Steve's death? And who, I wondered, had really suggested it? Katherine got on top of me and put me inside her and as she began to move her hips up and down I turned my head and saw we were making love with the curtains drawn back and the lights on. All of Manhattan, if it wanted to, could look in and watch us.

NINETEEN

THE NEXT DAY I MET Mickey Thompson at the Lion's Head. We said 6.30 but I got there early. I wanted a few minutes to gather my thoughts which had preoccupied me all day.

Before I left Katherine the night before she made omelets and we sat in her dimly lit dining room wearing bathrobes and eating slowly, our hunger deepened by the long hours of sex and the hollowness that comes after drinking on an empty stomach. She told me once again, between bites, that because of "certain things" between her and Steve, she wouldn't "cry at his funeral." As she finished her omelet she mentioned the convenience of a "fatal accident." And I was surprised, as I was earlier, at the oblique implication. In the sobering atmosphere of the dining room, with dim yellow light casting shadows across her face, I saw a deadly seriousness. A deadly seriousness to the tune of around fifteen million dollars. Was I surprised by her motive? More no than yes. Was I surprised that she would confide this in me? Maybe. Was I surprised that this woman, whom I had just made passionate love to, suddenly seemed capable of causing a fatal accident? A death? A murder? Absolutely.

I had been bothered all day by her implications, her inferences, regarding Steve and his money, about how she wanted it, about how she thought of getting it from him. It began to gnaw at me when I left her apartment in the early hours of the morning and even more when I got home to my own apartment. It bothered me when I woke up and bothered me all day while I was at work. And it bothered me now as I sat in the Lion's Head waiting for Mickey Thompson.

The fact that Katherine and Steve hadn't had the perfect marriage wasn't something new to me. During her divorce she had mentioned tales of unhappiness, Steve's sometimes cruel treatment of her, his arrogance, his frequent absences. Morris Bergman, who knew Steve vaguely from college but was introduced to Katherine by me, reiterated and confirmed those tales in her complaint as plaintiff. So yes, there was a history of unhappiness at which, I must admit, I had been secretly pleased. Crocodile tears and all that.

During the past year I had seen myself as a white knight of sorts, there for Katherine, supportive, on her side. But the fact that she confided in me her wishes for Steve's untimely death caught me by surprise. Even the subtle implication of it, the mere suggestion, was something I could not get myself around. And I wondered, sitting here in the Lion's Head waiting for Mickey Thompson, what Katherine really meant two nights ago when she asked me to help her. I loved her, to be sure, but I sensed she was right that just because she sat naked before an open window didn't mean she could be seen.

TWENTY

"IT'S THE J-MAN."

Mickey Thompson walked into the Lion's Head as I imagined he walked into any place. As if everyone here had been waiting for him, was glad he was finally here, and now they could back to their drinks and newspapers. Mickey nodded to Paul and two guys at the end of the bar I didn't know.

"Hey, Mick," I said, sticking out my hand. He shook it as he sat down heavily on the bar stool. He dropped his worn leather briefcase on the beer stained floor. He had oblong sweat stains under his armpits and his back had a racing stripe of sweat right down the middle. He took a bar napkin and dabbed at his forehead.

"Fuckin' hot out there, buddy. Man oh man. Stand on the platform of the number one and you'll lose ten pounds. Like a fuckin' Swedish sauna down there. How 'bout a cold one Paul?"

"Ain't seen you around, Mickey," Paul said, placing a perspiring mug of beer before him, white foam slipping down its sides.

"Ahhh, don't remind me, Paul. My wife says the same thing."

We touched glasses and drank. I nodded over to the corner where Katherine and I had sat two nights ago. Mickey stood up and grabbed his briefcase and we walked over with our drinks.

Mickey took a small black leather notebook out of his briefcase and flipped a few pages. I watched his eyes move up and down before he closed the notebook. He looked at me and said, "All right, Jed, what do you hear?"

"Nothing concrete, more than a rumor though. My department was told yesterday that we're having an evaluation. Eddie Carbone's too. He's circulation. The fear, of course, is cutbacks and lay-offs. I don't know when. I know you got a good nose for the media, the business side, and I thought you might know something. Joe Lieberman is shitting bricks. And Joe never shits bricks. I wouldn't be talking to you otherwise. If I'm going to get pushed down to the loading dock I'd like to know now rather than later. Give myself a shot somewhere else. Know what I'm saying?"

Mickey knew full well what I was saying. It's what he reported on, wrote about, made himself a name on. I knew for a fact Mickey had, at least once, tipped off two senior VP's who had been sources at a Fortune 500 company of their company's impending merger. Before they had gotten pink slips they found good jobs elsewhere, re-securing stability. They had come "clean" to their new company, not as "damaged goods." That was the key. To get laid off in your fifties can be devastating, not just to the employee, but to his family, his status, just about everything in his life. To look for a job as "damaged goods" meant you had little, if any, bargaining power. Mickey told me this story during a night of heavy drinking, most of it right here in the Lion's Head. It was a sympathetic moment and Mickey's tongue got loose and afterward he made me swear never to say a thing to anyone. It could cost him his credibility, the only currency a reporter really has, and I promised him I never would. A secret between Mickey and me. Also one of two reasons why I approached him about my department at the *Times.* Mickey, I knew, would give me a wink or a nod if I needed one.

"Okay," he said soberly, opening his notebook again. "The

paper is losing money, not too serious yet, but they're paying attention. Most divisions are pulling their weight but they've just finished modernizing plant and they've invested heavily in the internet. Online news. They believe it is the future. They haven't been able to generate any revenue from it yet and can't really pay for it by the print revenues. This website thing is like a vacuum cleaner in a room full of cash. They know it's the future, the *Journal* is doing it, so is the *News,* so they have to. They've hired a consulting firm, primarily focusing on operations. That's all I know. And what I know doesn't come from the office but a personal friend downtown, an analyst who specializes in media properties."

Mickey closed his notebook and sipped his beer. One of the guys he had nodded to when he walked in got up and walked by us on his way to the men's room.

"Hey, Mick," he said, his voice sounding like a bagful of loose stones. "Taking anyone for the play-offs?"

"Yanks all the way, Pete. And you know better than to ask me that."

"Sure, Mick," Pete said as the bathroom door slammed behind him.

Mickey winked at me. "Old writer from the *Sporting News.* Hates the Yankees." Mickey smiled and downed his beer, "Listen, Jed, you know as well as I if this gets out right now the other papers will have a field day. They'd love to do a number on us if they could, you know, big headlines, "TIMES DROPS HATCHET," or, "TIMES HEMORRHAGING." You'd have more defections at the paper than from Cuba in the last five years. The only way to control the story is if we report it first, take it and keep the lead. What I'm saying is it's in your interest to keep a lid on this." Mickey's voice had gotten low and I knew right now I was not Jed Chase his friend but Jed Chase his source.

"You develop a line on this?" he asked.

"What do you mean?"

"You know, you gotta a good source of information? Can you keep it coming?"

"Yeah, sure, anything happens I'll know before it comes down."

It was interesting to see Mickey operate as a professional. He said, "You talk to me and I'll keep you posted on what I hear, deal?"

"No problem, Mick, you got it." I stuck my hand out to him and he shook it. "But there's one other thing," I said.

"What's that?"

"I'm wondering if you could find out about a company, maybe a couple of companies. And some people, too. Down your neck of the woods."

"Sure, Jed, shoot."

"You ever hear of an outfit called Cahill and Company?"

TWENTY-ONE

EVERY SECRET HAS A HISTORY. Katherine's secret, her secret plan, didn't influence my feelings toward her. I was infatuated from the beginning. I clearly remember the evening in the Brighton Grill ten years ago when I first met her. I remember how the June sun cast shadows over us as we stood by the window in the moment before dusk. The early summer air was light and sweet and only moments before, when Katherine and Steve walked in, it was like he wasn't even there. I only saw her. Katherine's beauty had stunned me then, as it still does now, and her sly glances toward me that first time had cut through something that I still feel now. Steve, I remember, was barely able to contain himself. He, clearly, was as infatuated with her as I.

And that I had, in that instant, fallen in love with a woman I didn't even know frightened me. And excited me. My first fantasies about her began that night in the taxi home. And this I remember thinking, too. That judged by her flirting glances at me, her teasing smiles, she seemed to be encouraging me – *call me,* she seemed to be saying. *Steal me away from Steve.* This is what I thought ten years ago on the first night I met Katherine. But, of course, I didn't. I don't know why. Perhaps I was afraid, intimidated by that kind of beauty. It was that powerful.

But now Katherine and I had a secret. It involved Steve and he didn't know it. And the secret was what Steve's will meant to Katherine. If Steve had intended for her to find the will with the hope of keeping her he was gravely mistaken. Our secret, Katherine's and mine, was that her finding the will meant something all together different. Completely, totally, and perhaps even fatally different. That's what she wanted to share with me. What she meant when she said, "It's our secret." And now I wondered about that secret. Would it draw us together? Or pull us apart? All that was alive for me now was the need to know the future of my desires.

TWENTY-TWO

WHEN I GOT HOME FROM the Lion's Head there was a message from Katherine. "Call me," she said. "At Steve's." I felt the now familiar tingling. A bead of sweat ran down my neck. I turned the air conditioner full on and looked out the window at Tenth Street and remembered how her breasts looked yesterday when she sat across from me on the bed. Their roundness at the bottom, how perfectly curved they were where they met her ribs, how her nipples pointed at forty-five degree angles. No longer did I have to wonder what they looked like. Now I knew.

I stood before the air conditioner and remembered what Mickey had said about the heat. My shirt was damp just walking home from the Lion's Head, only a few blocks away. I hadn't really noticed but since yesterday a heat wave seemed to have invaded the city. I guess I was too preoccupied with my own heat wave to notice. The newspapers were saying it was the hottest day of the year. The last time the temperature reached a hundred, the papers said, was forty years ago.

But the weather could not distract me away from Katherine. I went into my bedroom and loosened my tie and thought of her body, her smooth, velvety skin, and the way her bottom curved away from her back. All day I had been dizzy with thoughts of her, of the sex we had yesterday. It was hard to do any work at the office. Even Marie noticed something and asked if everything was all right. Today was the first day of a new life with a woman I had been obsessed with for ten years. I felt like a teenager.

I undressed, took a quick shower, put on a fresh shirt and a pair of khakis. I went into the kitchen and replayed her message. Just hearing her voice was enough to arouse me now. Fantasy had become reality. I made a drink and called her.

"I've been thinking of you," she said. "About last night."

"Me too."

"I missed you today."

"Me too."

"You miss you, too?"

"No. I miss you."

"Ummm..."

"What are you doing?" I asked.

"Right now?"

"Yes."

"Sitting in my living room sipping a glass of champagne."

"Steve's living room."

"You're so precise. You could say my former living room."

"You could," I said, pausing for a moment, then, "what are you wearing?"

"Nothing," she whispered.

"Nothing?"

"Just my panties."

"Just your panties?"

"Just my panties."

"Are dressing or undressing?"

"Depends."

"On what?"

"On you."

"Oh," I said. "I see." I liked this game and I slowed it down by taking a long pull on my drink. I felt the dull coldness on my teeth. The ice tingled in the glass.

"You're having a drink, too."

"How do you know?"

"I can hear you." I heard her breathe into the phone and she said, "I want to see you."

"Me too."

"Last time I checked there were over ten thousand taxis in New York City. I'm sure a resourceful man such as yourself can manage to find one. What do you think?"

"I think I might be able to manage that," I said. I finished my drink. "Have you eaten?"

"No," she said. "I'll wait for you if you want."

"Yes," I said. "Wait. We'll get something," and I paused before I said, "later."

"We like to eat late, don't we?"

"Yes," I said. "We do."

There was silence and I could hear her breathing. I wondered what she was thinking. Then she said, "I want to show you something when you get here." Her voice took a turn, it was different in tone and her teasing words were now serious. I heard her light a cigarette and inhale deeply.

"What?" I asked.

"You'll see when you get here." I heard her exhale slowly and I thought I detected a mournful sadness in the way she sighed. Then she hung up.

TWENTY-THREE

WHEN I GOT TO KATHERINE'S there was a different doorman than the one the night before.

"What's your name?"

"Just say her cousin."

"I need a name," he said.

"Arthur," I told him. "Tell her it's Arthur."

And like the doorman the night before he had to repeat it twice before he said, "Go on up."

Katherine was at the door when I stepped out of the elevator. She looked surprised to see me.

"Don't do that," she said sternly. "I don't like it. It's not funny."

"Did you really think it was him?" I asked, surprised at her anger.

"Just don't do that," she snapped. Her voice was harsh and serious and I realized I upset her. She was dressed and I was disappointed. We walked into the living room and she made me a drink. She poured herself a glass of champagne.

"The first time I met you," I said, holding out an olive branch, "you were drinking champagne."

"I don't remember," she said, still cool.

"Yes. You were, it was June, I think. Brighton Grill. With Steve."

Katherine looked at me, the hardness dissipating, softening. "Oh yeah," she said slowly. "That place on Third Avenue we used to go to. I remember now."

The ice, it seemed, had broken a little but I was disappointed she didn't remember, at least right away. She seemed distracted. Perhaps my little prank with the doorman was a bad idea, I don't know, but whatever it was Katherine's mood had changed since our phone call an hour ago.

"Wait," she said, handing me my drink. "I remember now. Late spring or summer, one of my first dates with Steve. Brighton Grill. I never liked that place. Seventy-Fourth or Seventy-Fifth Street. Is it still there? You were wearing khakis and an oxford shirt, like you are now. You were drinking beer then. I remember thinking how much more handsome you were than Steve."

And just that quickly not only had the ice melted, it had evaporated, along with my disappointment. I smiled.

"Yes," I said. "That's right. You do remember after all." She looked at me and shot me a shy smile. Then she re-filled her champagne glass. I walked over to the wide window and looked out into the evening light. I looked down the avenue sixteen stories below and watched the stoplights change from green to yellow to red, one right after the other, like a row of dominos falling, all the way down Park Avenue to the old Pan Am building. It's now called the Metropolitan Life building or something like that but to me it will always be the Pan Am building. I think for a lot of people it will always be the Pan Am building. That's New York for me. The old Pan Am building at the bottom of Park Avenue and timed traffic lights changing and splintered sunlight slicing between tall buildings early on a spring morning. Wisps of steam escaping through manhole covers and bright yellow taxis whizzing by, the hollow sound of their shock absorbers laboring over crude potholes. The singing waiters at Asti or the uniformed doormen at the Waldorf dressed in their crisp gray suits with top hats and white gloves, hailing cabs by blowing whistles. Watching them blow up the balloons by the Museum of Natural History the night before the Thanksgiving Day parade. Or drinking at the bar on the 110th floor of the World Trade Center watching the sun set over New Jersey, tug boats and ferries plying the harbor, Brooklyn and Queens already in shadow, and the city suddenly lighting up like a pile of rough cut diamonds being lit from underneath. This was New York for me and I think for a lot of people who grew up here. Suddenly I felt Katherine slip her arms around me and I turned and kissed her.

"You said you wanted to show me something," I said. She hung her chin over my shoulder and we embraced. "I'm in love with you, Jed," she whispered. "You know that, don't you? I have been for years."

My heart felt like it had stopped and I just stood there. I don't know why but it was difficult to respond, my mouth wouldn't open, my throat seemed constricted, and all I could do was turn my head into her hair and kiss her on the ear. I felt her rub her hands down my back and onto my butt and she pushed me into her. Then she put her hand on me and said, "Before I show you the thing I mentioned – there's something else I want to show you first," she said.

"Oh?" I said. "You've piqued my curiosity." She took my hand and led me toward the bedroom.

"Follow me," she said.

Later, we washed each other in the shower. She was quiet, preoccupied, and I wondered what it really was she wanted to show me. Her attitude seemed to say, 'Just wait,' so I didn't ask. After we dressed we went back into the living room and she opened up some cabinets. There was a television and some speakers and a combination compact disc and video player.

Underneath the television Katherine pushed a hidden button and a door opened revealing rows and rows of video tapes. She reached in and took one out. There was some writing on it but I couldn't see what it said. She slipped it into the tape player, stood up, and turned out the lights. She sat across from me on a chair.

"Sit down," she said brusquely. "This is what I want to show you."

I sat on the couch and watched her play with the remote. Suddenly the screen lit blue and there was static and then the tape began. She paused the tape.

"You'll need a drink for this," she said. "I do, anyway."

"Okay."

She got up and made two drinks and then placed them on the coffee table. I reached for mine and took a big sip. I felt the vodka course through my stomach. Katherine sat back and held the remote and without looking at me said, "Don't hate me for this, Jed. Please. You have to understand, things were, well..." She stopped mid-sentence, looked over toward the window, and let out a slow sigh. She started the tape.

The blue screen disappeared and a dimly lit room came into view. There was a bed, a dressing table, a bureau, and a chair. It could have been a hotel room or the bedroom of a small apartment. I could hear a door open and I saw yellow light spill in from the left. The camera did not move. There was giggling. A man and a woman. I heard the man say, "Show me, show me."

The woman: "No." She laughed. It sounded like Katherine.

The man: "Come on, show me. I have to see you first."

The man came into view. White hair, a little aged, late sixties perhaps. He looked vaguely familiar in a New York sort of way. He could have been someone I did occasional business with, or someone who lives in my building, or even someone I'd seen on the elevator at work, I didn't know, a casual familiarity. I think that happens a lot in New York, familiar faces I mean.

Suddenly a hand, the woman's, came into view and reached for the man's crotch. He stood still and let her rub him.

The man: "You have to show me."

I turned to Katherine. She was looking out the window.

"Katherine," I said. "What is this?"

"Just watch," she said. "You have to see this to know what I'm talking about. About our secret." Her voice was as cold as the North River in January.

Then the woman came into view and I saw it was Katherine. I could tell from the way she looked, the way her hair was done in particular, that this could have been about five years ago. Maybe even around the time she married Steve.

"Katherine."

"Just watch," Katherine said. "Like a movie."

The man pulled Katherine close to him. They kissed. The man stepped back. "Show me," he said again.

Katherine stood before him. Slowly she began to undress. When she was naked the man said, "You are so young. Young and a very pretty girl. But you already know that, don't you? Yes, very pretty." He stepped to the side and blocked the camera. The screen was black.

The man: "How old are you?"

Katherine: "Twenty-four."

The man: "Put on your heels. Yes, that's it. Oh, so nice. Yes, turn a little, yes, oh yes. Okay. Bend over, like you want to pick something up. Yes, very, very, nice. You have a wonderful ass, simply perfect. And your breasts, too. Magnificent. Lovely indeed."

I saw Katherine's head come into view over his shoulder.

Katherine: "Oh, I see what you mean. You're so big."

She led him to the bed and he undressed. She got under the sheets and he followed. She flung the sheet back and put her mouth on him.

The man: "Oh, yes, nice, very nice. Oh baby, so, so nice. Lovely. Yes, oh, yes."

Katherine's head came up. He rolled over and got on top of her. They began to have intercourse and Katherine made a lot of noise, saying things to him, encouraging him. Katherine looked different, acted different, from the way I knew her. I felt like someone married to an actress who was watching his wife have sex on the big screen. Is this what it is like for them?

The man was breathing heavily, I could plainly hear him. Labored breaths, as if he were riding uphill on a bicycle. Katherine was saying, "Yes, yes, harder, fuck me, go ahead." Suddenly the man stopped. He was breathing fast.

Katherine: "No, don't stop, don't stop…"

The man: "Shit. Goddamn it."

Katherine: "What's the matter? Is it okay?"

The man rolled over and lay on his back. Katherine sat up and looked at him. She put her hand on him and rubbed his limp penis.

The man: "Just give me a minute."

Katherine: "Sure, take it easy. It's fine. It happens sometimes." Then she turned her head away from him and looked directly at the camera. She mouthed the word 'fuck' before turning back to the man. She kept rubbing him. They were both silent.

Katherine stopped the tape. She got up and turned on the light. I drained my drink and got up to make another. I was thinking and thinking and my mind was racing. What was she doing to me? Why would she show me something like this? Even if it was years ago? My ears were throbbing. I felt Katherine looking at me. I dropped some ice loudly into my glass. Without turning to her I said, "So what is it you want me to say?"

"Jed," she said, her voice cracking. "That's Steve's father."

TWENTY·FOUR

A SECRET IS A WEAPON and is often used as one. The way my head was reeling, spinning, I couldn't tell how Katherine was wielding this one. I felt like I'd been hit with friendly fire, a casualty of sorts. Was I simply collateral damage in Katherine's war with Steve?

I could clearly see this episode was painful and still had a residual effect on her, no matter how long ago. It was obvious to me now she had been thinking about this for some time, wondering whether or not to show me this tape. I wasn't sure if I was angry or hurt, certainly I was confused. I felt jealous too, but I wasn't sure if I was jealous simply because she had sex with another man or because the other man had something to do with Steve. Don't get me wrong. This is the nineties. And in the nineties sexual histories run deep by the time you are twenty and I knew Katherine was no exception. What was virginity anymore, anyway? A myth? Something that only existed in Saudi Arabia or Pakistan perhaps? A piece of history with medieval overtones? But talking about it and seeing it are two completely different things. To see on tape a woman you love, and loved at the time of the taping, having sex, was quite disturbing for me. That I watched her have sex with her future father-in-law, a man twice her age at least, made it all the more strange. My head was twisted. And the fact that it had been taped in the first place made it downright weird, pathological even.

Seeing it made me wonder whether I truly knew who Katherine was. It was as if the more I learned about her the less I knew. Was I simply being naïve? Did I know her past? For that matter, did I know her present? I thought I did. Or were there vast and profound areas of her life as unknown to me as our future? The tape challenged me to accept everything I didn't know about her. I suddenly felt disoriented. Was I capable of this? Was this too much for her to ask of me? I didn't know, of course, but I did know there had to be a reason why she decided to show me the tape. And there had to be a reason why this event was taped in the first place.

I turned and looked at her. She was quietly crying and she sniffled as she pushed a tear away. Then she turned back toward the window and said, "I'm sorry, Jed." I stood still and just looked at her. Through the window I could see the sky turning dark; lights were beginning to go on in the windows across the street. "I swear I didn't know it was him," she said. "I had no idea."

Suddenly I remembered something in a novel I had read recently. It was a love story, tragic of course, and it was about an affair between a married woman and a single man. At one point, as the man watches the woman leave his apartment to go back to her husband, the writer asks the rhetorical question, "Don't we forgive everything in a lover?" And suddenly I realized I knew what the answer was. Yes, I thought. Of course we do. Forgiveness protects lovers. Forgiveness is a shield, a coat of armor. When you lose the ability to forgive you lose the ability to love. I knew now exactly what the writer meant. It's the element most crucial when it comes to true love. And the element now that would help me to forgive Katherine for what I saw on the tape. Forgiving her kept the event in the past and away from our present. My forgiveness isolated it, like a cancer, and the next step would be to cut it out.

"Why were you there?" I asked.

"Oh God," she cried.

I stepped up to her and put my arms around her. I felt her go limp a little, resting her head on my shoulder. I held her.

"Oh Jed," she said. "Do you still love me?"

And although I had never told her I did I said, "Yes."

She stepped back and looked at me, her eyes wet, her nose runny. She pulled a tissue from her pocket, blew her nose, and dabbed at her eyes. "Steve," she said. "I didn't know it but he arranged the whole stupid thing."

"What?"

"He set it up. He and Arthur. They made me do it."

"I don't understand, Katherine. You mean you were part of the sex thing they had going? You were part of that?"

"No, but..." She turned away for a moment and when she turned back her eyes began to well up again. She put the tissue to her face. "I'm so ashamed," she cried. "I'm so awfully, awfully ashamed," she drew in her breath, "what he did to me."

"Come on," I said. "Let's get out of here. Go for a walk or something. Get some fresh air."

Katherine looked at me. "Yes," she said, "that would be nice, let's go somewhere else."

I finished my drink while Katherine went to the bathroom to clean herself up.

TWENTY-FIVE

IT WAS TOO HOT TO walk. We were perspiring by the time we reached the corner of Seventy-Fourth Street. Odors of ripe garbage and dog piss rose from the sidewalk and the air was thick like steam and stagnant like a swamp. We got a cab but it was no better. Even with the thin air conditioning it was cooler if we rolled the windows down. The driver wore a turban and had a long thick beard and I figured one hundred degrees heat and ninety percent humidity was probably normal where he came from. My shirt was already sticking to me. Strands of Katherine's hair stuck to her temples.

I told the driver to go to Eighty-First Street and Lexington Avenue. I knew a small place there but Katherine said, "No. Let's get out of this neighborhood. Especially Eighty-First Street."

"Okay," I said. "Where?"

"Take me anywhere. Just not up here. Take me away from here."

Katherine reached for my hand and held it in my lap. She squeezed it tight and stared blankly out the window. Her eyes looked strange in the orange and yellow street light, dark and hollow, a little empty. I leaned up and spoke through the plexiglass partition.

"Take us to West Tenth and West Fourth," I said. "In the Village."

Greenwich Village is the only area of Manhattan where the streets run rampant, outside of the grid that was the rest of Manhattan. In the rest of Manhattan the streets ran east and west and the avenues ran north and south, all in an orderly fashion. An organized pattern. A grid. Not in the Village. There they were a hodgepodge of both numbers and names, streets intersecting other streets, avenues intersecting other avenues, and plainly no rhyme or reason to any of it. There were alleys and mews, places and squares. If you wanted to go to where West Fourth Street, Grove Street, Seventh Avenue, Waverly Place, and Christopher Street intersected you said you wanted to go to Sheridan Square. There is a MacDougal Street and a MacDougal Alley, a Charles Street and a Charles Place, a Green-wich Avenue and a Greenwich Street, and so on. In the Village the streets were all crooked, reflecting the paths and roads as they were laid out a couple hundred years ago by the farmers who inhabited the area then. When the city implemented the street grid plan in the 19th Century the residents of the area petitioned the city to honor their existing roads and paths, perhaps the first non-conformist act by the area that later became famous for non-conformity. To this day, if you don't know the Village you will undoubtedly get lost. And in a sense, the name all New Yorkers call the area, 'The Village,' couldn't be more appropriate because of this hodgepodge of streets and avenues, of alleyways and mews. Sort of like the souks and medinas in the ancient cities of the Middle East.

The restaurant was called La Canard and was a few blocks from my apartment. I ate there often. It had a green awning with little white ducks on it and a white stucco façade and Philippe Michel, the owner, greeted us at the door. I introduced Katherine. I could tell he was impressed with her beauty. He led us to a table in the back, in the smoking section, where the lighting was only candles and the air conditioning good.

"I love it when you take me places, Jed. It's always something special, different."

"Jed is my best customer," Philippe said. "And when I go back to Paris he's promised to come and be my best customer there, too."

"Is that true, Jed?" Katherine cracked a shy smile, the first since the videotape.

"Only if you come with me," I said. Then, turning to Philippe, I said, "A bottle of your coldest champagne, please. We're trying to fight off the heat of the night."

"Very good."

We sat at the table and I looked at Katherine but before I could say anything she said, "Let me tell you what happened then you can ask me what you want."

"Fair enough."

She took in a deep breath, said, "Okay," and then folded her hands and rested them on the table in front of her. I took out my cigarettes knowing she wouldn't have hers and placed them between us. Philippe appeared with a perspiring bottle of Perrier-Jouet and opened it.

"This should be cold enough," he said, pouring our glasses.

I sipped mine. "Excellent," I said.

Katherine took a long sip and reached for my cigarettes. A waiter silently appeared with a lighter and held it before Katherine. She turned, her neck catching the candlelight causing it to look the color of sand, like a desert at sunset, and she said, "Thank you." Then she turned and faced me.

"Steve and I had been dating for some time. He and Arthur were doing the thing with the girls. Fixing up lonely executives in town for business, they told me; it's done all the time. If they get together that's between them, Steve used to say, it's their business. I sort of knew he was paying them, or Arthur was, whatever, it hadn't really registered with me yet. It was their business. Steve was making a lot of money, I saw that, and they way he mentioned the girls it always seemed to me it was more Arthur than him. I was impressed with Steve. He was older, smarter, confident, and operating in a world I knew little about. Wall Street. He was successful there. To be honest it dazzled me. I grew up on a farm, upstate, what did I know about Wall Street? Steve was obviously a player and he wasn't shy about it. You know him. Cocktail parties, charity events, the whole shebang. And spending money, boy he wasn't shy about that either. On me, on us, whatever. I liked that. I liked it a lot. I won't kid you. It was wonderful, it was New York, a world I had only known from television and magazines. He swept me away. Arthur did too, in weird way. He was much older, had taken Steve in under his wing, and walked around town as if he owned it. One time Arthur took us to dinner at Gracie Mansion and I sat next to the Mayor's wife. Can you imagine that? A woman like me? Twenty-two years old? This was heavy stuff. It blew me away. I wasn't interested in what other twenty-something's were doing, I didn't care about the clubs or singles bars, I was riding in limos, eating five hundred dollar dinners, shopping on Madison Avenue. Ann Taylor? Eileen Fisher? I didn't even know who they were; I shopped at Bergdorf's. If Steve fixed up clients with girls he knew from school or wherever, what did I care? I had a life. I was enjoying myself and I was having fun."

She paused and held her cigarette before her. The gray smoke curled in the candlelight. She reached for her glass, sipped it, then took another drag from her cigarette and blew the smoke out quickly before she continued.

"Anyway, Steve calls me one day and says, 'Look, you've got to do me a favor.' We'd been talking about getting married, nothing definite yet, no dates or anything, but it wasn't about if, it was about when. We knew it was going to happen, that we wanted it. I thought I loved him, I wanted to be a part of his world, I knew that, so when he asked me to do him a favor I'd drop anything to please him. That's me. 'Sure,' I said. 'What?' He says Arthur's got a client who is about to do the biggest IPO in Wall Street history. 'We're talking the big one here, babe,' Steve said. 'Arthur knows him and if we can get this guy we could make some real money. A couple million without even thinking about it.' This is when I knew Steve was going to ask me to go out with this guy and I said, 'No, Steve. Don't. I don't want to do that.' He begged me. He persisted. He was relentless. 'Steve,' I said, 'please don't do this. We're going to get married, how could you ask me this?' 'We're in a spot,' he said. 'Arthur's already got it lined up. We can't say no. I can't get anyone else. I don't want to lose this deal.' I knew how competitive Steve was, I knew all he was thinking about was the deal, but still."

Katherine put out her cigarette and sipped her champagne. She put the glass down and looked me in the eye.

"Then he said he'd give me ten thousand dollars if I did it."

I watched Katherine's eyes fall downward, avoiding mine. I never would have guessed in a million years that I'd hear Katherine tell me she got paid ten thousand dollars to have sex with someone. But it's the past, I kept saying to myself. It's history.

"So you did it," I said.

"Yes."

"How did you know it was Steve's father?"

"I didn't," she said. "I didn't know who it was. It was Arthur's client. Steve was happy, he said don't worry, it's only a night out. But yes, I did it. You saw the tape."

"Steve didn't care? I don't get it."

"No, he didn't. I think he enjoyed it. He has a strange relationship with his father, Jed. And of course, he could watch it on tape. I soon learned that's what he really likes. Watching."

Katherine paused, her voice was now a monotone, reciting

something rather than telling. She lit another cigarette. "Afterward I went home, took a shower, and, to be perfectly honest, felt absolutely terrible. I thought about all kinds of things; Steve, us, our wedding, would we still get married? That night I didn't know 'anymore. Was this some kind of test? I felt lonely and wanted to go home, back upstate. But then I began to think about the ten thousand dollars. I was twenty-four then, I had nothing. Ten thousand dollars was a fortune to me. It was more than a year's rent. I soon forgot about what I had done and thought about the money instead. That's the thing about money, Jed. It's powerful. It can push all kinds of things out of the way. Soon it was like it never happened. When I looked at my bank book it was like the money had always been there. What I had done had disappeared and only the money was real."

Another pause, another cigarette, more champagne.

"It didn't seem to have any effect on Steve at all. He was very nice, became very attentive. I began to wonder if he liked the idea of me having sex with someone else, you know, one of those weird fetish kind of things. Anyway, we never talked about it; it never came up, even if we'd have some kind of spat, an argument. And before I knew it we were married. We did it on our own. You remember that. I had never met his parents before we married. He refused. Said he didn't get along with them, he hated his father. We got married at City Hall, had the big reception at the Plaza, you were there, and then went to St. Maarten for a few weeks. After we got back he called his parents to tell them we got married. They were disappointed we didn't have a wedding. In a way I was too, but I didn't dwell on it. We were married now. Steve's parents wanted to host a small party for us up at their house in Connecticut. It was a quaint, catered affair, with music under a tent outside. We walked up to the house, Steve in a tuxedo (he insisted on it) and I in a long black velvet dress, pearls, white gloves, my hair all done and everything. I was nervous, shy, excited, and when I saw his father I almost choked. We recognized each other immediately. Steve seemed oblivious and I thought he hadn't known the guy Arthur lined up. Had never met him. He was Arthur's guy. First thing I did was run to the bathroom and puke my guts out. His father, of course, looked like he was about to have a heart attack. I was miserable and wanted to go home but was terrified of letting on to Steve. Of course his father avoided me like a leper. Then, during the course of the evening, the way Steve behaved with me and his father, kept telling us to dance, kept bringing me over to his father's table to talk, I realized Steve must know. And then I knew. I knew it was Steve who had set us up. There wasn't any IPO or anything. Steve paid me with *his* money. God knows what his father must have thought. But I knew from that day forward Steve had to have had something to do with setting me up. Through Arthur. Some weird thing between him and his father. I began to believe he married me because he wanted his father to think he had married some bimbo who'd had sex with both of them. And by the time we left his parents' house I knew our marriage was over before it even began."

I poured the rest of the champagne and pushed the bottle into the ice bucket neck first. I thought of Steve and his father and their hateful relationship. This was too strange for me and Steve, well, he seemed to me now simply a sicko. What had he been putting Katherine through all these years? I now saw Katherine as something of an innocent caught between a weirdly strange father son rivalry.

Katherine continued, "To this day I have no idea what that was about. I simply try and forget it. But back then, just when I thought I had made that fateful night disappear, it returned with a vengeance. It began to consume me and became an obsession. At first I treated it like a benign dislike and I tried to ignore it, like before. I thought about Steve's money, and spent it with abandon and total disregard. I soon began to hate him and our marriage became a trade-off. He could show me off at his parties, business functions and such, and I could live the life I wanted, lunch with friends, trips to Europe, anything I wished for. If Steve wanted to pay me to be his whore... well... you get my drift. It became an arranged marriage, a business relationship, as far as I was concerned." She reached over and took my hand. "I knew if I saw you any more than I did something would happen and Steve would get involved and I didn't want that. I wanted a divorce. That's when I found out about the tape. He threatened me with it but I didn't care. It meant nothing to me anymore. I have no idea why he taped us but I knew it had to do with his father, not me."

She squeezed my hand and her eyes got sad. She looked at me hard. "I hate what he did to me, Jed. What he did to us. I hate him so much I wish him dead. I could kill him myself and I sometimes fantasize about it. You know, push him in front of a subway, poison him. The best thing would be a plane crash or a car accident. You have no idea how it feels to be used the way he used me. This is why I asked you to help me. When I saw his will it made me even more angry, more mad. It made me crazy thinking he hid all of that from me. He owes me, Jed. He does. I'm willing to do anything to make him pay. After all, he has the money."

"You could blackmail him," I said and again I surprised myself by mentioning such things. With Katherine it had begun to seem easy.

"I thought about that, but no... it wouldn't work with him." Her voice trailed off as she put out her cigarette.

I realized Katherine was more serious than I thought. I could see that now. I couldn't blame her, either. I didn't know why Steve did what he did. I couldn't fathom anything like it myself and it made me sick just thinking about it. The truth is Steve used her like a tool. He had used a woman I had always loved to exact revenge on his father for God knows what. He used her like an instrument; a pawn in demented and sick scheme and it made me hate him more than Katherine did. Steve Cahill was no longer a friend, an old acquaintance. He had become my enemy.

TWENTY-SIX

AFTER WE ORDERED DINNER AND another bottle of champagne Katherine said, "There are other tapes."

"What?"

"There are other tapes. Steve made other tapes. Some are of me."

Her face was hard, taught, like a drum skin. I'd seen flashes of this before. Like when I told the doorman I was Arthur Barrett. This look was becoming more frequent now it seemed. A shadow passed over her and her eyes became shaded. Her voice was stiff, husky.

"You're not going to want to hear this, Jed. I'm warning you, you're going to hate me now but I won't blame you. I hate myself for it too. But I've not told anyone this and because now you know about Steve and his father you need to know this too. It'll have to be another one of our secrets. One, perhaps, that might ruin us."

Katherine whimpered. It caught me off guard. As if the tight hardened skin had cracked slightly. Her eyes dampened but no tears fell.

"It's all right," I said. "If it has to do with Steve I want to know."

"I'm warning you," she said, dropping her head down, as if

to an executioner. Her voice softened. "You'll not like this. It will make you think different of me. You'll not love me anymore, I am sure."

The waiters brought our appetizers, a plate of oysters on the half shell, lemons, horseradish, and cocktail sauce. I cut the muscle of one and handed it to Katherine. Then I cut one for myself and ate it and washed it down with the champagne, the metallic taste of the oyster battling the wine, and it left my mouth tingling and fresh. Then Katherine began to speak in a drab monotone.

"The apartment has a two-way mirror between rooms. As you saw, the camera is set up in the other bedroom. Steve set all this up. Early on, when he and Arthur started the stuff with the girls, they thought they had a deal with a particular guy they'd set up on a date. He came to the apartment with the girl and that was that. But when his merger happened and they didn't get the deal, Steve got pissed. That's when he decided to set up the camera. If someone wanted to back out of a deal Steve would blackmail them by telling them about the tapes. The tapes were Steve's insurance. He and Arthur used to joke that they had 'self-insured' themselves. Believe me, they used this threat more than a few times. And it worked."

"Where do you come in?" I asked.

"After the thing with Steve's father it wasn't long before I felt like I was simply a hired wife. An ornament for Steve, like a fancy car or a diamond studded watch or something. And the episode involving the ten thousand dollars stayed with me. Then one time I was away, I forget, Florida I think, it was winter, and I came home a day early for some reason. When I walked in Steve was sitting on the couch, naked, his dick in his hand, watching one of the tapes on the TV. I walked right by him and went into the bedroom and unpacked."

"Jesus, Katherine. What did he say?"

"Nothing. Not a word. Acted like I wasn't even there."

Katherine shook her head in disgust. "I knew then that we were done. Only problem was it seemed I was the only one who thought so."

"You wanted out then? What did he say about that?"

"Refused. Wouldn't hear of it. We argued. He went to work. Ignored me. Was afraid he wouldn't have me on his arm anymore. But it got me thinking. I knew at some point it would happen, the divorce, it had to. So I thought why don't I make good use of the time between now and then, whenever that is? Steve thought of me as an employee when you got right down to it. So, I thought, if that's the case I'll act like one. I needed money. One day I would leave him, be gone, divorce or not, and I needed my own money. Especially if he wouldn't give me a divorce. He had paid me ten thousand dollars for one night already, why not more? He can tape it for all I care, just like he did with his father. The hell with him, I thought. Screw Steve, I'll play his game. So I told him I'd be one of his girls, I told him I'd be his *best* girl. But I wanted ten thousand every time. He had it, he was making it, and if I was going to date these big shots I wanted a piece of the action too."

No, Katherine, I thought. *Don't tell me this.* But I didn't say anything. I just listened.

"I was shocked. He loved the idea. Went nuts over it. Of course he'd be in the next room watching. That's what he was into, Jed. Watching. I couldn't believe his reaction. But then I realized that's what turns him on. Simply watching. I always suspected he was fucking around, you know with the girls he had for the dates but then I realized, yeah he was fucking them all right – *mind* fucking them. Sitting on the other side of the two-way mirror. Anyway, that's what I did. I was one of his girls. I eventually saved two hundred and fifty thousand dollars. That's when I started to press him for a divorce. I told him if he didn't give me a divorce I'd quit working for him. He laughed. 'You'll be back,' he said. 'Two hundred fifty thousand is nothing.

Chump change. You'll go through it before you know it and then you'll be back.' Eventually he relented. Took two years but here I am. That's why he left his will out for me to find. I know Steve. He did it on purpose and I hate the bastard even more for it." Those last words she spit out.

If watching the tape back in Steve's apartment left me spinning and reeling, this left me numb. My ears were ringing and I was unable to hear anymore. It sounded too fantastic. Katherine? Doing this? A high priced prostitute? When you got right down to it that's what it was. No getting around it. And at the same time my mind was resisting this information it was doing some cruel calculations. Two hundred fifty thousand. Twenty five men. Two and a half, maybe three years. One a month. No wonder she didn't want to see me. Could I forgive her that? Who were these men? CEO's of big corporations? No, I thought. Don't go there. Don't even think about it. It's not something you want to know about. But in all honesty what she had done by telling me this was to devalue our own physical relationship. Was I just another man for her? This was too much for me. Things were changing. Fast. Was forgiveness even a part of this anymore? But then I thought maybe she was doing this purposely, pushing me, forcing me to choose, to leave her now or commit even stronger to this thing we have. Was she putting the ball into my lap? Is that what this was? Warts, blemishes, flaws and all?

She reached across the table and took my hand. The waiter came and cleared our plates. Katherine squeezed my hand and said, "I'm sorry."

"No," I said. "Don't be. It's something you did, a part of your past. Somehow you felt you had to, because of Steve perhaps, I don't know. I'm trying to understand it. To be honest, I don't like it, I'd prefer not to hear about this but it's done and over with."

"You hate me now, don't you?"

"No, of course not." I looked away. "I don't hate you."

"You're mad, I can tell."

"No, Katherine, I'm not mad. Disappointed maybe. But I'm not mad. It disturbs me to think of you like that. I wouldn't be honest if I didn't tell you that. Do I hate you? No. Of course not. I'll learn to accept what you did, that's all. I don't hate you. No. I hate Steve for doing this to you, allowing you, pushing you into it, that's what I hate. It's like he did it to me, took a part of you away from me. That's what I think. But it's over now, gone. It's the past. The present is us now and what our thoughts are about what our future should be. That's what counts, I think. As for Steve, I hate him for what he took pleasure in. His pleasure is my pain. I hate him for that and for how he used you against his father and for the other things he's done. I feel bad for you, I'm angry for the way I feel about all this, angry at Steve, mad as hell actually, for his role in all of this. I could kill him."

Katherine took my other hand and held them together and kissed them.

"I know," she said. "I could too."

TWENTY-SEVEN

HOW DOES ONE DECIDE TO kill someone? When does one cross that fateful line, make the commitment, cross the Rubicon, so to speak? When does the exact moment occur? Before you cross? In the crossing? Or perhaps not until you are on the other side when events out of your control have forced you to realize it is too late, you are now beyond the point of no return.

For Katherine I think it happened long before she got to the other side. In fact, her early decision led her directly to the other side without any difficulty at all. Katherine, I was convinced, had been contemplating this murder for a long time. She had been on the other side of the Rubicon for quite a while and now she was simply waiting for me to cross, to come to her side. I realized of course I was in her boat for this journey and not mine. But, admittedly, I was there willingly for I loved her, had loved her, and now she needed me. My moral compass? After all, what was morality in this case? Had Steve not used and abused her for his own schemes? Was that not reason enough to give her good cause? Did it justify murder? Probably not, but at least it eliminated the morality issue from the picture.

She had made her decision, was the captain on this journey, and as I stepped on her boat I felt the current carrying us swiftly, faster than it appeared from shore, and by then I was somehow convinced that I should be there, be her first mate as it was. Was it a conscious decision on my part to join her? Or did I simply allow myself to be swept up by her, by the current beneath these seemingly still waters? I don't know the truth in the answer to that question. It is still a mystery to me. But she was steering and navigating this voyage, and I would be her confidant, her first mate, her alibi. Could I love a murderess? I forgave Katherine everything. And Steve? Well, Steve had taken away any kind of sympathy from me. Certainly from Katherine. I loved Katherine and she loved me. In the end that's all that mattered. We were in this together and the world, our world, would suffer just a little less if Steve Cahill were no longer in it. This is what had become, truly, our secret.

Our plan was simple. I would buy a gun. When Steve came home from London Katherine would arrange to meet him at the Eighty-Second Street apartment where she would shoot him. She would make it look like a business associate Steve taped had decided on revenge, did not want to be blackmailed into one of Cahill's IPO's. To be written off as one of Steve's attempts gone wrong. She'd throw around a bunch of tapes (of course, we would destroy all the ones of Katherine), the tapes of the girls and other businessmen, collateral damage to the others who certainly would be caught up in this mess, she'd leave the camera set up, the bed unmade, maybe some condoms and sex toys, maybe some drugs if we could find some. All in all, the ingredients for a tabloid field day. ***WALL STREET MAVERICK SLAIN IN SEX DEN*** perhaps or, ***SOCIETY EXEC SUFFERS SEX SLAYING.*** I knew enough about the newspaper business to know this would be an irresistible story that would play for days. Weeks even. But, ultimately, Steve would be dead, Katherine would be left with millions of dollars, and we would be left with the rest of our lives. Together. This was my desire. This was my future. This is what I wanted.

To be sure, I had never thought of killing someone. But the way I felt about Steve it didn't seem to matter. I felt nothing toward him. Besides, I reminded myself, somewhat cowardly, Katherine would be the one doing the shooting. My role though, as her white knight, would undoubtedly be established and our big decision would be; where to spend the rest of our lives? New York? Europe? The Caribbean? The South Pacific? There were endless possibilities and we tossed them around like cards in a game of black-jack.

After dinner at La Canard we walked over to my place and Katherine spent the night. This was the first time she'd been to my apartment and I was relieved my housekeeper had been in the day before. With the hum of the air conditioner blanketing us we made long, languid, almost bittersweet love until we were damp with sweat and the sheets stuck to our legs. At first it was difficult, for me at least, there seemed to be an edge somewhere. I kept thinking about those twenty-five guys. But somehow Katherine's body, her softness and the way she seemed to know what I was thinking helped push it away. She caressed me in both body and spirit and soon we were asleep in each other's arms until the middle of the night when the chill of the air conditioner gave her goose bumps. I pulled the sheet up over us and we made love again, this time even slower than before, but more passionate and not as lonely, rubbing gently, licking the taste of our last love off each other, probing with fingers and tongues, bringing ourselves up and down as slowly, as softly, as possible.

It wasn't until we saw the gray sultry sky of yet another steamy morning appear before we fell asleep. I woke at 9.30 and called Marie to tell her I would be late.

"Joe wants to see you when you come in," she said. I heard the penetrating floor noise of the office on the other end of the line and I realized the other world was still there, still around me, and as I spoke to Marie I remembered Katherine and I had decided to murder Steve Cahill the night before.

"Tell him I'm on my way, should be there by 10.30."

"Right, see you in a bit."

Katherine reached up sleepily and pulled me back into bed. She put her hand on me.

"No," I said. "I have to go."

"Just a minute," she said. "A little something to remember me by."

TWENTY-EIGHT

I ARRIVED AT MY OFFICE at 11.15. Marie handed me a note from Joe Lieberman that said we were having lunch together.

"Okay," I said when I called his extension. "When and where?"

"I don't know, just a quick bite. I'll come by your office around 12.30."

I knew this wasn't going to be a business lunch so much as an office politics lunch. Joe wanted to talk to me in private. I looked through my messages and the only important one was from Mickey Thompson. I rang his extension.

"I got some dope for you on that company," Mickey said. "I'm on my way downtown right now, got something going on in Silicon Alley. Want to meet later?"

"Sure," I said. "Where?"

"There's a bar on Eighteenth Street off Broadway called the Old Town. I'll be there at 6.00."

"See you then."

At 12.30 Joe and I grabbed some sandwiches and containers of coffee from a vendor in Bryant Park but it was too hot to eat outside so we gave them to a couple of kids and went across the street to a luncheonette. The air conditioner above the door leaked like a sieve and we both got dripped on as we walked in. We sat at the counter and Joe ordered a hamburger and I ordered a tuna sandwich and we both had coffee. I felt a growing ache in the back of my head and I asked the counterman for a couple of aspirin. I was beginning to feel the few hours' sleep I'd had. The counterman took a greasy bottle from under the register and Joe said, "They're not waiting for Christmas."

"Huh?"

"Just what I said. I met with Lefkowitz last night. It's all hush-hush but they want to shape up the numbers before the end of the year. Show it on the statement. The evaluation thing is just for show. They're starting with circulation and us, modernizing they're calling it. I'm calling it slash and burn. They want to integrate us with the website ad guys. They want us together, in the same room, Lefkowitz wants half of our department gone, throw those resources into the joint ad group. Severance, early retirement, contract buyout, whatever. He even gave me a budget. I got no say in this, Jed. This came down as an order. It's a done deal. Carbone doesn't even know yet, they want to push him out. Lefkowitz told me to keep my mouth shut, he's only telling me because he owes me big and doesn't want to see me get blindsided. It's all going to be official Labor Day anyway. You know what that fuck said? Justify yourself. Can you believe it? Fucking justify myself? I've been here twenty fucking years for chrissakes and fuckin' Abe Lefkowitz says justify myself."

Joe's face sagged, the creases around his eyes and forehead seemed more pronounced than ever and suddenly I felt sorry for him. It was true. He had given twenty years to the *Times.* You'd think that was justification enough. Christ, he must have brought in a billion dollars of revenue in that time. But now, from the sound of it, he was going to have to work under a twenty-five year old web page designer if he wanted to keep his job. I wondered where that left me but for some reason I didn't really care. I was working with a different agenda where something so pedestrian as job security seemed trite. Besides, I remember thinking in a moment of self-justification about my plans with Katherine, I knew nothing about computers or web pages or the internet. The only thing I knew about computers was the one on my desk where the only time I used it was to fill out those stupid forms when one of my accounts placed an ad. That was relatively new, too. But at the end of the day that was it. I sold advertising space for a newspaper. There wasn't anything high tech about it. I was beginning to feel like the buggy whip salesman when he saw the first Model T car dealership spring up. But when I thought about it, it was okay. I had another option I was exercising. Joe, I could tell, was lost.

"What do I look like?" I asked.

"You're with me, Jed. I stay, you stay. I just don't know if I want to stay anymore. Not if they're going to treat me like this. Lisa's got a good job. Maybe I'll take my twenty and run with it. Do something else. Consult. Work for an agency. I know a lot of guys; there's stuff out there for me. I'm not that old. But if I go you're on your own."

Then my options became crystal clear. Keep my wagon hitched to Joe, or hitch it up to Katherine.

"Don't worry about me, Joe. I'm healthy, younger than you for chrissakes. I can take care of myself. You know how I feel about everything you've done for me, how grateful I am. That goes without saying. Without you I wouldn't even be here. You do what you have to. And you know what? Fuck Abe Lefkowitz. If he hadn't married into the family we wouldn't even know him for god's sake. Maybe it *is* time you moved on. Fuck 'em all."

"Jeez, Jed, where's all this coming from? It isn't like you." Joe bit into his hamburger and a line of juice ran down his chin.

"Ahh," I said, between bites of my own sandwich. "I hate to see stuff like this, that's all. It's too common these days. And what gets me is no one says anything. Guys like us roll over and play dead, and the other guys left standing just watch. Who's gonna tell old Abe he ain't cutting it? I mean, for chrissakes, who built the goddamn advertising department, anyway? Huh? You did, pal. And this is what happens after twenty years? Now we got computers. Big fucking deal. Twenty-five-year-old whiz kids, who'll work for nothing, work for stock, for chrissakes, who find more reward in the latest technology than reading a good book or taking his girlfriend out to dinner. This is who we are competing with, Joe. Don't kid yourself. That's what Abe fucking Lefkowitz sees. Why pay us the big bucks when he can get a couple of whiz kids out of school for much less money? Managing accounts the way we do, Joe, is old world. They want a new world now, do it on the computer, do it online, do it on the internet. No need for human interaction any more, it takes too much time. And time is money. You know what, Joe? You're right. Time to move on, go take Lisa out to dinner, read a good book, smell the fucking flowers, for chrissakes. Forget the goddamn *Times*."

"Yeah," Joe said wistfully, his juice-stained chin resting in his hand, his eyes gazing through the window out onto Forty-Second Street. "Maybe you're right."

TWENTY-NINE

THE OLD TOWN BAR IS true New York. It's a saloon in the traditional sense. More than a hundred years old it sits in the middle of a block that a hundred years ago was lined with stables and carriage houses and repair shops for the horse drawn delivery trucks owned by the merchants and stores that lined Broadway. When the blacksmiths and drivers and mechanics and stablemen needed a place to eat and drink and play cards they went to the Old Town. Today the area is called the 'Flatiron' district after the building of the same name on Twenty-Third Street and it has recently attracted New York's version of Silicon Valley. In fact the Flatiron's new nickname is Silicon Alley because of all the internet start-up companies that have moved there. Today, when the web designers and software engineers and managers of internet start-up companies need a place to eat and drink and swap ideas they go to the Old Town.

There are other bars in New York like the Old Town. The Ear Inn on Spring Street or Pete's Tavern on Irving Place where O. Henry supposedly drank. The White Horse Tavern on Hudson Street where John Belushi used to get trashed and where Dylan Thomas fell off his barstool one night and died. One of my favorites is McSorley's Old Ale House on East Seventh

Street which didn't allow women until 1970 when a court ruling forced them to. The owner wasn't too pleased about that and he refused to put a ladies bathroom in the place so women had to share the men's room. I think it was the only co-ed bathroom in New York until the owner finally put one in about ten years ago. In any event, every bar in New York has a story but the older bars have the more interesting ones. The Old Town was no different and I came to hear another piece of the story I now found myself a part of. I saw Mickey Thompson in a booth reading the paper and drinking a pint. I slid in across from him.

Mickey glanced up, a tired look on his face. "Ahh," he said, reaching for his glass. "These internet guys frazzle me." He folded up his paper and pushed it aside. "They seem so scatter-brained it's amazing anything gets done. I just came from a place where they are developing a new start-up, a company that guarantees delivery of anything, *anything,* a car, a book, a five course meal, a pack of condoms, in an hour, anywhere in New York City, as long as you order it through their site. The place is packed with kids designing the website, researching infor-mation, establishing links to other services, lining up the advertising, that's where the money is by the way, but, you know, it's all this mumbo-jumbo techno-geek website-internet-software stuff and everyone runs around like pinballs bouncing off each other. Somebody suddenly does something interesting and bells and whistles ring and instead of taking the crew out to lunch the boss orders a dozen pizzas so they can work through lunch. Talk about living the moment, these guys *are* the moment."

I was thinking about my lunch with Joe. "The question is," I said, "is it a lasting moment, or a fleeting one?"

"If I was a betting man," Mickey smiled wide. I knew he'd won and lost a few in his time. "If I was a betting man," he said again, "I'd say lasting. There's a bunch of kinks and wrinkles that need to be ironed out, could take a while, lots of time and flops and lost money, but the truth is this is the future. Make no mistake about it, Jed. The internet, the world-wide web, is just the tip of the iceberg. Its impact on business and how things run will be huge. Really huge. Like the light bulb or the printing press."

I ordered a beer and took out my cigarettes. I offered one to Mickey and as he gave me a sarcastic look said, "Are you kidding? All you gotta do in this place is sit back and breathe." He waved his hand over his head. He was right. There were thick ribbons of blue and gray smoke wafting overhead like low clouds in a valley. I lit one anyway.

Suddenly I thought of Katherine and wondered what she was doing right then. In a way I wanted to talk to Mickey about her. I wanted to tell him how I loved her and how she loved me and how we were going to have a life together. How would I describe her to Mickey? That she was young and beautiful? That she had just gotten divorced? That she had been in a bad marriage with a horribly perverted and despicable ogre? Mickey had heard that story a thousand times and I didn't want Katherine classified with all those others. It felt weird to have such a strong desire to talk about her with a good friend and yet at the same time be afraid. Like it would jinx something. Mickey is married with two daughters. He lives in a house in a nice town in New Jersey, has a good job at the paper, pays his taxes, and takes a two week vacation in the summer. What would describing someone like Katherine mean to him? No, I thought. Best to keep my mouth shut.

"So," he said. "You want to know about Cahill and Company?"

"Yes."

"I'm curious first. Why?"

"I knew Steve Cahill in college. We were friendly then but lost touch. Coincidentally I'm seeing his ex-wife now and she claims she knows nothing of his business. Thinks she got screwed in the divorce. I figured if anyone could tell me about the company you could."

"Not a particularly good way to re-establish old ties, Jed. But I'm sure you know what you are doing." Mickey paused, looked around the room, and sipped his beer. "Interesting character this Steve Cahill," Mickey continued, "appears to be somewhat of an independent operator. This is rare on Wall Street. Relationships are vital and Cahill isn't famous for that. He has few friends and even fewer who will speak about him. But the few friends he does have seem to be the right ones. Guys who are in very good positions to steer him some very heavy business. No one can quite tell me why. He's got a godfather. Guy by the name of Arthur Barrett of Goldstone, Meyer. Very big cheese. And very definitely *not* an independent operator. Perhaps the reason Cahill feels free to not nurture any friendships, I don't know. The few pieces I have seem to indicate Cahill and Company is like a front, a set-up of sorts, to do business outside of Goldstone. Cahill travels a lot, isn't around as much as Barrett. I don't exactly know where he goes or who he sees, it doesn't make a whole lot of sense yet. The other interesting thing is Barrett is the only other principal in Cahill. Major violation of his employment contract with Goldstone so it tells me this isn't just for kicks." Mickey took a long pull on his beer and licked his lips. "Cahill takes companies public, sells them, mergers, acquisitions, the usual stuff which in and of itself is no big deal. But a company like Cahill is too young, too small, to be doing the kind of deals they are doing. I'm sure that's the Barrett angle. They've done some big ones. Made some enemies along the way and there's some bad blood. But the bottom line is they've made some pretty hefty profits, too. Don't have any numbers on 'em yet but they're up there. Cahill is privately held so it's tough. SEC filings on the IPO's, mergers, etc. are about it. Word on the street also points to his father, Cahill, White and Company, as pushing deals his way but I haven't really found any evidence to support that yet. Talk around the street today is that they're about to bring a big one out after Labor Day. Supposedly their biggest."

"Why would a guy like Barrett, big shot at Goldstone already, want to risk it all to be involved with Cahill like this?"

"Lot's of reasons, money being the main one. Goldstone is big and old and conservative; they don't have to do every deal that comes along. They don't like huge risk. And they don't like internet companies. You know, the Warren Buffett school of investing. Long term, businesses you can understand, something you can touch and feel. Not they way Steve Cahill and Arthur Barrett operate. They roll the big dice it seems. And they win more than they lose. As matter of fact they don't lose that often at all, so whatever they're doing seems to work. They don't do an extraordinary number of deals but the ones they do, Christ, some big fucking winners, Jed. They know how to pick 'em. A lot of small Defense Department sub-contractors, software companies, emerging technologies, stuff like that. A lot of them government related."

"Steve had a lot of friends in college," I said. "Odd he doesn't now."

"Most common comments are 'aloof, a loner, not around much...'"

"Is that not acceptable if you're a good businessman on Wall Street?"

"Yeah, but there's a way to finesse it; Steve Cahill doesn't care. You've got to understand something, Jed; there is a culture down there. A club, a private club with an exclusive membership, clubs within clubs. And like any club there is a code, a certain ethic. Like a fraternity – a place where friends count. Guy throws you a bone, you throw one back. Not Steve. Not unless Barrett says so, at least from what I hear. Barrett's reputation is good, impeccable really, old school and all that, but Cahill is known as an independent, a maverick. Something you definitely don't want to be on Wall Street. It's okay in a rising market, like now. But when the bubble eventually bursts Steve Cahill, I'm afraid, will be standing on the corner of Broad and Wall with his hand out and not a friend in sight. Barrett not withstanding."

The waitress came up and I ordered two more beers and a plate of cold shrimp. Mickey took out his cigarettes and lit one. I put mine out.

"What's the story with this Arthur Barrett?" I asked.

"Interesting guy," Mickey said, squinting through the smoke. "A legend in the making. They used to call him the 'Mad Wolf.' But that's from the eighties. He made Goldstone a ton of money then. But he's also an overgrown frat boy hootin' and hollerin' about deals, winning is everything, there is no second place, push the envelope, you know, all that bullshit. But he's a rainmaker, no doubt about that. Big kickin' ass taking names kind of guy. Used to run the trading floor for Goldstone in the eighties, his so called 'Mad Wolf' days. Evidently some kind of hero during the Vietnam War; Navy Seals, Special Ops, CIA, you hear all kinds of snippets but who knows, part of the legend I suppose. One story I heard more than once was when he was a year out of the Marine Corps and had been hired on as a rookie trader with Salomon Brothers. They gave him a client who absolutely refused to do business with Salomon, deal gone bad or something. Barrett somehow got into this guy's office and stood out on the window ledge thirty stories up and refused to come in until the guy gave him an order. Later, when he was running the floor for Goldstone, he was known for taking ten, twelve traders out to dinner at Le Cirque or the Four Seasons after a particularly profitable day and running up ten thousand dollar tabs."

"Ten grand for dinner?"

"Wine. He's a real wine head. Loves the stuff and is a minor expert on it. Holds lectures and wine tastings, rents out large rooms, invitation only, producers from Napa, Burgundy, Bordeaux, the works. Evidently it's his main avocation outside of Wall Street. Apparently writes articles and reviews for publication."

The waitress came with the beer and shrimp. Mickey reached for one, dipped it in the cocktail sauce, and ate it shell and all.

"Shells?"

"Good for your digestive," he said, matter of fact. He ate a few more.

"Barrett sounds like a real character," I said as I peeled my shrimp. I wasn't sure about the shells.

"I get the feeling I'm just scratching the surface," Mickey said. "Oh, listen to this, you'll like this one. I got this confirmed today. When Barrett was running the trading floor at Goldstone apparently their building was across an alleyway from a gym. The ladies locker room was across the alley from Barrett's office. In the summer they'd open the windows and you could see the women getting dressed and undressed. Barrett set up a telescope in his office, across from the window, camouflaged his own window so you couldn't see from outside, and if a trader was having a good day Barrett would give them ten, fifteen minutes at the window. It became a perk if you worked for Barrett. Oh," Mickey smiled mischievously, "I almost forgot. Five or six years ago, '91 or '92, I forget, he had sexual harassment charges brought against him."

"Really? At Goldstone? For the telescope?" And then I thought about the camera Steve had set up in the apartment on Eighty-Second Street. Is this what gave him the idea?

"No, something else. Serious stuff. Created quite a scandal. Goldstone being Goldstone they managed to keep it in house, none of the papers got hold of it, and very few if any, apparently, know about it outside Goldstone. Barrett settled it and it seems to have calmed him down quite considerably. Matter of fact, right after this harassment thing was when he and Cahill started Cahill and Company. Absolutely discreet of course but that's when Barrett got below the radar. No more 'Mad Wolf.'"

"So what was it," I asked. "Secretary or something?"

"No, it wasn't a secretary. It wasn't even a woman. Get this, some intern working there for the summer, a college kid in business school. Claimed Barrett assaulted him in the men's room one Saturday morning during a seminar. Word is it cost Barrett and Goldstone a hefty chunk of change to settle. Couldn't get any more on it, though."

"Geez, Mickey. You got some contacts."

"Got to, Jed old boy. I write for the *Times*." Mickey drained his glass and lit another cigarette. "All right," he said. "Fill me in on what's happening back at the ranch."

I told him about my lunch with Joe Lieberman. Mickey didn't take any notes. He just listened, nodding his head.

THIRTY

WHEN I LEFT THE OLD Town I walked home. It was very humid. The beer filled me up and I began to sweat it out in streams and my shirt was soon striped. When I got home there was a message from Katherine. Before I called her back I undressed and took a cold shower. Afterward I made a drink and dialed her number.

"Hi."

"Happy hour?"

"Met a friend for a beer."

"Business or pleasure?"

"Both," I said, letting her voice infiltrate me. Some people have a naturally good phone voice. Katherine was one of them. Her voice eminently suggested sex, authority, coyness, seduction, all with a dash of flirtatiousness thrown in for good measure.

"When can I see you?"

"Whenever you want.'

"Whenever I want?"

"Your place or mine?"

"I don't care. Mine. Don't gentlemen do the calling?"

"I'm on my way."

I went downstairs and on the street I felt a sudden coolness in the air and a building breeze. I looked up and saw thick clouds bunched up like lumps of charcoal in the thin darkness. The silvery light of the city was reflected off their bulging bottoms and the sharp contrasts reminded me of Cezanne's rock paintings. The clouds were moving very fast and the breeze stiffened and I knew a front was coming through. A cold front and there would be rain, maybe a thunderstorm. Perhaps the heat wave was finally broken.

I went back upstairs and got my umbrella and then walked to Fourteenth Street where it would be easier to find a cab. I was excited because I knew the approaching storm would change the weather and push this miserable heat wave away. Change was always exciting, but, I knew, not necessarily for the better.

The air smelled electric, musk-like, and the street and sidewalk felt steamy, warmer than the air. I loved summer thunderstorms. When I was a young boy I'd sit in the window of our apartment and watch the streets flood and the lightning flash and listen to the thunder roll away. I always liked the way the city smelled after a good thunderstorm, clean and fresh. Especially at night with the headlights and taillights and street lights all reflecting off the wet black streets and the storefront neon glistening; the traffic lights incandescent and somewhat magical to me.

When I got to Katherine's I had a head full of good summer smells and all the memories those smells evoked and I was feeling pretty good. If you had a happy childhood, as I did, these things happened. At Katherine's the doorman recognized me and without asking rang up Katherine and said, "You cousin is here," and he sent me right up.

"Jed," Katherine whispered as she embraced me. Her arms felt good around my back and I felt for the first time she really did need me, that it came from inside her. She kissed me and her breath was sweet on my face.

She went to the wet bar and made drinks and I walked over to the window and watched the clouds roll over the city. Big fat thick ones that resembled goose down comforters. To the south the tops of the Twin Towers pierced through the bottom of the cloud cover and were completely hidden from view. Closer to us stood the Chrysler and Empire State buildings, lit up, their thin lightning rods pointing, defiant, ready to defend the city against any incoming storm. I went over and turned out the light. Katherine looked at me.

"Better to see the lightning," I said.

"Ummm…"

We stood together at the window sipping our drinks in silence. Soon little pellets of water began to splat against the window and then hard pieces of hail, like sand, and soon it seemed as if a wall of water had come up to us and the rain dropped in sheets and it dimmed the street lights below and made everything look fuzzy. Katherine put her drink down on the windowsill.

"I'm going away for a few days," she said.

"Oh? Where?"

"Home. I mean upstate. To see my mother. I want to see her before Steve comes back. Before we do our plan." Katherine looked at me and I had the feeling she didn't think I believed her. I sipped my drink and a sudden clap of thunder cracked across the city.

"You're still sure you want to do this, go through with it?"

"Absolutely." She turned toward the window and a bolt of lightning flashed. It lit her face. "I'm looking forward to it, actually. You're not having second thoughts, are you?"

"No. I told you. I'm with you, Katherine. All the way. But you have the hard part. You're the one who's going to do it, that's all. That's all I mean. And if you're not completely sure then I'd say…"

Katherine didn't let me finish. "I'm sure," she said.

I stepped next to her and put my drink on the windowsill beside hers. I embraced her and she rested her head on my shoulder. We stood that way for a few minutes, distant thunder rolling away. An errant flash of lightning now far, far away. The rain began to let up. The storm was passing. Her hair snapped with static electricity and smelled like violets.

"While you're away," I said, "I'll try and find a gun. I've never bought one before."

"I'm sure you'll figure it out," Katherine said, her head still against my shoulder. Her hands slowly rubbed my back. "I can get one in Windham. It's easy there. Maybe I should get it."

"No. We talked about that. There can't be any connection to you. Besides, there are too many people in your home town that know you. Somebody might remember something."

"Right."

"Come on, Katherine. You can't forget these things. This is important. If you're going to do this, if we're going to do this, you can't make any mistakes. This is a serious business we have going here." Her carelessness annoyed me.

"I know," she said. "You're right." She kissed me long and slow on the lips and her cool tongue tasted like her drink. "I'm so glad I have you now, Jed." She squeezed me into her. "I don't know what I'd do without you." She paused. "I love you."

I hugged her and Katherine threw her head back and smiled at me.

"Do you love me?" she asked.

"Yes," I said. "I do." And then I paused before saying, "I always have."

She reached down and touched me and at the same time I felt her tongue darting around my ear. It tingled and gave me shivers. Another distant flash of lightning lit the room and then it got very dark.

THIRTY-ONE

I DIDN'T SEE KATHERINE UNTIL the following week. I decided to make good use of her time away and focused on obtaining a gun. I went to one of those places near Times Square and got some phony identification made up. I couldn't think of a name so I had them made up in the name of Steven Cahill. I got a Social Security card, a New York State driver's license, and a birth certificate. If they ever traced the bullets or the gun somehow I figured it would be a good idea if they came up with Steve's name.

On Saturday I drove down to North Carolina. I was always reading in the papers how gangs from New York went down to North Carolina and bought trunk loads of guns and sold them on the streets of Brooklyn or the Bronx. Especially back during the big crack wars of the eighties. I figured it should be pretty easy for a respectable looking guy like me to walk into a gun store and buy a pistol. It was. It was probably the simplest purchase I've ever made outside of shoving a few quarters into a Coke machine. I couldn't believe it. The guy in the store barely looked at my ID and simply copied Steve's name onto a form he had to fill out. I had to sign something that said I had never been convicted of a crime and that I was an American citizen. I walked out with a Smith & Wesson .38 caliber pistol. "Best stopping power for the money," he had said. "Anybody gets too close to you up there in that jungle you can depend on this." I told him it was really for my wife. "A favorite with the ladies," he went on. "They find it easy to use. Just be sure to tell her to get up close before she shoots. Ladies tend to have weak wrists, if you know what I mean." He winked at me. I bought a box of bullets and as I was leaving he said, "Ain't no accident the .38 is standard equipment in most police departments." It was the way he said police. PO-leece.

That night I took a room in a motel off the highway. Like the pistol I paid in cash. I read somewhere that if anyone wanted to trace your movements, credit card use was a dead giveaway. Cash, on the other hand, was untraceable. There were mostly semi's and pick-up trucks in the parking lot. A lot of them had Confederate flag stickers in their windows. For dinner I went to a place that had "the best fried chicken in Dixie" and it was good except they only served iced tea or Coca Cola. I was dying for a beer but I had an iced tea instead.

The next morning on my way back to New York I had the pistol wrapped up and buried inside my suitcase. I made sure to drive the speed limit which was hard because everybody drove much faster than the speed limit. I wondered what the punishment was for gun smuggling. Then I began to have doubts about how well I was cut out for this business. Every time I saw a police car or what I thought was an unmarked police car I broke out into a sweat and my heart pounded my chest. It wasn't until I was back in New York that I finally felt safe and relaxed.

In my apartment I sat on my bed and held the .38. It scared me a little, sitting there, holding it heavy in my hand, the hard steel gleaming blue-black, and feeling its heft made me think of its power. If someone walked into my apartment with bad intentions right now I could kill him. Easily. That was the thing with guns. They made killing easy. Without guns killing would be much harder. You would have to really work at it. You would have to spend a lot of time thinking about what you were doing before killing someone. A lot of people would probably have second thoughts about it. Maybe only smart, ruthless people would be successful killers, I don't know, but without guns it would certainly be more difficult, definitely messier, and would require a lot of effort. You might change your mind. With a gun, though, it's just point and shoot. Like a camera.

The next morning Marie called me at 8.00 and said Joe Lieberman wanted to talk to me right away.

"Now?" I asked, startled by the early hour of her call.

"Kind of," Marie said.

"What's the matter?"

"Buy the paper before you come in."

I hung up puzzled. I quickly showered and dressed and wondered where I was going to buy a paper. I work at the *Times*. I don't buy newspapers. I can get any newspaper I want at the office. The only time I buy a newspaper is when I am out of town. So it was odd for me to buy one now and I had to think for a moment where the nearest stand was. The subway station. Of course.

At the newsstand I saw the headline without even picking the paper up.

IN MOVE TO CUT COSTS
TIMES TO LAY OFF UP TO 300
3 Departments to Merge –
Move Toward Internet Seen
Middle Management Stunned

The by-line was Mickey Thompson's. I quickly glanced at the other local papers and did not see anything except in the *Post*. In a box at the bottom of the front page was a small headline: "Trouble at the *Times*?" When I got to the office all Marie said was, "He's angry." I headed upstairs.

"Who the fuck is Mickey fucking Thompson's source, Jed?" Lieberman paced back and forth behind his desk. "Huh? Would it be you by any fucking chance?"

"No, Joe," I lied. "It's not. I swear. I know nothing about it. He's a business writer. He knows a lot of people."

"Don't give me that shit, Jed. He's your fucking friend. Everybody at the fucking paper knows that. Marie says you guys been talking the last couple weeks. That's too goddamn coincidental for me, Jed. You fucked me. I trusted you. I'm your friend; I took you into my confidence for chrissakes. I looked out for you. I took care of you. Fucking Lefkowitz thinks I'm the fucking source, okay? You lousy son of a bitch. Thanks a lot, pal."

"Joe..."

"I don't want to hear it, okay? All right? Forget it."

"Joe..."

"Goodbye, Jed. I don't want to talk to you any more. Have a nice fucking day." Lieberman turned his back on me and stared out the window. Outside a passive blue sky hung above the skyscrapers of midtown and in the distance I could see a green and white blimp with FUJI FILM written across it. It was heading east toward Queens and I remembered the U.S. Tennis Open was about to start in Flushing. They always sent blimps to the Open.

"Joe, listen..."

"Get out, Jed."

I went back to my office feeling pretty rotten and Marie came in.

"I'm sorry, Jed," she said. "I hadn't seen the paper when he asked about Mickey Thompson. I told him you guys talked a few times the last couple weeks, that maybe you went out for a few beers, but that you guys always do that. Then I saw the paper. I didn't know, Jed. I'm sorry. Did I really screw up?"

"No, it's okay, Marie. It isn't your fault or anything. Just a bad day, that's all."

"What does all this mean?" she asked.

I looked at her and shook my head. "I have no idea," I told her.

By the end of the day the whole advertising department was in complete disarray. It was like everyone had been blindsided by an unexpected death. Word spread like a bad virus that Joe Lieberman had resigned, effective immediately. Marie told me she heard through the secretarial pool that the *Times* bought out his remaining contract and gave him a nice severance along with his pension. But no matter how I cut it I felt like a heel. Joe was my friend. An old friend. It was something I knew I shouldn't have done. Bad judgment on my part and now there was nothing I could do about it. Joe was gone. Either way, I shouldn't have told Mickey so much and I shouldn't have lied to Joe about it. But I did. And I still feel awful about it.

THIRTY-TWO

THE NEXT DAY I WENT into the office and met with Abe Lefkowitz. I told him Joe Lieberman had asked me to take some vacation time and that I wanted to take my week now.

"How about both weeks?" Lefkowitz asked. He looked like a cartoon character. His features were all exaggerated with creases and deep wrinkles and his ears and nose were way too big for his face. In all the years I've known Abe Lefkowitz I've never liked him too much, he's not the sort of fellow you warm to, and all I knew was he had grown up poor on the Lower East Side and still carried a big chip on his shoulder. That he had married a niece of the family that owned the paper seemed to have made that chip bigger. Especially with guys like me. He always had an unlit cigar stuck in the corner of his mouth and his lips and teeth were stained dark by it.

"I don't want to lose my job, Abe," I said.

"Nothing's been decided, contrary to what some people are saying, and the vacation will have no effect. We're slow as shit, Chase, you know that. And you read the goddamn paper this morning. Doesn't take a fucking rocket scientist to see we need some breathing room here."

"All right then," I said. "I'll take my two. You can include today. I don't have anything going on Marie can't handle."

I went over some stuff with Marie, nothing too heavy, August by far is our lightest month, and by lunchtime I went home. It kind of threw me for a loop. I had already bought Katherine's gun. Steve wouldn't be home until Labor Day, as always. Katherine was still away. I had nothing to do. There was nothing else until Steve came home. The end of next week. When he does get home Katherine will call him, say she needs to see him, needs to get a few things out of the Eighty-Second Street apartment. She'll get him to meet her there. Katherine will do the business with him. I'll pick her up and we'll go home, hers or mine, and stay in the city for a few days. Show a lot of shock and sympathy, she'll be the grieving widow, or ex-widow, or whatever you call the ex-wife of a dead guy. We'll bury him somewhere, tidy up loose ends, and decide where we were going to go. Where we were going to go, that is, with all those millions of dollars.

I was thinking all these things when I got out of the subway at the Christopher Street station. I bought a sandwich at a deli on the corner and went over to the Lion's Head to have a beer. Mike's wife Shirley was behind the bar and was surprised to see me.

"You're in early today, Jed. Holiday or something?"

"Vacation."

"Oh. Sticking around, huh?"

"Yeah. Where's Mike?" I opened my sandwich as Shirley placed a beer before me. I reached for a copy of the *News* that was sprawled across the end of the bar.

"Downtown. Business. Bad business. Taxes, permits, license fees, code violations, you name it. Threatening to shut us down. And to be honest Jed I don't think we can make it much longer. The landlord is talking about raising the rent. It's getting to be too much. It's simply a local place, we're not growing. You know that. Who comes here besides you guys?"

"What?" I said. "Shut down? The Lion's Head? You can't do

that. That's impossible. You're an institution. They ought to pass a law to keep you open. Landmark it or something."

"Tell that to the IRS. Bunch of Nazi's if you ask me. Mike's down there pleading with them now. But to be honest, Jed," Shirley's rheumy eyes turned toward me, "I wouldn't mind a rest. It's been nearly thirty years. I'm tired…"

"But still, sell it to someone. Someone will buy it. Think of all the good times here."

Shirley looked away and silently wiped beer mugs and glasses with a dirty bar rag. I stopped eating my sandwich and closed the newspaper. I couldn't believe it. The Lion's Head shut down? That'd be a huge loss. Another legendary piece of New York dead. And the truth is it was happening all over the city. It was as if McDonald's, Walt Disney, Eddie Bauer, Hooters, and Barnes and Noble had conspired with the mayor to take over the city. New Yorkers didn't go to these places. Tourists did. And the idea was that in order to get tourists to come to your city you had to make them comfortable. And to make them comfortable you made your city familiar to them by encouraging all the stores and bars and restaurants to be just like the ones back home. It was our own fault. This was the price we paid to rid ourselves of the all the crime and drugs and corruption that had taken over the city in the seventies and eighties; the reason why no one came here to visit in the first place. In fact, were scared to death to even think about it. Now it was discovered tourism was big bucks, a money maker for the city. Places like the Lion's Head and the corner book store and the neighborhood shoe store and the local coffee shop had become remnants, things of the past, and were closing up all over the city. None of them could pay the rising rents based on a strictly local economy anymore. And the reality was that tourists didn't go to these places, one of the main reasons why people like me, *New Yorkers*, still went to them. It was a new age now. Chain stores and fast food franchises. The mall mentality.

The millennium was approaching. And New York, it seemed, was preparing itself.

The truth is I miss the New York of my youth. The gritty streets, uncrowded restaurants, no lines at museum openings. Sure there was some crime, but crime in New York was like packs of wolves in Montana, or prairie dogs in Nebraska or South Dakota or wherever prairie dogs are from. You just deal with it. No, the tourists were ruining New York; there was no doubt about it. We were whoring ourselves for the money, that's all. And people like Mike and Shirley, the moms and pops of this world, of this city, were the victims.

I drank my beer and felt myself sinking. I was getting depressed. Suddenly I wanted to leave the city. I wanted to get out and think. I felt overwhelmed by everything. The city. The *Times*. Katherine's plan. There was so much going on and all I was doing was sitting here in a run down bar drinking a beer in the middle of the afternoon. By myself, for chrissakes. No wonder I felt bad. I'm not doing anything at all, just fucking off, simply letting events take hold of me and push me along. Lefkowitz was right. Some breathing room would indeed be helpful. I needed to get out of here. I needed to do some thinking.

I decided to drive upstate to the little town of Windham and find Katherine. I'll surprise her, I thought. I started to feel better and I thought, yes, that's exactly what I'll do. It's not that far away. I'll drive up this afternoon and find her. It's a small town. Someone will know where she is. I knew the place from when I was a kid skiing there with my father. If I didn't fool around I could be there before dinner. I finished my sandwich and went home and threw a few things into a bag. I was feeling pretty good again. I felt like I was doing something. I left my apartment and headed to the car rental place over on Sixth Avenue.

THIRTY-THREE

THE LAST TIME I WAS in Windham was probably twenty years ago. It's beautiful country, soft hills and mountains, rivers and streams, good hiking and skiing and fishing and general outdoor activities. It smells good. The air is clean. There is no traffic except on Sunday afternoons during ski season. And that's because of all the New Yorkers driving back to the city. As I drove off the parkway and across the Hudson River I reminded myself that this time the purpose of my trip was to find the person I loved in order to pursue a risky and dangerous path that would forever change our lives. But still, as I drove through the rolling countryside, I marveled at how this piece of the past had re-entered my life in an entirely different way.

At 5.00 I drove into town and I could see all kinds of changes. The town had grown, there were new buildings, new signs, even some old dirt roads had been paved over, but the Windham Arms Hotel still stood which was reassuring. My father and I used to stay there. I went in and took a room for the night. I asked the deskman if a Katherine Cahill, by chance, was staying there.

"No," he said. "No one by that name."

"How about Katherine Hall?"

"No," he replied again, looking over the tops of his glasses, his hands resting on the registry. "No one with the name Katherine at all. No singles. Except you."

I figured Katherine was staying with her mother but on the off chance she wasn't this was the most likely place.

My room was spacious and neat and had a balcony that faced south. I could see the ski area, the slopes like big brown birthmarks on the landscape and the chair lifts stood still like power lines running up the mountainside. In the clearings I could see some hikers and mountain bikers and since the sun was still high I figured I might as well try and find Katherine.

I found an old phone book in a drawer with a Gideon's Bible and in the section for Windham there was only one listing for Hall. I went down and asked the deskman where the road was and he gave me directions. Then he looked over the rim of his glasses and said, "It's an old dirt road and I don't know anyone lives out there. They must be the only ones."

I found the road easy enough and as I slowly drove down it in the fading sunlight I was suddenly anxious to find Katherine. Maybe I'd find her and we could have dinner or something. Maybe, I thought, Katherine would come back with me to my room at the Windham Arms.

I passed an old abandoned house. It was rundown, rotting in sections and the chimney was toppled over and most of the windows were broken. The gray clapboard siding was cracked and curling up. In some parts it was gone altogether. Shingles were missing on the roof and at one corner there was a big hole, as if it had simply fallen into the house. The grass was grown up all over and there was an old rusting Buick in the back up on cinder blocks with the windows smashed in and the wheels missing. I drove on past the house but soon came to a dead end. That couldn't possibly be the Hall residence, I thought. But it was the only one on the road.

I went back to the abandoned house and drove up to it. I could hear the grass scraping against the floorboards under the car. A couple of crows flew off the roof as I approached. I parked in what I thought was the driveway and got out.

I walked over to the house and stood on the wavy dilapidated porch and saw the door ajar. I don't know if it was technically ajar. It looked like it had been open like that for centuries. I stepped in. The room was empty except for an old couch and some milk crates. There were beer cans and liquor bottles and cigarette butts all over the floor and it looked to me like a hang out for the local kids. The place smelled damp and moldy and like stale tobacco. There were cobwebs in the corners and thick dust covered the moldings and window sills. I walked around and entered what was probably the den. I saw a stack of old newspapers beside an old desk with all the drawers missing. The newspapers were brown with age and also damp and moldy. The top one said November 21, 1976. Behind the desk on the floor I saw more papers. Not newspapers but stationery, writing paper and envelopes. I pushed the desk aside and squeezed behind it. I picked up a sheet of the writing paper and saw a name and address engraved across the top. It said:

Thomas and Dorothy Hall

Box 12

Windham, New York

12554

Well, it seemed like I had found the Hall residence all right. But it didn't look like Katherine or her mother was here. Obviously no one lived here and hadn't, apparently, for decades. Strange, I thought. They must have moved or something. I walked from room to room but with the light fading fast I was losing my sight and of course none of the lights worked.

I drove back to the Windham Arms and spoke to the deskman again. Now his glasses were perched on the very tip of his nose so he could look straight at me without tipping his head.

"Like I told you, I don't know that anyone ever lived out there recently. Used to, I guess, in that old place you probably saw but that's been abandoned for years, as long as I've been here and that's five years. Originally from Catskill so I don't know much about who lived here back then."

"Well," I said. "I'm pretty sure that used to be the Hall place. I'm wondering how I could find out where they went."

The deskman shook his head.

"I don't know," he said. "Maybe go to the post office in the morning."

The phone rang. The deskman answered it and while he spoke I thought, damn, what rotten luck. When the deskman hung up he pushed his glasses up on top of his head and said, "Wait, you know something? Maybe Virginia might know. She's our cook. She grew up here. I'll go and ask."

He left and went through a door behind the check-in counter. After a few minutes he returned.

"You're in luck," he said. "She's busy with dinner so if you want to talk with her you'll have to go back there in the kitchen. If you want I'll take you in."

"Sure," I said and I followed him to the kitchen.

THIRTY·FOUR

IN THE KITCHEN I PICKED Virginia out immediately. She was waving a spoon and yelling at one of the line cooks.

"I tol' ya a hunert times already. It's TABLEspoons, not TEAspoons. Now go on an' do it again." She turned and saw us.

"Virginia," the deskman said. "This is Mr. Chase, the man I told you about."

"Yes, all right." She looked at me from head to toe. "City boy, ain't ya?"

"Yes," I said. I smiled politely and said, "I was wondering if you could help me."

"Maybe. He says you're lookin' for the Halls."

"Yes, that's right."

"Well, can't help you none there."

"Oh? Why not?"

"Ain't any Halls been in this town nearly twenty years. Maybe twenty-five. Not the family anyways. The girl, though, she was here till about twelve years ago, maybe fourteen. Little Katy, that is. But that's history about now I reckon, isn't it?"

The deskman left and I stood on the greasy black and white tiled floor looking at Virginia. I was trying to understand exactly what she was saying. Virginia looked old, late sixties maybe. Her wiry hair stuck out in tufts from under her white cap, like steel wool. She wore thick black framed glasses that magnified her eyes. She probably never married and had survived her whole life in the kitchen.

"But they're still listed in the phone book," I said. "Out on the road up past town."

"Are they now?" Virginia eyed me suspiciously. "Well maybe because no one told the phone company in Albany what happened. Maybe because the land was never sold after the accident."

"Accident? What accident?"

"What are you lookin' for, mister?"

"Well," I said. "To be perfectly honest Katherine Hall is a friend from New York and she told me she came from here. I've been up in the Adirondacks on vacation and I'm now on my way back to New York. I was talking with some friends yesterday and they told me Katherine was here in Windham visiting. I thought I'd stop by and see her, that's all."

"That girl ain't been here in ten years, at least. I don't know who'd tell you something like that."

"What was the accident?"

Virginia shook her head impatiently and took me by the arm and led me to a table that had flour and balls of pastry dough all over it. She turned to me and said, "Look, I'm gonna get real busy in a few minutes so listen up. Dorothy Hall was a friend of mine and if Katy is a friend of yours it don't surprise me none she ain't tol' you all this, so don't tell her it came from me, ya hear?"

"Sure," I said, still confused.

"'Bout twenty some years ago," Virginia paused and scratched her chin, "twenty-three now last November I reckon, Dorothy and her husband Tom and their two little boys went over to Cairo to have dinner with friends. Cairo is a town about fifteen miles from here. It was a Saturday night. First Saturday of deer season, don't ya know, a pretty darn big deal around here. Young Katy was sick with a flu or something and they left her home with a family friend, Mary Sheridan and her daughter. Mary ran the Sportsman Motel over toward Hensonville there. Anyway, they was killed by a drunk driver. Never made it to Cairo. Bunch a deer hunters on their way home, big ol' buck tied on the roof and everything. Drinkin' like their life depended on it. Dorothy, Katy's mom, lived. Paralyzed from the neck down and in a coma. Been in Green County Hospital ever since. Little Katy was around five years old then. Mary Sheridan over at the Sportsman took her in and raised her. Raised her like her own with her daughter Rebecca. Never married, though. Mary, that is. Raised them girls by herself. Ain't seen Katy, like I said, ten, fifteen years. Don't think she'd ever wanna come back here, no sir. She's gone from here far as I know. That's all I can tell you, mister."

I didn't know what to think. I had no reason to doubt Virginia's story. She had no reason to lie to me and it all sounded tragically true. It was just so completely out of the realm of what I expected or what I thought I knew about Katherine. It knocked me off balance. We never specifically talked about her childhood but I always had the impression, from Steve now that I think about it, that she grew up in a middle to upper middle class family, went to a private school, and had a warm and loving family. Now it seemed, even though her mother was alive, she had essentially grown up an orphan. Then it dawned on me that Steve was the kind of guy who wanted people to believe Katherine had the kind of upbringing I thought she had.

"Well," I said, clearing my throat. "I didn't know that. I appreciate you telling me this. It's very sad. I didn't know."

"Well, yes, ya know, bad things happen to good people and the Halls was good people. That's how God works, don't ya know. Now, don't mind but I gotta get to work."

Virginia walked back toward the stove and lifted some lids

and smelled the insides of the pots and I got a strong whiff of tomato sauce.

"One more thing," I called over to her. "Is this Rebecca Sheridan still around?"

Without turning back toward me she said, "Should be workin' over at Jimmy's. Windham Mountain Inn. Bar down the road across from the bowling alley." She stuck her big spoon in the pot and started stirring. I turned and left.

THIRTY-FIVE

THE SUN WAS GONE NOW and it was dark. There was no moon. The stars showed sharp and clear and deep up there in the mountains and I saw one shooting star streak across the sky above me. I heard the rising and falling cadence of crickets as I walked to my car. I knew where Jimmy's Windham Mountain Inn was. My father and I used to stop there for a hamburger before driving back to the city after a weekend of skiing. It was out along the golf course and, like Virginia said, across from the bowling alley.

I pulled into the parking lot and saw a pick up truck under the big spotlight by the front window. As I walked up to the door I saw in the back of the pick up some fishing rods and tackle boxes and mud stained coolers and a lot of crumpled beer cans. Inside Jimmy's I saw it hadn't changed one iota in the twenty years since I'd last been here. Above the bar, as before, were green paper shamrocks tacked to the wall and Irish flags and pictures of Irish soccer teams and rugby teams and a sign that said, "Erin Go Bragh" and a bigger sign that said, "Russian Vodka Not Served Here." A remnant of the seventies, I recalled. The Cold War.

There were two men sitting at the end of the bar and I could see the pick up truck behind them, through the window. They were wearing mud-caked rubber boots and had mud on their pants and I figured they sat near the window to keep an eye on their truck and their fishing gear. They were drinking shots of whiskey and mugs of beer and they glanced up at me as I stepped to the bar.

Jimmy Gallagher, the owner, stood behind the bar snapping the pages of a newspaper and he waited until I sat down before looking up. He was a tall, thin, bald man with a basketball paunch above the belt and he had no hips or ass. It looked like his pants would slide right down his legs if he didn't have a belt on and I remembered he had looked exactly the same way last time I saw him. His face had more wrinkles now, though, and his skin was ash gray from standing in a bar all his life, and his nose was redder than before but otherwise he looked the same.

"What can I get ya, mister?"

"How about a martini, vodka martini, dry, up, with a twist. Thanks."

He made my drink and the two guys at the end of the bar held up their empty mugs and Jimmy went and filled them from the tap.

Jimmy walked back to his newspaper near where I was sitting.

"Excuse me," I said to Jimmy. "I was wondering if you could help me."

"Sure," he said. "What's up?"

"I'm looking for Rebecca Sheridan. Virginia over at the Arms said I might find her here."

"Sorry, she's off tonight."

"Oh," I said. "I see." I sipped my martini. Jimmy watched me. I could tell I got his curiosity. Stranger asking about a local. Midweek in a country bar. Might be the only interesting conversation he'd have all week. Maybe all month.

"Visiting a friend, I think," he volunteered.

"That's too bad. I was hoping to ask her about a mutual friend of ours."

Jimmy contemplated that with the studied face of a true bartender. Talk or not talk. If talk, how much? Who wants to know, he might ask. Or he may simply choose to dominate the direction of the conversation. Either way, it was a bartender's choice. "Well," he said. "I know pretty damn well nearly every-one around here. Nearly everyone that's ever breathed, anyway."

Jimmy closed his newspaper and poured himself a beer. A bell rang from the kitchen and he turned and took two plates from the pass through. I could see fried fish and fried potatoes on them and he served the two men at the end of the bar. The fried fish smelled good and made me hungry. I took another sip of my drink. Jimmy refilled their beers and then came back and stood by me.

"Anyway," he said. "You were asking about Becky?"

"Well, kind of," I said. "Actually about a friend of hers who used to live here. Katherine Hall. She's a friend of mine and I was passing through on my way home and I heard she was visiting up here so I thought I'd try and look her up. Virginia said Rebecca might know where she is."

"Katy?" Jimmy shook his head. "Nah, she ain't here. She ain't been here in years." He sipped his beer. "If she's up here she's visiting her mother over in Cairo at the hospital. That's almost twenty miles from here. She goes there some but she don't come around here no more."

"Oh? Why not? She's still got friends here, no?"

"Oh, I don't know. She got into a little bit of trouble here about fifteen years ago, she and Becky did, and they left after that but Becky came back after a while. Katy never did. Don't know exactly why. People move on, I guess. She had no family here no more, nothing keeping her here. She and Becky stayed friendly, though. Sees her sometimes when Katy comes up to visit her mother. Maybe that's where she is tonight if you say Katy's up here. She had a bad beginning here, Katy did, so I guess it's good she got out, if you know what I mean."

"What kind of trouble they get in, if you don't mind my asking?"

"Maybe you ought to talk to Becky about that. I don't know all the details. Stole some money and got caught, stuff like that." Jimmy looked away. "It was kids stuff, really. They were good kids."

"Well, come on. Sounds like a good story."

"I don't know the details, Becky can tell you better." Jimmy looked at me as he lifted his glass. He kept his eyes on me as he drained it. Then he let out a soft burp and said, "What's your name, anyway?"

"Jed. Jed Chase."

"Well, Jed," Jimmy said slowly, like he was intentionally teasing me. "I shouldn't really be telling tales out of school but that gal left town a long time ago so I guess it don't matter much no more. How do you know her, anyway?"

"Know her husband, really. Went to school with him. That's how Katherine and I met. I'm leaving tomorrow, anyway, so I guess I won't be able to look her up. Be interesting to hear about her little trouble here, though. Give me something for my effort, if you know what I mean." I didn't want to seem like I was pushing him but now my curiosity was piqued.

Jimmy poured himself another beer. Put the glass down and inched closer to me. Leaned over and let his head drop a notch. "Oh, I think Katy always knew she was going to leave Windham. She talked about it all the time. She was going to go to California or New York or Paris, always someplace big like that. She was sixteen, seventeen. It was just a matter of when, I guess. And, of course, money. That turned out to be all it was."

I finished my drink. Jimmy nodded at the glass and I nodded

back. He made me another. "On me," he said as he slid it back in front of me.

"What do you mean, money turned out to be all it was?"

"Becky's mother, Mary, ran the old Sportsman Motel down the road in Hensonville. They took in mostly over the road truckers and traveling salesmen. No one around here would go there, see; everyone would know it, if you follow my meaning. Mary was – what shall I say? She was a service-oriented person, if you get my drift. She had regulars that'd pass through on their way to Albany or Boston or Syracuse or Utica. By the time Becky and Katy were fifteen or sixteen they kind of caught on to Mary's business. Of course around here no one ever talked about it. Mary was raising them girls all alone, she had to make ends meet. Took in Katy at a rough time, people round here never really judged her for it. As long as their husbands stayed away, that is. Anyway, Becky and Katy began to steal money from the customers. They worked for Mary cleaning rooms and stuff so they had room keys. When someone was busy with Mary they'd go in and clean them out. At night they'd go into the trucks. They'd find the truck keys in the room, go into the truck and look for the lockbox. Them girls was pretty smart when it came to stealing money. Went on for quite a while before they got caught. They saved up and when they got caught they ran away to California. Hollywood, I heard. After a while Becky came back. Katy never did."

I looked at Jimmy like he was from another planet. In the last two hours I had heard stuff about Katherine that was the polar opposite of what I thought I knew. Not only was she an orphan, I thought, she grew up in a whorehouse. If I weren't up here in Windham hearing it first hand from eye witnesses I would never have believed it.

"Well," I said as I drained my second martini. "Sounds pretty harmless compared to what you hear about today. What happened to Mary Sheridan?"

"Got real sick. Cancer. It's why Becky came back. Looked after her until she died. Buried her and sold the Sportsman. Stayed here ever since. Been working for me about five years."

I was hungry. I asked Jimmy to make me a hamburger and fried potatoes and another drink. I began to think about Katherine and what she might have been like at sixteen years old. When she was sixteen I'd have been twenty-five, twenty-six, and working at the Times already. She was a teenager stealing money from Mary Sheridan's customers so she could get out of Windham and chase her dreams. I wanted to be a novelist. She wanted to go to California or New York. She got what she wanted and although I never became a novelist I eventually got what I wanted. I got Katherine. The difference between us, I had to admit, was she did something about it, took risks, which was more than I did, to realize her dreams. Me? Well, it seemed to me that I simply drifted along, still dreaming, and whatever I got, Katherine included, came to me rather than me going after it. This was, I admitted, the harsh difference between Katherine and me.

THIRTY-SIX

THE NEXT MORNING I GOT up early. I stood on the balcony and smelled the dew on the grass and the leaves drying in the sun and the pockets of cool shadows warming. It was a pungent smell, damp and earthy, and I thought I could smell the autumn coming. I heard birds singing and I saw a young woman jogging down the road, her feet softly slapping the pavement and her hair tied back in a ponytail swaying like a horse's tail across her sweaty shoulders. I watched her until she went around the bend. I stood for a moment looking at the empty road in the early morning light when suddenly a car, a black Lincoln Town Car, swung by, its tires squealing as it headed toward the bend. A little too fast, I thought. I hope they see that woman running in the road. And then I saw through the open window the driver whom I could have sworn was Arthur Barrett. The silver hair and tanned face with etched lines in all the right places was unmistakable. There was a passenger too and I could tell it was a woman by the blonde hair blowing around. The woman had her head thrown back like she was laughing but I could not see her face. Then the car was gone before I knew it, it all happened in a split second, and I was not exactly sure what I saw. I stood on the balcony staring at the empty road and then pushed the whole thing out of my mind. There was nothing else I could do.

It wasn't them, it couldn't be. I suddenly felt weak and helpless and although I wanted to I knew I would never ask Katherine if she was in Windham with Arthur Barrett. It was absurd. It was just a moment of insecurity, that's all. After the stories I heard last night I was a little confused. My mind was playing games with me. It couldn't have been them. It was somebody else. It had to be.

I quickly packed my things. I wanted to leave. I wanted to get back to the city. There was nothing left for me in Windham. Katherine wasn't here, she was visiting her mother twenty miles away, but somehow it didn't seem right for me to go to the hospital and find her. Not now. Wouldn't seem appropriate. Not after all I heard yesterday. I wanted to see her, though. Now more than ever. I needed some kind of reassurance. I felt an ache in the back of my head and suddenly I had this uncontrollable sense of urgency that Katherine and I needed to talk. We needed to get our heads together, get on the same page so to speak. I needed her to reaffirm we were in this together. She and I alone and nobody else. Steve will be home in a week. I was worried now. It seemed to me we were simply drifting towards the end of this plan, our plan, Katherine and me, like a rudderless boat in a fast moving river. We weren't, I began to fear, in control. It was momentum that carried us. Plain and simple. Like the Lincoln barreling down the road. But now I couldn't help but worry about it.

And then it all seemed, for the first time really, to sink in. We were talking about killing someone – murder – a capital offense in New York State. A death penalty crime. How did I truly feel about that? Not too good, to be honest, Katherine notwithstanding. Is this really me? Thinking and talking about killing someone? The truth is Katherine would be the one who did the actual deed, but still, I was an accomplice, a co-conspirator, a willing partner. Any judge and jury would see that.

On the other hand, Katherine did have some kind of case, when you got right down to it. Domestic violence, abuse, cruelty, all kinds of things when you looked beneath the surface. There were tapes. There was evidence. There had been recently, in New York, some cases where the wife had killed the husband and gotten off on that kind of defense. Self-defense. There were all kinds of psychiatrists and psychologists and social workers who testified to the emotional veracity of such an action. For every action there is an opposite and equal reaction. Something like that. Could Katherine warrant the same defense?

And the truth was I never had any real feelings for Steve, even in college. He was a cold fish to me. And learning what he did to Katherine certainly didn't endear me to him. The thing with his father would sway any jury, I was sure. Knowing what I know now, about him and Barrett and Katherine, my feelings for him had certainly hardened. I despised him. And knowing he'd been with Katherine all these years doing what he was doing with her made me despise him even more. When you got right down to it, if Katherine wanted to kill him that was fine with me. I had no feelings one way or the other about it. It was Katherine who was important to me. It was our future that really mattered. And if Steve Cahill was the only thing in the way then it had to be cleared.

Katherine, I now knew, had had her own fair share of pain and suffering. Before Steve began to inflict his own on her. What I had learned here in Windham in the last twenty-four hours was testimony to the cruel and unusual punishment she had been enduring most of her life. No one in their right mind could say she deserved it. Practically orphaned at five, her mother incapable of functioning, being raised by a roadside prostitute, seventeen-year-old runaway, first Hollywood then New York, abused at the hands of Steve Cahill, who knows what I didn't know. Who could blame her? Killing Steve would be cathartic, a final cut from the cruel life she's had for the last twenty-five years. Katherine had survived. I admired her for it. She deserved everything Steve Cahill had kept from her. It *was* hers. She had earned it. I could see that now. This is why I needed to help her. She *needed* to kill Steve. His death would be the action that gave her back her life. This is why she deserved the money. It was her reward for surviving, it represented all that she had suffered through, it was why she had kept on going, struggling to make it somehow, and now it was here. And it had to be me; I was the only one who could help her. Who else would? She needed me. I was convinced now more than ever.

Later, on the drive back down through the Hudson River Valley, the green and brown hills rolling out with the parkway curving and cutting along and big white cotton ball clouds hovering in a sky so blue it reflected off your skin, I thought again about Katherine and decided I would not tell her I had come up to Windham to find her. I respected her life, maybe even a little more now than before, and I thought if she wanted me to know these things she would have told me. Perhaps one day she will. But the truth is some things are best left unsaid. I was selfish in wanting to find her when all along she, unselfishly, had come to visit her invalided mother. It was not my place to intrude on her private, personal affairs at this stage of our relationship, and considering what was going to happen in the next week I guess Katherine figured it might be a while before she saw her mom again. Yes, I thought, some things are best left alone.

THIRTY-SEVEN

WHEN I GOT BACK TO the city it was late afternoon. There were two phone messages from Katherine. The first one had come just after noon and the second one only moments ago. I called her.

"Hi."

"Where have you been? I was worried," Katherine said. "Are you home? Your office said you took a vacation."

I heard her walking, her shoes tapping the tiled kitchen floor, then the clinking of glasses, then more walking. The image of the Lincoln screeching around the bend flashed like an igniting match but I quickly extinguished it.

"What are you doing?" I asked.

"Emptying the dishwasher."

"I took a little trip."

"Oh? Where?"

"To get something we need."

"Let me guess."

"No. Not till I see you."

"What, my dear, are you waiting for?"

"See you in a bit."

I changed my shirt and grabbed a pack of cigarettes from the refrigerator. I always kept them in the refrigerator. It was trick I learned while in Florida once. It kept them fresh. Then I went into my bedroom and reached under the bed for the leather briefcase I kept my manuscripts in, my unfinished novel and some short stories, and removed them and stuck them in a drawer. Then I took the .38 and the box of bullets and wrapped them in a towel and stuffed them in the briefcase.

When I got to Katherine's the doorman recognized me and rang up Katherine.

"Your cousin is here," he said. He turned and nodded at me.

I wondered if the doorman really thought I was Katherine's cousin. I doubted it. These guys see everything. He knows every married woman's lover and every married man's mistress. He probably thinks because Steve is away I'm here to boff his gorgeous lonely wife; that is, ex-wife.

As I walked through the elegant lobby I wondered how many guns have passed through here. Probably not too many, I thought. But I bet somebody has walked through here with one. Just because its Park Avenue doesn't mean the extremes people suffer don't happen here.

"Oh, Jed, darling," Katherine said, standing at the door. She smiled at me and her eyes wrinkled up in that familiar way. "I've missed you." We embraced and kissed. I smelled her and tasted her tongue and all the familiar tingling came back. I felt a little lightheaded and a soft ache enveloped my heart. I had missed her too. She ran her fingers through my hair.

"How's your mother?" I asked.

"She's fine. She was glad to see me. She always is. I don't get up there much any more and it means so much to her. I'm all she's got."

"I'd like to meet her one day."

She kissed me again and said, "Where have you been?" Her arms pulled me into her and I felt her breasts flatten against my chest. I ran my hand up her back and discovered she was not wearing a bra.

"While you've been away I've been working for the common good."

"Oh, that's sweet. Did anyone ever tell you you'd make a good husband?"

"I don't know about husband. Partner, maybe. But husband? That's another story."

"Every husband has a story."

"And every wife," I said.

"That's true," Katherine said, winking at me. "And you know mine, don't you?"

"I don't know, Katherine. Do I?"

Katherine looked away, then stepped back.

"Well," she said, reaching for my hand. "Tell me about your adventures." She led me into the living room. It was so familiar to me now it was like my own.

I sat down and Katherine went into the kitchen and returned with an ice bucket and a bottle of champagne.

"You open this and I'll get the glasses."

I lay my briefcase on the couch and opened the bottle. Katherine set two champagne flutes on the coffee table. I poured.

"Well?" Katherine held up her glass.

"To us," I said.

"To our future."

"To our future," Katherine said.

We drank and held each other's eyes. Her face was flushed with color and her tight fitting knit pullover hugged her body like another layer of skin and I could see the outline of her breasts and nipples, hard and pointing up, and the fine lines of her waist and arms and neck. Some women, when you meet them, seem awfully good looking but more often than not as you get familiar with their bodies, after making love, after having examined the hidden places, after seeing them without clothes, watching them from behind walk naked into the bathroom, they lose their luster, their sheen. Not Katherine. To me Katherine's beauty seemed only to improve, as if it were still developing. I've never known a woman past the age of twenty-five where this was true.

She leaned over, ran her fingers through my hair, then kissed me. She seemed anxious. A good anxious. Anticipation. A rushing sensation like you feel before something big is going to happen.

"So, darling. What's in the briefcase? The fruits of your labor?"

I reached over and opened it. I pulled out the bundle and unwrapped it. I held the gun in my hand and placed the box of bullets on the coffee table.

"Jed, my God. You've got a gun."

Katherine sat up and reached for it. She held it sideways in her open palm. She slowly wrapped her fingers around it and with her other hand she stroked it, stroked the barrel, the chamber, the tiny bumps on the grip. She brought it to her nose and smelled it.

"It smells strong. Powerful. Metallic. Like oiled steel that's been heated. Like a machine, an engine. It smells clean." She continued to stare at it, her eyes wide and curious. She spun the chamber, like they do in the movies, and it clicked smooth and sounded solid. Comforting in an odd way.

"How does it feel?" I asked.

"Good. It feels good." She looked at me. "It feels sexy." She giggled and put it in her lap. She reached for the box of bullets. The box said, ".38 Caliber."

"This is a .38?" she asked.

"Yes."

"Is that good?"

"Yes. All the cops use them."

She opened a box and took out a single bullet. She held it up between her fingers. The light glinted off the copper head and brass casing. She looked at me.

"Even the bullets look sexy," she said.

"You should only need one, two at the most," I said. "But we'll fill the chamber anyway. Just in case. The less shot the better, though."

"Wow," Katherine said. "This is it, isn't it? Now we just wait."

"Yes. We wait."

All the anxiety I had felt that morning dissipated. I felt in total control of everything. Sitting here with Katherine and holding the gun and bullets replenished my confidence in our plan, in our future. It's going to be all right, I thought. Everything is going to work out just fine. Katherine picked up the gun again and held it between us.

"How do you put the bullets in?" she asked.

"I'll show you but not now. You should never load a gun unless you are about to use it."

"Yes, right. Of course." She seemed disappointed.

Katherine took the pistol in her two hands and aimed it out the window. Then she drew it in to her and rubbed it up against her breasts. She giggled again. We reached for our glasses and she said, "The future of us." We drank. I poured.

"God, Jed. This makes me feel so, so, ooh, so…" She was staring at the pistol.

"What?"

"You know, I don't know how to explain it. It's electric, you know, high voltage, powerful in a deep, strong way. Very strong way. In an erotic way, too. It's sexy, you know? It makes me feel so, so, ahhh…"

Katherine drank some more and rubbed the gun against her leg and inside her thigh. She looked at me and said, "It's making me so horny. Is that weird, or what?"

Then she stood up and smiled. It was a dopey smile, like she had just smoked opium or something. Her eyes changed. They were dull and glazed over. She drained her glass and her face deepened in color. She reached and took my hand. I stood up and she led me toward the bedroom. I carried the champagne and Katherine held the pistol.

"If I had known what kind of an effect a gun would have on you I would have bought one years ago," I said, as we went down the hallway.

We walked into the bedroom, Katherine ahead of me. I put the champagne on the bureau and unbuttoned my shirt. Katherine had already slipped out of her clothes.

"Look," she said, holding up her underwear. "I'm soaking wet."

We got in bed and Katherine placed the gun between us, the blue-black gunmetal stood sharp against the white linen sheets. We kissed and Katherine's hand went down and held me and I quickly became hard. I put my hand between her legs and she was right. She was dripping. I could feel in her kisses a passion, a fury unlike any I had seen before, as though she was so heated up she was about to burst into flames. She kissed me hard on the lips and opened her legs and pushed her hips up over mine. She was like a starved animal leaping onto a table full of food. It was beyond hunger. She couldn't get enough of me and she rode me like a horse, like a wild mustang, holding my shoulders like a horse's mane, barely in control, not at all concerned about falling off. She leaned forward working herself up and down into a frenzy. I could feel the gun against my side. She moved quickly and let out a sharp cry and then slowed. She reached for the pistol and as she slid off me she rubbed herself against my leg and then got beside me and took the pistol between us and stroked it before she pulled me on top of her and put me inside of her again. She lay on her back, her legs spread wide, knees slightly raised, and she put the pistol on the flat of her stomach, the barrel touching the top of where we met, my hardness sliding in and out, the barrel rubbing against her too and she began to whimper, then long, slow moans.

"Oh, oh," she cried softly. "Oh, Jed, oh God, oh, oh,.."

She let out a faint, almost plaintive sigh before suddenly jerking sharply, twice, her body twitching like a frayed electric cable, her left knee banging into my side, then she let out a deep, low grunt as her body became still.

She lay below me breathing hard, her stomach and chest warm and moist and the gun now warm between us. I watched a bead of sweat roll down her neck and another run between her breasts. She moved and I was still hard as I slipped out of her. She pulled me down and came around on top of me. She put the gun between us again and I felt her move over it and she pushed down on it against me so I felt the gun hard between us. She moved back and forth with the gun between her legs and it hurt a little as she pushed it into me. Then she bent over and started kissing me ferociously. "I love you, Jed Chase. I love you, I love you, I love you." Then she moved back and started kissing my chest moving down to my stomach. She took the gun from between us and held it in her hand as she continued to kiss me and then she saw I was still hard and she said, "Oh, Jed. You haven't even come yet." She put her mouth on me and as she held the pistol in one hand she held me with the other and moved her mouth up and down on me.

Her extraordinary passion and lust fascinated me. I had never seen her like this before. Strangely I felt more like an observer than a participant. She was possessed, as if an alien force, a power outside of her, had taken over her body. I was amazed and curious by her behavior. But she was wrong about me. She was so caught up in her own rushing rapture she hadn't realized I had come. I was so overwhelmed by her passion, so excited watching her, I remained hard. As she worked her mouth on me it felt so good, so perfect, I thought I had never felt so good before in my life.

Katherine, her mouth still on me, looked up. Her eyes were glassy, her mouth wet, her hair draped over my thigh. Then she lifted her head and smiled devilishly, her face flushed and damp, her pink lips full, and she crawled up my body and kissed me. She still held the pistol in her other hand. She stopped kissing me and whispered, "Fuck me, Jed. Fuck me with the gun. I want you to put bullets in it, load it up, and fuck me with it. I'll show you how. Please, do it for me."

"For real?" I asked. "Are you sure?"

"Oh yes, Jed. Please, oh please. I trust you. Do it. I want you to do it. Please do it."

So I did. She held me until I was hard again and I rolled over and got on top of her and I fucked her hard and slow and as long as I could until I couldn't hold back any more. The whole time Katherine groaned and cracked tiny, sudden smiles as she looked at me with distant eyes. She reached over and wrapped her fingers around the barrel of the gun. She let out tiny bursts of noise, not screams, rather moaning pants until I finally came again. We lay still a few minutes. Then she got up and still holding the gun went into the living room and returned with the box of bullets. She handed me the box and sat beside me and watched wide-eyed, her body trembling, shivering as if she were cold, while I loaded the gun, slipping a bright, shiny bullet into each chamber. Her eyes held mine as she lay back on the bed spreading her legs wide. I made sure the safety was on before I handed her the gun. I watched her put the barrel in her mouth and wet it. Then she put it between her legs and slowly, delicately, moved it around, rubbing the barrel first against the inside of her thighs, and then inside her. I became hard again just watching her. She reached for my hand and placed it on the gun and showed me what she wanted, slowly moving the barrel in and out, then let go as I continued and Katherine began rubbing herself. She moaned and her legs began to jerk slightly.

Then her body began to jump and jolt and her hips started

jerking up and down and she drew her knees as far back as she could. She cried my name out and began to hyperventilate and she started whispering, "Yes, yes, yes," in a sort of frenzied rhythm and then long groaning animal grunts and as I continued to stroke her with the gun and with the fingers of my other hand she went into an uncontrolled and completely frantic epileptic-like fit. Her body jerked erratically and I saw her eyes, her lids half closed, and they rolled all the way back so that only the whites showed like dull, faded china. Then she threw her head back and let out a scream so loud I thought all of Park Avenue could hear her. And then she was still.

Thoroughly exhausted she lay on her back with her eyes closed and I placed the pistol on the pillow next to her, the barrel wet and gleaming as if it had just been oiled. I watched her body relax, her eyes lazily closed as she drifted into sleep, her leg muscles twitching, trembling, her breathing heavy and deep, her breasts moving sideways as her chest rose and fell, and her skin seemed to glow, a sheen of perspiration covering her. Her body shuddered, as if each twitch, each flutter, were aftershocks in the wake of a huge, powerful earthquake.

I quietly rose off the bed and went into the kitchen and made myself a drink. Then I went into the bathroom and took a long shower.

THIRTY-EIGHT

DURING THE WEEK BEFORE STEVE Cahill returned from London Katherine and I finished moving the last of her stuff into the new apartment she had rented on Seventy-Second Street. We washed the sheets and towels and vacuumed all the floors and wiped everything down but Katherine still wasn't satisfied and she insisted we hire an industrial cleaning service. When the team of uniformed cleaners came the next afternoon they were puzzled why we had called them. The place was immaculate.

The day before Steve came home we sat on boxes in Katherine's new apartment and talked about what was to occur the next day. Our plan was for her to call Steve at his office and tell him she had to see him. She would tell him that in his absence she was unable to stop thinking about him and their divorce, hint a little about maybe missing him. Perhaps, she'd imply but not actually say, they had made a mistake. A bout of second thoughts, and all that. Suggest, covertly of course, she had seen his will. Katherine hoped somehow this would lure him away from the office on his first day back. The trick was to get him to the Eighty-Second Street apartment.

"I know," she said. "I don't have the keys. I gave them back a

195

while ago. I'll tell him I left some things there. I want to get them."

"Maybe he'll think you're coming on to him," I said stiffly.

"Maybe," Katherine said. "But who cares? Whatever works, right?"

"Of course," I said, thinking of the business at hand. "Do you think it will?"

"Sure. If not we'll think of something else." Katherine was confident.

Our plan was for Steve to meet Katherine at the apartment. Under the guise of looking for some of her things she'd get him to a closet to pull down a heavy box. Then she'd shoot him. We figured the closet would muffle any sound the gun would make. Then she'd mess up the place, the bed, other things, and make sure the camera was set up with the one way mirror. She'd throw a bunch of the video tapes around, the ones Steve had of different girls with various men. We'd already collected the ones of Katherine from Steve's apartment and Katherine said there were none at Eighty-Second Street. I was to wait for her in a coffee shop on the corner. When she was done she'd meet me there and we'd go to lunch in a very public place, the Carlyle we decided, and afterward I'd take her back to her apartment. Then I'd go on back to mine.

We decided it would be best for us to stay in the city. The police would probably want to interview her and we thought we'd make it easy for them. Her alibi would be that she was with me, an old friend, having lunch. If it looked as if Katherine were not a suspect I'd escort her at the funeral and afterward we'd go somewhere. We talked about Europe or South America but eventually we decided on Steve's place in St. Maarten. For the time being at least, until we settled on a permanent place. Our reasoning was that if Katherine were even slightly suspected she wouldn't go to a place her dead husband had owned. That was too easy. Also, we thought it fit the picture of a distraught young woman who has tragically lost a husband, or ex-husband as it would be, someone she had deeply loved once, and perhaps still did. I would be there as a close friend and confidant of the family, there to comfort her in her time of mourning.

We agreed on the plan, the sequence of events, and I left Katherine unpacking her boxes and went home. I walked down Seventy-Second Street and across Fifth Avenue to the park and walked through it over to Columbus Circle to catch the train. It was quite pleasant in the park but my mind remained unsettled. We were entering yet another phase and I was anxious about where we'd end up. Since the evening when I gave Katherine the gun (and the night we had sex with it) something got stuck in the front of my brain that wouldn't go away. I wasn't sure exactly what it was but it was all about that night, how Katherine had been, how she had behaved after I showed her the pistol, and since then I had been replaying our lovemaking over and over searching for some kind of clue.

To be sure, in the last three weeks we made love a lot. More than a lot. Nearly every day. And not just a series of quickies, either. Long afternoons that segued into evenings. Late nights seamlessly woven into early mornings. For me they were a series of moments, events, loaded with passion, filled with a timelessness I had never known before. Afternoons and evenings that fulfilled my every wish, my secret desires. And all the time spent cementing my love for a woman I had been secretly in love with for years. Once just a dream and a fantasy, but now a reality. But that night with the gun was different.

We'd had sex a few more times since that night with the gun (and I refer to it as sex rather than making love). Yet every time we had sex since the gun I'd been unable to maintain an erection. Katherine had been fine about it, I had the feeling she had been through something like this before, and I remembered the tape of Steve's father. She did her best to comfort me.

"You're nervous," she said. "About Steve. About our plan. Relax." But it bothered me. It still bothers me. I can't explain why. It never happened to me before. For some odd reason I think it had to do with the gun.

I kept apologizing to her. I felt humiliated. I was sorry I failed her and did not know what else to say. I felt a sense of powerlessness to her power. Believe me, it was humbling experience. One I don't think any woman can ever truly understand. Katherine was good, though. "Don't worry about it, for God's sake," she said. "Maybe it was me." "No," I told her. "It's me." I apologized again but she just kissed me and said, "Shhh, you're wonderful. We'll just have to practice more, that's all. Get you back into shape."

But there was something else that night in bed with the gun. It was the first time I'd actually seen Katherine lose herself in sex, really enjoy it purely for her own pleasure. She wasn't concerned with me or my desires. It was all about her. As though she had gone into some kind of trance and her focus was on only one thing; self gratification with the overwhelmingly erotic experience she found herself having with the loaded gun and me. What bothered me most, I realized afterward, was that I could have been anybody. It wasn't me that got her so excited, it was the pistol. I was an equal with the gun. Not more, not less. Anyone with a penis could have taken my place. As long as there was the gun. It wasn't planned, she had no foreknowledge of it, it was a complete surprise, a sudden moment. But from the minute I pulled the .38 from my briefcase and watched her hold it for the first time I knew something had happened to Katherine.

What really disturbed me was when I began thinking about her past sexual partners, particularly the ones Steve had singled out for her, the anonymous strangers. I felt a hot stab of jealousy burn in my chest. I suspected she may have been the same way with them. A sudden moment turned into an erotic fantasy of sexual frenzy. A surprise, a complete and totally unexpected moment of mystery, suspense, eroticism, pure pleasure. And Steve got off on watching this. Watching the kind of thing I had witnessed the other night with the gun. I could see, in a weird way, why Steve liked to watch. I could also see how Katherine could want this. I saw what it did to her. Maybe it was more than just strangers and guns. Maybe there were certain "tools" involved. Maybe certain "toys" or "locations." Maybe, maybe, maybe. Who knew? But the fact that I was now thinking these things bothered me and then these last few nights when I could not keep an erection, when I could not even *enter* her, I knew something had happened. Something in me had changed. It was about how I looked at Katherine. Her past, her present, our future. Our unknown future.

When I got out of the subway at Christopher Street I walked over to the Lion's Head. It was early still, 5.00, but I felt like a drink. I'd told Katherine I would call her at 7.00 and make plans for dinner. I had a couple of hours to kill.

When I walked in I saw they had taken all the framed book covers off the walls. Even the pictures of Mike's sailboats that hung over the bar were gone.

"What's going on?" I asked Mike as he made me a martini.

"This is it, pal," Mike said. "Last of the Lion's Head. Drink up. Everything's on the house."

"You're kidding."

"No, Jed. Not kidding. This is it. We're shutting down. Actually, we've been shut down. Marshall's orders. Tax liens, creditors, code violations, the city, you name it. Everybody, it seems, wants a piece of me. They're going to auction everything. I'm just taking a few things before the Gestapo arrives. Drink up, it's on the government."

"Jesus, Mike. I can't believe it. Where am I gonna go? Where is everybody gonna go?"

"Can't help you there, buddy, but me an' Shirley are goin'

down to Florida. Bringin' my boat down and sail a bit and see what happens. Rather go against the wind and sea than the goddamned IRS." Mike tilted his head toward me and looked over the top of his thick glasses, "Not as many sharks in the ocean as there are right here in New York City."

"Jesus Christ, Mike, I'll miss you guys. What about Paul?"

"Charlie's taking him over at the Corner Bistro on West Fourth. They need a good night guy over there."

"Hell, Mike, I still can't believe it. After all these years. Good luck."

"Thanks, Jed."

Well, there it was. The end of something. I felt empty inside thinking about it. I don't get emotional or sentimental over many things, especially bars, but when I think of all the nights spent here, the good times, the laughs, the parties, the goddamn history of the place with all the writers and everything it just made me feel lousy that it was all coming to an end. I, like untold others I'm sure, felt like we were a part of this place and now they were taking it away. Like losing a piece of your identity or something. But then I thought of all that was happening with me now, my questionable future and every-thing else, and I figured it was probably as good a time as any for a part of my life to be shut down. Make room for something else. I drained my glass and put it out for another.

"It's the Jed-ster."

I hated it when Mickey Thompson called me that. He was the only one who did and thank God for that. I've told him for years to quit it but it's a habit he can't seem to break.

"You know something," I said. "Every time you call me that you finger yourself as an aging yuppie, a product of boarding school, an old school preppie. It's out of vogue, pal. Get with the program."

"Can't help it, Jed. Besides, you *are* the Jed-ster."

"You're labeling yourself."

"Old habits die hard. Especially figures of speech and nicknames. You should know that, being the frustrated writer that you are."

Mike put a pint draft in front of Mickey and a fresh martini in front of me. Mickey sucked the foam off the top and then took a long pull. He turned to me and said, "I've been looking for you. You didn't tell me you were going on vacation."

"Yeah, well, with all the crap back at the farm, no thanks to you, *pal,* they're looking for guys to take time off. Give 'em a chance to do their so-called evaluation. I've got a funny feeling my days as Vice President of Advertising Sales are about to come to an end."

"Maybe. Maybe not."

"Come on, Mickey. You wrote the story. You know better than I do. Sure, they won't lay me off but come on, get real. Can you see me working for some kid selling advertising through a web page or web site or whatever those things are?"

"I heard Lieberman resigned."

"Yeah, well, he seemed ready for a change anyway. Call it collateral damage. It was a bad business, Mick. You should have given me some warning. Joe knew you and I talked. He knew I was your source. Abe Lefkowitz is convinced Joe leaked the story to save his ass. There was bad blood all the way around."

"That's why I wouldn't discount your job." Mickey sat silent for a moment while he drank his beer. Then he shook his head and said, "Yeah, I know, Jed. I'm sorry. I should have tipped you off but I had to call the shot. I was worried someone else was on it. Better we broke it than some other paper."

"Not for me it wasn't better. I've lost Joe as a friend, he won't even talk to me. Lefkowitz is pissed it got out before he could control it. The department is all fucked up. My future is totally up in the air."

"Sorry, Jed. You know what they say."

"What?"

"Never trust a writer."

"Fuck you, Mickey."

"Listen," Mickey said, lowering his voice. "I'm working up a story on your buddy Cahill and Company."

Oh, Christ, I thought. I turned and faced him.

"On what?"

"I'm not sure yet but there's something real fishy over there. I can't figure it. I go to the SEC and half the requests I make are 'classified.' Classified? They're taking companies public, for chrissakes. So, I say, why are they classified? They tell me I need a security clearance for them to tell me anything. A security clearance? From who? I never heard of such a thing. So I start asking around, you know, people I know, old contacts. Nobody knows anything. Cahill is a mystery, very few friends, rubbed a few guys the wrong way, etc. Stuff I know already. Two things, though, caught my interest beside the classified angle. One is an old Wall Street guy I know, a heavy hitter who has been around a long time. He tells me Cahill and Barrett have a source of unlimited funds for certain kinds of deals. Unlimited, I ask? Off the Street, he says. Generally that means offshore money or international investors. Very interesting, I think. The other is Cahill maintains a number of accounts in London and in Jersey. Not New Jersey, old Jersey. The island. It's a tax haven off the coast of England. Sort of like a little Switzerland, but even more secretive, total anonymity, numbered accounts, the whole ball of wax. After he does a deal there's a stream of funds that go in and, like clockwork, go out. Fifty million. Maybe a hundred. Disappear into all kinds of accounts under all kinds of names all over the place. Middle East, Eastern Europe, the Balkans, Asia. To companies like Indo Air Charter, East-West Grain Company, Ltd., Turkish-Syrian Trading Company. Nothing to do with the companies he is supposedly taking public here in the States. Go figure. Money trail disappears after that. And for some reason the United States government is keeping a lid on it."

"Jesus, Mickey."

"I know." He tapped his nose and said, "There's a big deal in Cahill's hopper right now, some kind of military subcontractor into RFID; radio frequency identification equipment. The technology is big right now with the Department of Defense, big contracts, hundreds of millions. Supposed to happen next month, after Labor Day. I'm going down to Washington. I've some friends there. See what I can dig up." Mickey finished his beer and stood up to go. "By the way," he said as he put his arm around my shoulder. "You still see his ex-wife?"

"Yeah. Why?"

"Think maybe I could talk to her?"

"No," I said. Fuck him, I thought. If he thinks I'm going to let him get to Katherine he's crazy, especially after the Lieberman thing. "She doesn't know anything anyway."

"That's not what I'm hearing."

"Get the fuck out of here, Mickey."

He smiled at me and left. I looked at my watch. Just after 6.00. Enough time to take a shower and call Katherine.

THIRTY-NINE

THE COFFEE SHOP WAS ON Third Avenue and cater-corner to the apartment building on East Eighty-Second Street. The avenue was wet from rain. From where I sat inside I could see Katherine come out of the building and walk toward me. She looked good. Pretty. More than pretty. An all too common scene in the city. Any city. Paris, London, Milan, New York. An attractive young woman in a navy skirt, white summer blouse, expensive shoes, a black handbag. I watched her beige raincoat flap back at the knees as she crossed the street against the light. Her hair whipped across her shoulders as she stepped quickly. I saw two guys on the corner follow her with their eyes. One hit the other on the arm and nodded at Katherine. The other smiled and said something to him. A bus passed slowly before her and for a second I lost her. Then, as the bus passed, she reappeared, her head now turned the other way and she quickly stepped up onto the curb and into the coffee shop. She did not look like she had just killed someone.

It had rained earlier and it looked like it was about to again. The gray sky bulged like a loaded sack of coal and the daylight had a silvery sheen like moonlight. Katherine came straight to my table.

"God," she whispered. Her voice was husky, thick. "I did it, Jed. I can't believe it. I did it."

"Shhh," I said. "We'll talk about it later. Sit down a minute, catch your breath. You want something? Coffee? Water?"

"I don't care."

The waitress came over. I ordered two coffees. When the waitress left I said, "How was it?"

"Jesus," she said. "I can't believe I did it." Katherine bit her lip. "It was easy, Jed. Too easy."

"How many shots?"

"One. Just one."

"Good."

"He's dead, Jed. Steve's dead."

"That's what you wanted, right? It's what we wanted."

"Yes," she said. "Yes, it is. I just can't believe how fast it happened. It doesn't even seem like I did it."

The waitress came with the coffee. Her fingernails were so red they caught my eye. They matched her lipstick – a bright, bold red. Like blood, I thought. Katherine asked for some water. We both lit cigarettes. I saw Katherine's hand tremble as she brought the cigarette to her mouth. Her foot was tapping the floor. She reached into her handbag and took out a small pill bottle.

"What's that?"

"Valium."

She put one in her mouth and drank some water. Then she ate another one.

"Oh Christ, Jed. I'm a wreck. How do I look?"

"Fine. You look fine."

I reached for her hand and held it. It felt very cold. Like it had just been in a bucket of ice. It trembled. She pulled her hand back and started fumbling in her handbag. Then reached into the pockets of her raincoat, checking each one. My heart skipped a beat.

"Shit," she said as she turned away. She looked out the window at the apartment building across the street.

"What?"

"I left it upstairs."

"What?" I knew the answer but I had to ask.

"The gun."

Katherine's face was white. She looked at her watch.

"We have to get it, Katherine."

"Damn it," she said. "I was in such a rush, the videos, the camera, everything. Damn it."

"Katherine," I said. "Get a hold of yourself."

"I can't go back up there." She looked at the floor.

I suddenly had an incredible sensation of déjà vu. How could I not be surprised at this turn of events?

"Give me the keys," I said.

"I don't have them."

"What? Christ, Katherine, now what?" I was having trouble keeping my voice down and looked about to see if anyone could hear us.

"The door's open," she said. "I didn't lock it. Steve has the keys, remember? I don't have them. I couldn't take them with me, remember? We talked about this."

She was right. That's how we got Steve to the apartment. Katherine didn't have the keys. I drew deep on my cigarette. "You're right," I said. "I forgot."

"It's a walk up," she said. "Third floor. Apartment 3B."

"No doorman?"

"No."

"Where did you leave it?"

She thought for a moment and bit her lip again. "In the bedroom," she said, looking at the floor again. "I left it on the bed across from the closet. I shot him in the closet and then I put it down so I could arrange the camera and everything. It's on the bed."

"Stay here," I said. I stood up, lit another cigarette, and left.

FORTY

KATHERINE WAS RIGHT. THE DOOR was not locked. I walked in and locked it behind me. I caught a faint whiff of cordite and, strangely, Steve's aftershave. Polo. Ralph Lauren. It was easy to recognize, he'd worn it for years. I used it myself sometimes.

I could see Katherine had done a good job of messing up the place. Stuff was knocked over, a lamp, an empty vase. I was still in the foyer and suddenly I realized I didn't want to get my fingerprints on anything. I didn't have any gloves. I looked for the kitchen. I'd need a dishtowel or something if I was going to pick anything up, like the gun. It was off to the right and I went in. On the counter next to the sink was the .38. That's strange, I thought. Katherine said she left it on the bed. She was certain of it. I went over to the sink and looked for a dishtowel. I opened some drawers and found some linen napkins. I took one, wrapped my hand in it, and picked up the gun. She was probably too nervous and anxious to remember correctly, I thought. All that adrenaline pumping through her veins and everything. Then I turned and looked for a bag, a shopping bag or a garbage bag or something to put the gun in. I held the pistol in my right hand but it was hard to hold with the napkin around my hand so I undid the napkin and wrapped it around the gun. Then I held the gun normally, my hand on the grip, and it felt more natural. I thought I heard a sound come from inside the apartment and I stood still a moment. There was nothing and I began opening and closing drawers looking for a bag. Then I heard the distinct sound of footsteps and I turned around. Had Katherine returned? No, she couldn't have, I locked the door. Then the footsteps stopped and suddenly a man appeared in the doorway to the kitchen. I couldn't quite see him; he stood back and to the side, obscuring his face. But his body was there and he looked big, tall. Was it Steve Cahill? Then I saw him holding a gun.

"Mr. Chase..." His voice was deep, gravelly, and he spoke as if he were expecting me. He moved forward, towards me, and I saw the gun raise up and point right at me. And then I shot him. I don't know why. I was scared. He had a gun. It was aimed at me. I clearly panicked. He stood for a moment and I wasn't sure I'd hit him. Then he let out a heavy gasp, like a deflating tire, and fell to the floor, collapsed really, like a puppet that'd lost its strings. I looked down. He was wearing gloves and then I saw the gun in his hand. A .38. Just like mine. He looked familiar somehow. The white hair, the tanned skin, but his face was turned away from me. I walked over to him and I found myself shaking uncontrollably. I was afraid I was going to drop the gun so I went back to the sink and set it on the counter. I put the napkin in my pocket and for some stupid reason I washed my hands. Then I walked over to the body and stepped over it and saw it was Arthur Barrett. I had shot Arthur Barrett. What was he doing here? How did he get in? He must have been in here before me. Even if he had keys I would have heard him open the door. And if he was in here before me then he must have been here when Katherine was here. My head was spinning now. This was certainly not part of the plan, of *our* plan. What the hell did all this mean?

I couldn't think straight but my instinct told me I ought to walk through the apartment to make sure there weren't any other surprises. Christ, I thought again, what the hell was Barrett doing here? In the hallway I could see the doors to the two bedrooms, one right next to the other. In the first I saw cut into the common wall with the other bedroom what appeared to be a casement window looking into the other bedroom. There was a video camera set up on a tripod in front of it. Through the mirrored window I could see Steve's two legs sticking out from inside the closet. I reminded myself again not to touch anything. I was still shaking from shooting Arthur Barrett and I felt nauseous, my mouth was suddenly very dry, and my heart was pounding my chest. Then I thought I could see one of Steve's legs move. His shoe turned inward. It was dim. No, I thought. It can't be. He's dead. Katherine shot him. Then his foot moved again.

I went into the other bedroom and walked over to the closet where Steve's legs stuck out and I saw his torso and the back of his head and there was a lot of blood. I decided I didn't want to look. The less I saw the better. Then his leg moved again and I felt my heart jump into my throat and a cold shiver run up my spine.

I leaned into the closet, took the napkin out of my pocket, and turned on the light. There was a pool of blood around his torso and his head, his shirt and pants were soaked with it. His head was flat against the floor facing me; he was looking at me. His eyes blinked twice. He recognized me. He was still alive.

I could see his wound. It was on the left side of the neck, near where the shoulder and spine meet, below the skull. I'm no expert but it seemed the bullet may have hit his spine, or a part of it, and he was partly paralyzed or something. He might still be alive, I thought, but he was bleeding fast and badly.

He coughed and there was a gurgling sound. "Jed," he said, in a hoarse whisper. I squatted down beside him. "What are you doing here?" His eyes widened and some blood began to trickle out of his mouth.

I didn't say anything at first. I looked at him and thought about all the weirdness he perpetrated in this room, the weirdness he perpetrated on Katherine, the weirdness he perpetrated on himself. His eyes looked into mine now. They were worried eyes. The eyes of someone who knows he is in deep, deep trouble. Suddenly I felt sorry for him.

"What happened Steve?" I asked him. "Who did this?"

"Barrett," he whispered. "Barrett and Katherine."

"Why?"

"The accounts," he said, his voice barely audible. "Barrett is controlling the accounts now... the... Dakota... the... money..."

"What accounts?"

Steve's eyes looked up at me. He was struggling. His mouth opened but nothing was coming out. Even in his last moments, I thought, he was thinking about his business. I stood up and watched Steve's eyes. They suddenly dulled and stared blankly into nothing, not blinking. I bent over and tried to hear if he was breathing. Nothing. I put my finger to his neck. There was no pulse. The blood had almost filled the floor around him and I knew it would start seeping into the bedroom. Could I have saved him? Probably not. Did I want to? If I could have, would I have? Why? The reason I was here was to save Katherine, not Steve. I turned off the closet light and walked back into the hallway. I saw Barrett lying in the entranceway to the kitchen. His blood, like Steve's, filled the floor. I could smell it, now. Metallic, coppery, sort of sweet, like burnt sugar cane after it rains.

I walked quickly through the apartment. I took the linen napkin out of my pocket and I wiped everything I thought I touched. Door knobs, drawer handles. Then I let myself out, left the door unlocked, wiped the door knob, and took the stairs two at a time down to the street. There was no one in the building and, fortunately, no one on the sidewalk in front of the building. It was raining again. The sky was dark. I slipped out the door and walked as calmly as I could toward the coffee shop. Deep inside though, I had a bad feeling. Very bad feeling.

I walked into the coffee shop but I did not see Katherine. I looked at every table. She was gone. And then I remembered I left the gun upstairs in the apartment by the kitchen sink. Just where Katherine had left it. With her fingerprints on it.

FORTY·ONE

I NEEDED TO WALK. I needed to do something physical. My nerves felt like an unraveling bundle of live wires, broken and frayed with sparks flying all over the place. It was still raining and my clothes were wet. I bought one of those two dollar umbrellas from a strange looking vendor on the corner. Whenever it rains in New York these guys come out of the woodwork. Big ones for ten dollars, medium for five dollars, small for two dollars. Disposable umbrellas I call them. You get about five uses out of them before they break. Like disposable razors. Probably made in the same factories over in China. I kept walking down Third Avenue. I did not want to think about Katherine and it was all I could not to. I thought about Barrett. I thought about Steve. I crossed Seventy-Ninth Street. Why was Barrett there? Steve said 'Barrett and Katherine' had shot him. Did Barrett shoot him? Or did Katherine, as she claimed? Did it matter? And for chrissakes, I killed Barrett. Katherine was right. It *was* too easy. Like I've said before, that's the problem with guns. It's too easy. I don't think I even meant to. It was a bad reaction, that's all. I panicked. I thought it was Steve. But still, the poor bastard was dead. And for some reason I didn't seem to care all that much about him either.

I came to Seventy-Second Street. Suddenly I found myself

walking past Katherine's new apartment building where twelve hours earlier I had been sleeping, my arm lazily flung across her back. I walked up to the entrance and asked the doorman if Katherine was in. He rang up. I waited. He pushed the buzzer again. After a minute he shook his head. I walked back to Third Avenue and continued south.

It was raining hard now and my shoes were soaked through. They squeaked as I walked. I wondered what Steve meant when I asked him why he thought he was shot. What did he mean about the accounts? What accounts? Then I remembered what Mickey Thompson had said about Cahill and Company's bank accounts in London and some other place. What was it? Jersey, he said. Jersey? Where the hell was that? Off the coast of England, Mickey had said. Numbered accounting system. Private. Secure. No names. Like Switzerland, only better. That's what Mickey had said. Money went there from New York and London and then disappeared. Something like that.

And Steve also said something about 'Dakota.' The Dakota? The apartment building over on the West Side? Seventy-Second Street and Central Park West? What did that have to do with anything? Did they keep another apartment there too? I had too many questions now, none of which I had any answers for.

The wet streets shined black like mirrors and reflected white headlights and red taillights and before I knew it I was down near Gramercy. I cut over toward the Flatiron building and then down Fifth Avenue to Greenwich Village. The rain had let up some but I was thoroughly soaked. I needed a shower and dry clothes. And a drink. By the time I got home to West Tenth Street it was late afternoon. After a shower and more than a couple of drinks I ordered some Chinese food to be delivered. I finished the bottle and had opened another one before I passed out.

FORTY·TWO

I WOKE UP MID-MORNING WITH the worst hangover I've ever had. Worse than any I suffered in college or on any New Year's Day morning. My head was throbbing and it seemed no amount of aspirin could put a dent into it. A bottle and a half of vodka and Chinese food – Jesus, what was I thinking? Even my hair hurt. I showered and dressed and walked over to the diner on Sixth Avenue for some eggs. What I needed was a good old greasy American breakfast: eggs, bacon, potatoes, toast, and coffee. Lots of it. As I passed Christopher Street I saw the Lion's Head. It had yellow caution tape all across the front and a big black and white notice glued to the door. It said, "Closed by Order of the Marshall's Office."

After breakfast I felt only marginally better, the waves of nausea had abated but my head still throbbed. I decided to take the train up to Columbus Circle and walk over to the Dakota and ask the doorman if Steve Cahill lived there. Or Arthur Barrett. Or Katherine Cahill. Maybe I could start making sense of this. This was the the first time since yesterday I had thought about Katherine.

Why did she leave? Why did she leave me there all alone? Leave me holding the gun? The gun that shot Steve Cahill. And Arthur Barrett. It was obvious she and Barrett had something going on; they were in the apartment before me. But what? I still had a hard time believing she ditched me. Were they in this together like Steve said? Barrett and Katherine? Was I simply a fall guy, part of a larger set up? She played me good, that's for sure. Boy, did she play me good. She fucked my lights right out. I didn't see a goddamn thing. I should have known better. The Lincoln in Windham, for instance. That should have said something to me but I was stupid. I ignored it when I shouldn't have. That was like a big neon billboard screaming 'Hey idiot!' But why me? Why did she, or Barrett, pick me? And then it all seemed to suddenly make some kind of sense.

Obviously there was some kind of monkey business going on with Steve's company, Cahill and Company. I didn't know what it was but it had to do with secret bank accounts and offshore money. Katherine must have had an inside scoop on them. Or discovered them in the course of the divorce. But no, she couldn't have as they were secret. And because they were secret a lawyer, her lawyer, wouldn't have known about them. That was the point of having numbered bank accounts in Switzerland or the Caymans or Jersey. It was Barrett. Barrett told her. He must have. But, no matter, at some point she knew there was a lot of money somewhere. Steve said Barrett controlled the accounts 'now.' *Now.* That was the operative word. It implied there had been a struggle between Steve and Barrett. And so it only made sense that Barrett and Katherine had gotten control of the secret accounts in Jersey and either Steve found out or was about to do something about it. They decided to kill him. They needed someone to take the blame, to be Steve's murderer. They needed a fall guy. So they could run off with the money. They picked me. Katherine knew I was an easy mark. She knew I was infatuated with her. She knew I'd go back up into the apartment to get the gun, her gun, the gun she got me to buy. All she had to do was ask. *I can't go back up there,* she had said. Of course. She knew *I* would. And Barrett would be waiting there to kill me. With another .38, just like the one I had bought. What would he do? Make it look like suicide? Like I killed Steve and then myself? Or were they planning to make it appear to be a robbery gone bad? Or would it be what Katherine had said about our plan from the beginning, an act of revenge by one of the businessmen on one of the tapes? I didn't know exactly but I knew there had to have been a plan. A plan I had no part in creating. I was a part of it certainly, but as a component not as a planner. I was to go up to the apartment to get the gun, Barrett would shoot me, and Katherine would go off to meet Barrett at some prearranged place. Then they would fly off to live happily ever after somewhere. Something like that.

Only Barrett getting killed was definitely not part of their plan. Katherine must have gone to the prearranged place to meet Barrett and waited. And waited. And waited. I wonder what she thought when he didn't show up. She must have freaked out. Was that it? Were they supposed to meet at the Dakota? Would I find her there? Where was Katherine now? What did she think about Barrett? Did she think he was dead? That I killed him? Or did she think I was dead, that Barrett had bolted and left her, ditched her like she ditched me? Or even worse, that he never killed me to begin with, that he bolted right after Katherine, leaving my plan intact, except he had the money. And then, again, I remembered the gun... Katherine's gun. The gun with her fingerprints on it. It was sitting on the kitchen counter. In the apartment on Eighty-Second Street. With two dead people in there. Was Barrett supposed to get it for her? After he killed me was he supposed to retrieve the gun and leave his there? After wiping his prints off it, and then perhaps wrap my hand around it? Actually, he was wearing gloves so no prints of his would be found. Was that the real plan? Or had he planned to leave Katherine's gun there all along?

I got out at Columbus Circle and walked by the old Coliseum

which was closed now, like one big white brick left over from another era. I remembered as a kid my father used to take me there for the Automobile show every year which was a funny thing since we never owned a car. My father was born and raised in Manhattan, like his father and me, and whenever we left the city he would rent one. But he loved to go to the car show every year. He liked looking at the new models, the sports cars, the big Bentleys and Rolls Royces. I remember all the pretty women that would stand by the cars, wearing practically nothing, and try and get you interested in that particular Ford or Chevy. As if when you bought the car the girl came with it. But that was a long time ago and like the Lion's Head the Coliseum was done and over with.

I walked up on the park side of Central Park West toward Seventy-Second Street. The Dakota was on the corner, across from Central Park. A lot of famous people lived there. Lauren Bacall, Leonard Bernstein, Judy Garland, and many other movie stars, rock stars, and people famous for being famous. John Lennon had lived there. It was where he was murdered by some nutcase who had a copy of "The Catcher in the Rye" in his back pocket. How weird is that? Anyway the Dakota was one of the first co-operative apartment buildings built in New York City back in the Nineteenth Century. 1880's or 1890's. A lot of people think it was called the Dakota because back then this area, Central Park and the surrounding streets, was so barren and empty, development had not come here yet, that people referred to the building as being "out in the Dakotas." I've heard that story isn't true, that in fact the building's developer liked western Indian names and actually had a statue of a Dakota Indian put somewhere on the façade of the building.

The entrance to the building is on the north side of West Seventy-Second Street. It's a big driveway, a courtyard really, that was originally built for horse and carriages to drive into to let their passengers out. There is a big iron gate and a small walkway beside it. This is the spot where Lennon was shot, by the way, and crowds of people from all over the world, his fans and such, still come here to mourn him. People take pictures and throw flowers on the ground. Seeing the crowds there always reminded me of the kind of people who slow down on the highway to look at a car wreck. This is why, for example, Park Avenue buildings don't want rock stars or movie stars living in their buildings. They draw too much unwanted attention and messiness.

Anyway, I walked through the narrow walkway. There is a little security house there and doormen, concierges, porters, more staff than a hotel practically, and all of them kind of hang out around there. I asked one of the doormen if a Steve Cahill was in.

"Who?"

"Steve Cahill."

"No such person here," he said.

"Maybe it's his wife, Katherine Cahill," I said.

"No," he said. "She doesn't live here either. Maybe next door?" He pointed down the street.

"I'm sorry," I said. "I must be confused. It might be a company apartment, Cahill and Company? Or Arthur Barrett?"

The doorman looked at me strangely. "Companies don't own apartments here," he said. "And neither does a Mr. Barrett."

I left the Dakota disappointed and crossed the street back toward Columbus Circle. Obviously Dakota had another meaning for Steve Cahill. I tried to think of all the ways in which the word Dakota might have some meaning for Steve or Katherine. I couldn't think of any. As I stepped up onto the curb I passed a newsstand. There were piles of newspapers and magazines and rows of candy and gum. There are many papers in New York beside the *Times*. There are three tabloids, a lot of business papers, and in many newsstands, depending on the neighborhood, you can get foreign newspapers and magazines.

In Spanish neighborhoods you can get all the Spanish papers, Italian neighborhoods all the Italian papers, and so on. The first thing I noticed in this newsstand was the three local tabloids, each stacked up against one another in a row on the sidewalk. Each one had the same banner headline in bold letters.

WALL STREET EXECS FOUND SLAIN
IN EAST SIDE APT

One paper had a picture of the Eighty-Second Street apartment building. Another had pictures of both Barrett and Cahill in what looked to be old photographs. I quickly turned my head and began walking down Central Park West. The bright September sun was above the tip of Manhattan and I could see its yellow reflection off the silver sides of the Twin Towers. I looked away from the glare and wondered where Katherine was and for the first time since yesterday I was scared.

FORTY-THREE

"SO THEN WHAT HAPPENED?" MORRIS Bergman asked. He re-lit the remainder of his cigar which resembled a thick stubby plug. His collar was unbuttoned and his tie hung loose, like a noose around his neck. The only thing I hadn't told Morris, the parts I left out, were how Katherine had planned to kill Steve right from the beginning and my shooting Arthur Barrett. I left that stuff out, at least for now anyway. I simply told Morris that Katherine had shot Barrett dead as well. That when I went up to the apartment and saw the bodies I got scared and left, forgetting the gun.

"I walked home," I said. "All the way. Lost myself in the crowds, just like the day before. To Tenth Street. When I got there two police cars were waiting out front."

"Man, they got to her fast. At least now you know where Katherine is. She must have told them something. Told them about you," Morris said. He leaned back on the bench. The waning afternoon light put a warm glow on his face. I could see him thinking, as if this were a math problem and he hadn't quite completed the equation yet. I pulled out my last cigarette and lit it. There was a small pile of crushed butts at my feet. It was rush hour now, the traffic was thickening, and the sidewalks were filled with office workers going home.

"That's what I figured," I said. "When I saw the police cars I turned right around and went back uptown, up to my club on Central Park South intending to spend the night but then I got paranoid. The police commissioner is a member there and hangs out quite often. It felt like cops were everywhere. So I figured the best way to hide was to find the biggest crowd I could and completely disappear in it. I went over to Times Square and checked into the Marriott Marquis under a phony name. Of course I couldn't eat or sleep, wondering what Katherine had said to the cops. Even the four or five martinis had no effect. When I left this morning I went to a coffee shop and then came here."

"Adrenaline," Morris said. He paused a moment and looked at his fingernails. "Why did you feel like you had to hide? Katherine was the one who shot them, right?"

"Morris," I said, looking him in the eye. "I was in the apartment. I was with Katherine right up to the moment she went in there. I went in afterwards to get the gun. Isn't that conspiracy or something?"

"Well, they don't know you're actually hiding. You sought out your lawyer, that's all." Morris threw his cigar stub into the street and rubbed his eyes. "Come on," he said. "Let's go back upstairs."

I had gotten to Morris' office just before lunchtime but now, as we went back up, it seemed like a hundred years ago. We got off the elevator and stepped into his office. Morris closed the door and sat behind his desk.

"Okay," he said. "If they're looking for you you're going to have to talk to them. Avoiding the police will only make matters worse. If you've told me everything then at worst you're facing, as you say, conspiracy and accessory charges. But conspiracy to murder is no cakewalk. We're talking jail time. Unless we can figure a case for reasonable doubt. Or something else. Katherine's manipulation of you would be a good place to start. The fact that this firm handled her divorce, you're her friend, the discovery of hidden money, somehow you got sucked into helping her get more money, and we try to establish there was no intention of murder. At least in the beginning. It was a rash act on her part. I don't know. We'll have to see how it plays out with the police. What they know. But if Katherine is talking to them you can be sure she isn't praising your virtues."

Suddenly the weight of all this bore down on me like an unexpected tsunami. It hadn't quite overwhelmed me yet but it was pushing me so fast I couldn't grab onto anything. I couldn't stop and start all over again. I had to ride this out the best I could. Katherine had betrayed me. Yes, I could say that now. She had betrayed me in the worst possible way and that, to be honest, is what hit me hardest. It's finally sunk in. I wasn't fucking her all these weeks, she was fucking me.

Morris opened a drawer and pulled out a black leather folder. An address book. He leafed through it.

"I've got a good contact, a friend, in the One-Nine from my days as an assistant D.A. The One-Nine is the one that has jurisdiction here, jurisdiction for Eighty-Second Street, most of the Upper East Side. I'm going to call him and tell him you're in my office. See what he has to say. See if there is any wiggle room."

Morris dialed the phone. "Lieutenant Rodriguez, please..."

I intentionally blocked out Morris' conversation, a small if not feeble attempt at slowing this thing down, and gazed about his office. I would learn soon enough what the police had to say, I knew. Behind Morris' desk I could see framed pictures of his family, his wife, his kids, two girls and a boy; on the beach, skiing, playing in the park, school photos, all of them fresh faced, happy, cheerful.

I looked at these pictures and wondered what the hell was I thinking with Katherine? Did I think we were going to have pictures like that someday? Is that why I went along with her?

Was I really that stupid and foolish? I had loved her, to be sure. Blinded, I now knew, to the point of going along with her cockamamie plan to murder Steve over his will. And she betrayed me certainly. And now I am in deep shit. To be sure, if there is any lesson in this it's that I deserve everything that is coming to me. Who could argue with that? The only person in the world right now who could was Morris. And that, I knew, was the truth behind my harsh reality. This is what my life had finally come to: Morris Bergman's ability to persuasively argue. And how would Morris argue if he ever found out I killed Arthur Barrett? Surely Katherine would claim that. She hadn't shot him. We both knew that. So in the end it would be my word against hers. Was that enough?

Morris hung up the phone. "They definitely want to talk to you," he said. "Tonight. Now."

"Is Katherine there?"

"No. They've got her somewhere else. They won't tell me where."

"What did he say? Anything? Do they want to arrest me?"

"Not yet. Depends, I guess, on what you say. You may have to surrender your passport. Katherine, of course, is denying everything. Claims you murdered both of them. Says the whole thing was your idea. Fortunately the police don't believe her. Not yet, anyway. They have a gun. Two actually. Apparently Barrett had one too. They also have something that connects you."

"They do? What?"

"He wouldn't tell me. Said we'll find out when we get there." Morris reached into his desk and pulled out another cigar. I suddenly remembered I had smoked my last cigarette.

"Can I pick up a pack along the way?" I asked.

"Sure," Morris said. He reached into a drawer and pulled out a legal pad. "All right," he said. "Let's write up a statement first.

Then, when they begin to question you, don't answer anything unless I tell you to."

We wrote the statement and then Morris and I talked for about an hour.

FORTY·FOUR

OUTSIDE AN EARLY SEPTEMBER EVENING had arrived. It was pleasantly cool and squares and rectangles of white and yellow light started to appear and the sky began its rapid descent into darkness; from pink to blue to gray. I picked up a pack of smokes at a newsstand on the corner and Morris and I hopped a cab. Lieutenant Rodriguez was waiting for us. He was a trim looking man, combed thick black hair, neat moustache, crisp white shirt and brown sport jacket, no tie. His black shoes were shined bright and he had a warm smile.

"Been a while, Morris," he said taking Morris' hand.

"I know," Morris said. "We're on different teams now."

"Our loss," Rodriguez said. I took that as a good omen.

My statement essentially said everything I told Morris; I'd known Steve Cahill in school, met Katherine through him, friends ever since, when Katherine and Steve separated I remained friends with Katherine, we started a relationship recently, I agreed to help her with some sort of an appeal to her divorce settlement. I detailed the information Katherine had told me about Steve and Arthur Barrett, their business relationship, the sex scheme with the girls, how Steve made video tapes of the sexual encounters, to be used if necessary to gain business. Basically everything except the part Morris didn't know, me shooting Barrett, and the part he did, me buying the gun. Morris felt if the gun issue arose we wouldn't deny it but until then there was no point in giving that piece of information to them. Morris said to me in private, before the interview started, that depending on how the questioning unfolded we might be able to formulate some kind of deal. I wasn't exactly sure what he meant by that but at this point the relationship between Morris and me was one of God to servant. What ever Morris said as far as I was concerned was the Golden Rule.

Lieutenant Rodriguez led us into a room. It was a small, dingy place, with a table and four chairs. It looked like what I had always imagined an interrogation room in a police station would look like; a scuffed and worn light green linoleum tiled floor, faded green walls with dark olive trim, and a cracked plaster ceiling with ancient rust stained water leaks. It had government issued metal table and chairs and harsh white fluorescent lights that had a slight hum to them. There was an old coffee machine in the corner that looked like it had not been used in years. There was a bakelite ashtray in the center of the table. Then the door opened again and a rumpled, craggy-looking man walked in. He looked tired and disheveled, like he'd been up all night. His shirt collar was unbuttoned, his tie loose, his shirt sleeves rolled up, and he had a cigarette dangling from the corner of his mouth.

"This is Lieutenant Pederale," Rodriguez said. "He'll be joining us."

Morris' eyes widened and he looked surprised as he shook hands with him and then we all sat down at the table. Standard operating procedure, I thought. Every interrogation needs a witness. On both sides.

Pederale sat like a sack of potatoes, leaning to one side and seemingly uninterested, and his dark eyes stared blankly into space. He stubbed out his cigarette in the ashtray without looking at it, as if he did this a hundred times a day. Rodriguez opened a medium sized notebook, worn and used, and he leafed through it until he came to the page he wanted. He glanced at it for a few minutes then looked up. "Can I get anyone coffee or anything? Water?" he asked.

We shook our heads. Pederale sat motionless. He reached into his pocket and pulled out a crushed pack of cigarettes, delicately pulled a crooked one out, and lit it. I reached for mine and did the same. Rodriguez then took my statement, read it carefully, and handed it to Pederale. Pederale barely glanced at it.

"Okay," Rodriguez said. "Mr. Jared Chase. Let's just take care of some formalities for a minute. You reside at 55 West Tenth Street, Manhattan, correct?"

"Yes."

"You are employed by the *Times* and work in their headquarters in midtown, is that correct?"

"Yes."

"How long have been there?"

"About fifteen years."

"Position?"

"Senior Vice President for Advertising Sales."

"Where were you born?"

"Here. New York. Lenox Hill Hospital."

"D.O.B.?"

"January 12, 1958."

Rodriguez lazily wrote my vital statistics in his notebook.

"Tell me how you spent the day on Tuesday last. From the moment you woke up," Rodriguez asked. The Monday was Labor Day, of course. The day Steve got home from London. Tuesday was the day Katherine met him in the apartment on Eighty-Second Street. Today was Thursday.

I looked at Morris. He nodded. I took a long drag on my cigarette and let the smoke run through my nose. Pederale looked me in the eye for the first time. He had the look of curiosity, like a scientist at a lab table.

"I had spent the night at Katherine's, her new place on Seventy-Second Street. We woke up and I went out for some bagels and coffee. She left her place around 11.00, maybe 11.15. She was to go meet Steve Cahill at an apartment he owned on Eighty-Second Street. Katherine had some things there. She wanted them. I was to meet her at a coffee shop on the corner. Around 12.30, 12.45. We had a lunch date at 1.00 at the Carlyle. When she came into the coffee shop she looked terrible, I asked her what was wrong. She said she had shot Steve," I paused a moment and took another drag off my butt. "Steve and his partner, Arthur Barrett."

"She told you that?"

"Yes," I said. I looked at Morris.

"It's in his statement," Morris said.

"I know," Rodriguez said. "I want him to tell it. You know the routine, Morris." Rodriguez turned back to me. "When was your lunch date?"

"1.00.

"The Carlyle?"

"It was where we had our first date," I said.

"Why didn't you meet there?"

"She was picking up some things at the apartment, I forget, shoes I think, some handbags. She wanted me to help her carry them."

"Where did she get the gun?"

"I don't know."

"Did you know she had a gun?"

"She told me she had a gun some time ago. For protection, she said. I never saw it."

"Were you surprised when she told you she shot them?"

"Yes. Very surprised. It seemed to come completely out of the blue. I was shocked, to put it mildly."

"What do you mean, shocked?"

"I never dreamed she could be capable of such a thing."

Rodriguez looked at me a moment and then wrote something in his notebook.

"Why do you think she shot them?"

"I don't know," I said. "There was no love lost between her and Steve, I can say that."

Morris gave me a look. "Just answer the questions, Jed," he said stiffly. "Try and keep them to 'yes' or 'no.'" Pederale looked at me again.

"Okay," Rodriguez said. "She told you she shot them. Then what?"

"She was panicked, shaking. I don't think she fully realized what she had done. It made me think she hadn't thought this through, like it might have been an accident, that she hadn't meant to do it. A waitress came over and I ordered some coffee. Katherine was upset, very upset. She ate some valium to calm her down."

"Valium?

"Yes."

"How do you know it was valium?"

"I saw the bottle."

"Did she always carry a bottle of valium with her?"

"I don't know."

"Did you ever see her take valium before?"

"No."

Rodriguez was writing in his notebook. Morris was making some notes on his legal pad. Pederale stubbed out his cigarette. The clock on the wall said 9.30.

"Then what?" Rodriguez asked.

"She told me she left the gun upstairs."

"Where?"

"In the apartment. In the bedroom. Like I said, she was panicked, kind of freaking out. Said she couldn't go back up there. I knew if she left the gun there, the gun she shot Steve and Barrett with, she'd be nailed. I loved her. I didn't want her to get caught, to be perfectly honest."

"So you went up to the apartment to get the gun."

"Yes."

Pederale slowly shook his head, clearly indicating he thought I was some kind of idiot.

"Willingly went to get the gun." Rodriguez stated as he wrote. He obviously agreed with Pederale.

I nodded my head.

"Yes or no?" he asked.

"Yes," I said. "Willingly."

"Okay. So you willingly went up to the apartment to retrieve the gun. What happened next?"

"I went into the apartment. It was open. I saw Barrett on the floor by the kitchen. There was blood everywhere. It scared me. I went into the bedroom, there were two. Two bedrooms. The first one had some kind of camera set up. A video camera. On a tripod. There was a window looking into the other bedroom. There were cassette tapes, video tapes, scattered all around. Five or six, maybe seven. Maybe more. I didn't understand why. I went into the second bedroom and saw Steve on the floor, half in the closet. Blood everywhere also. Like I said, I was starting to freak out a little; I've never seen anything like this before. I went to college with him you know, I've known him a long time. Katherine told me the gun was on the bed. I looked on the bed. I didn't see a gun. I looked under the bed, under the pillows, nothing. Steve lying there dead was getting me crazy. I didn't want to be there. I wanted to get out of there, gun or no gun. Then I realized about my fingerprints. I took my handkerchief and wiped everything I thought I touched and left. I wanted to leave. I walked down to the street, went into the coffee shop, and Katherine was gone."

"What did you think of that?" Rodriguez asked. "When you saw she wasn't there?"

"I didn't know at first. I was puzzled. Everything happened so fast, it was confusing in a way, and when I saw she wasn't there I tried not to think of what the implications were. It wasn't until yesterday, really, that I finally accepted the fact that she was trying to set me up. That she had betrayed me." I felt Pederale's eyes on me as I spoke. He was watching me.

Rodriguez studied his notes. He flipped a few pages and studied some more. Then he said, "Katherine Cahill says you came up with a plan to murder Steve Cahill when she told you about his will, that she was to inherit everything in the event of his death. What do you say to that?"

I looked at Morris. He nodded.

"It's not true," I said. "There was never any plan to do any such thing. The only plan we talked about was how she could go about appealing her recent divorce. She wanted me to help her with that."

"What sort of help?"

"You know, sit with her when she spoke to lawyers, give her advice, that kind of thing. She wasn't completely confident in dealing with lawyers and Wall Street businessmen. She knew I'd known Steve a long time, she thought that'd help. That maybe I could get to him somehow."

"Why did she want to appeal her divorce settlement?"

"She found out Steve Cahill had a lot more money than he admitted to in the divorce proceedings."

"How much more?"

"We weren't exactly sure. When she found the will it appeared to be about twenty-five million. Later I received information that suggested perhaps closer to a hundred million."

Pederale's eyebrows raised and he cleared his throat. He lit another cigarette. Rodriguez wrote quickly. Greed, as a motivator, has probably passed through this room a hundred thousand times.

"How did you find that out?" Rodriguez asked.

"I have a friend at the *Times*, a reporter." Pederale sat up now and leaned against the table. He quickly rubbed his eyes and folded his hands and placed them on the table before him. Rodriguez looked at me between scribbling notes. I said, "When Katherine found Steve's will she learned he had more money than he led her to believe. She was surprised to learn that. In the separation agreement she had agreed to a lump sum settlement of around two million cash plus Steve was to buy her an apartment. It was like a no-fault divorce, a mild arbitration you could say, a friendly buy-out. She didn't want to contest anything, make him prove his assets, all that stuff. She just wanted out. When she found his will while he was away it got her thinking, she changed her mind. This is what she told me. She thought maybe Steve purposely misled her, cheated her. That's when I asked my friend at the *Times* to look into Cahill and Company. I thought if Katherine hadn't known about her husband's personal finances she certainly wouldn't know anything about his business finances. I simply thought it would help her in her appeal."

"What did your friend find out?"

"He's still looking into it," I said. Pederale pulled out another cigarette but kept his eyes on me as he lit it. "But he told me last week he suspected Cahill and Company was hiding money in secret bank accounts offshore, money, my friend said, that had suspicious origins. Apparently Cahill would take a company private or do a raise up, or an IPO, and the money would covertly appear in one of these secret accounts. From there it disappeared."

"How does your friend know this?"

"He's a reporter, that's his job. He's in Washington now; apparently there is another one of these big deals about to happen. With Cahill and Company. It was supposed to happen when Steve got back from London."

Pederale was sucking on his cigarette anxiously. He took a long drag and placed it in the ashtray, the smoke curling up into the crudely bright fluorescent light. He took a thick notepad from his pocket and opened it. He looked right at me and asked, "What is your friend's name?"

"Mickey Thompson."

Pederale and Rodriguez wrote this down.

"Why is he in Washington?" Pederale asked. His voice was calm, soft.

"When he started to look into Cahill and Company he went to the SEC, you know, look into some of the deals Cahill was doing, try and develop some kind of profile. For some reason they told him some of those deals were classified. A lot of them apparently. Seemed sort of contradictory, you know. The SEC? Classified? That got him interested."

Pederale shook his head slowly and closed his notebook. He stood up and left the room, his cigarette still burning in the ashtray.

Morris turned to Rodriguez. "What's he doing here?" he whispered.

"They have an interest in this case."

Rodriguez turned to me. "Do you want to take a break? You want coffee or anything?"

"Coffee would be good," I said.

Rodriguez stood up. "Morris?"

"Sure," he said. "Black, no sugar."

"Same for me." I said.

Rodriguez left the room. When the door was closed I turned to Morris.

"Who was the other guy?" I asked.

"Lieutenant Pederale. Officially he's the NYPD liaison to the

FBI's Joint Counter-Terrorism Task Force. Unofficially he is the NYPD's liaison to the CIA."

"CIA? New York City cops work with the CIA?"

"Well, the UN is here for starters. So are intelligence agents for about 180 other countries. CIA has a huge counter-intelligence challenge here. Legally they are constrained so they work through the NYPD. In fact, NYPD has their own Intelligence division, sort of like a shadow CIA. That's where Pederale is from. It's not that surprising when you think about it."

I looked at Morris. I was puzzled. "Why," I asked, "would they be interested in this?"

"Good question," Morris replied.

FORTY-FIVE

RODRIGUEZ RETURNED WITH THE COFFEE. It smelled good in the stale air of the smoke-filled room. He placed the cups before us and he had one for himself. He sat down and took out his notebook and studied it. Morris took his cigar out of his inside pocket and tapped it on the table before running it under his nose.

"You said you have something that connects my client," Morris said.

"Yes," Rodriguez said, looking up from his notebook. He shifted in his seat. "Tapes. Video tapes. Pretty intimate ones. Of your client and Katherine Cahill."

What? I was stunned. How did that happen? Who took them? Where?

"What does that prove?" Morris asked. "He's already stated that he and Katherine Cahill had a relationship, an affair, if you will."

"I know," Rodriguez said. "I'm more interested in why they were taken. And by whom."

"Well, they certainly weren't taken by my client," Morris said, in a gamble. This was new information. He turned toward me. "Do you know about this?" he asked. I shook my head. It was a safe bet, I indicated. I had nothing to do with it.

"Right now we don't think they were either. It was a pretty sophisticated set up. Not something you put together overnight. Automatic focus. Motion detectors. Automatic light adjustment. Trailing technology. Super high tech. A professional job. The kind of stuff some of the agencies use. Looked like it had been installed some time ago. One thing disturbs me, though, Mr. Chase," Rodriguez said.

"What's that?"

"What you said about the gun, that all you knew was that she told you she had one but that you'd never seen it. Didn't you say that?"

My heart jumped. I knew where this was leading. "Yes," I said. I swallowed hard, ready for Rodriguez to reply.

"Well one of the tapes indicates otherwise," he said. He looked at me, his face hard, unmoving.

"Well," I stammered. I could feel my face reddening. "I, uh, if it's of what I think it is, perhaps, uh, you can understand my reluctance to mention it." Morris looked at me. He was clearly puzzled.

Rodriguez smiled. "Yes," he said. "I can understand that. But you must also understand that as a police officer it causes me to wonder what other information you may be withholding. That's what disturbs me."

I looked at Morris and back at Rodriguez. He knew this was my weak spot. "Nothing," I said. "I'm not withholding anything. I mean, the gun, you know, the only time I saw it was that afternoon and under the circumstances, well, you know, it's kind of embarrassing. I didn't think that was the kind of context you were looking for. But honestly, there is nothing else. It's all in my statement."

"Well," Rodriguez said. "I hope so. We'll see."

Rodriguez looked at me in an odd way, as if he had just thought of something. Then I remembered all the tapes in the apartment thrown across the floor. The ones of the girls and various businessmen Katherine and I decided to toss around.

"When I was in the apartment," I said, "when I went back to get the gun, there were maybe a half dozen tapes strewn about the floor. What were those?"

"Those are the tapes I'm talking about," Rodriguez said. "Those are the ones we found. All of them were of you and Katherine Cahill."

"But I'd never been in that apartment before," I said, not sure he had understood me.

"They weren't filmed there," Rodriguez said. "They were filmed at Steve Cahill's apartment on Park Avenue. We established that this afternoon. That's the equipment I was describing."

"What were they doing in the apartment on Eighty-Second Street?" I asked.

"That's one of the things we'd like to know."

"I saw a video camera in one of the bedrooms pointing through a window that looked into the other bedroom," I said. "Was there a videotape in the camera?"

"Yes," Rodriguez said.

"Of what?" I asked.

Rodriguez simply looked at me. Morris took the cigar out of his mouth and cleared his throat.

"May we go outside for a moment?" Morris asked Rodriguez.

"Of course," Rodriguez said. They stood up and left the room.

I sipped my coffee and looked at the clock on the wall. 10.15. I'd been here since 8.00. I was tired. I couldn't believe the tapes. How the hell could that have been? Did Katherine know? She must have. Maybe. Maybe not. Maybe it was Steve's thing. How many could there be? High tech, Rodriguez said, motion detection, automatic focus, light adjustment. Whenever anyone went into the room the camera started rolling. Steve liked to watch, Katherine had said. That means every time we were in her bedroom it was recorded on tape. Was there sound? Probably. Jesus Christ, how many times were we in there? Rodriguez said all of the tapes were of us. There were at least five or six I saw in the apartment. Maybe there were more in the room with the camera, I just didn't see them. Christ, how many times did we have sex at Katherine's? We've been together the last three weeks, twenty-one days. At least half that, say ten times, we'd been in her bedroom. There must be others. What did we talk about? The high tech aspect made it sound a little scary. This wasn't simply a camera set up on the other side of two-way mirror. But had Katherine known about it? Rodriguez said it had been installed a while ago. Was this something different than anything else I had learned about Katherine and Steve? Was this a whole new wrinkle?

I tried to remember exactly what we talked about in her bedroom. I don't ever remember talking about Steve. It was something I just don't think I'd do given the circumstances, being in his bed and all. I was pretty certain of that. But what about the gun? What did we talk about that afternoon in the bedroom with the gun? I had to assume there was sound. To the best of my knowledge we didn't mention anything other than Katherine asking me to fuck her with the gun. Loaded. That's right. I loaded the bullets. That's what Rodriguez was disturbed about. Were my prints on those bullets? On the gun? My God, they had to be. Did Katherine do that purposely? Of course she did, I decided. It was part of her plan. Hers and Barrett's. Get my prints on the bullets and the gun. The trip up to the Eighty-Second Street apartment was merely to finish me off. Somehow make it appear I killed Steve Cahill; jealous rage perhaps, Steve found the tapes, confronted me, I shot him, then shot myself. Murder – suicide. It happens all the time. Between the best of friends. I read somewhere once that something like eighty or ninety percent of all homicides are crimes of passion, between people who know each other. Well, the way Katherine and Barrett set this up it would certainly have filled that bill. Love triangle and all. And the way Katherine and Barrett planned to show that, to have it appear, was to have Katherine shoot Steve, go down and send me up, Barrett shoots me, puts the .38 in my hand, takes Katherine's gun, and he and Katherine take off and disappear... with a ton of money. That was their plan. Had to be.

Except that I shot Barrett and now, given the new circumstances, I needed to behave, *to think, to act like* Katherine did it. That she must have had a change of heart and decided to keep the money herself. Decided to get rid of Barrett, too. And to leave me holding the gun, so to speak. And somehow Morris had to suggest the conspiracy gone bad and get Lieutenant Rodriguez to buy into that. That's the way I saw it now. I had to behave like that is what happened. It was Katherine's and Barrett's conspiracy and Katherine changed it at the end. My role was essentially the same. I was the fall guy. Except in the original I was to be dead and in the revised version, Katherine's version, I had to be left alive. Left alive and holding the gun.

Rodriguez and Morris came back into the room. Morris said, "All right, Jed. Lieutenant Rodriguez and I have made an agreement. You can go home for now. You're free on your own recognizance but you'll have to surrender your passport, you can give it to me tomorrow and I'll get it over here. You can't leave the city and you have to be available for further questioning. I don't think you'll object to that."

"No," I said. I was curious about what Morris and Rodriguez spoke about. I looked at the clock. It said 10.30. "That's all fine with me."

"You are a person of interest," Rodriguez said. "This means we may arrest you at any time we feel there's enough evidence linking you to the crime. You understand?"

I swallowed hard. "Yes," I said. "I do."

After another half an hour of paperwork, fingerprinting, and photographing me Morris and I left the station house.

FORTY-SIX

THE NEXT MORNING I WAS awakened by the phone. It was 6.30.

"Jesus, Jed," Mickey Thompson said. I heard a lot of throbbing background noise. "I just saw the story about Steve Cahill and Arthur Barrett. What happened?"

"Where are you?" I asked.

"D.C., Union Station. I'm catching the 7.00 back to New York. There's a story in the Post, front page, about the murders. What's going on?"

"I don't know," I lied. I could hear cavernous echo's in Union Station. It was noisy. Rush hour, I thought. The rest of the world moves on.

"Where's the ex, Katherine?" Mickey was a true, instinctual reporter. He went right to the heart of the matter.

"The police have arrested her," I said.

"No shit."

"Yeah." I could hear Mickey thinking.

"You get anything on the company?" I quickly asked, before his mind began to make leaps and bounds.

"Yeah," he said. "I did. Heavy stuff."

"Yeah? Like what?

"I'll be in New York in three hours. Let's meet."

"Sure. Where?"

"You got a decent diner near you?"

"Sure. Sixth Avenue and Waverly Place. On the corner. Across the street from the subway. You can catch the E or the F out of Penn Station. I think they stop there. West 4th Street Station. You know it?"

"Yeah," he said. "I'll meet you there in three hours."

"Okay."

"Jed?"

"Yes?"

"You got anything to do with this?"

"I don't know," I said.

I lay in bed and thought about last night, the questioning, and what Morris told me after we left the station house, about what he and Rodriguez spoke about. For starters Morris vouched for me. Said Rodriguez held off keeping me overnight on Morris' word. I was grateful for that. He said Lieutenant Rodriguez didn't think I killed anyone, not yet anyway, but he suspected I knew more than I was saying. Because of Katherine. Because of our relationship, particularly our romance over the last month. His instinct, Morris said, was that I had some kind of idea, knowledge even, of Katherine's actions. What was throwing him was Barrett and why he was there. What also threw him were the tapes. Why were they there?

Rodriguez had gathered up the history of Steve Cahill and Arthur Barrett, had done enough digging to know there was something big going on with the offshore bank accounts, the ones in London and Jersey. He also knew what Mickey Thompson already told me, that Cahill and Company had some kind of involvement with the government. Some kind of financial relationship, not necessarily above board, Rodriguez told Morris. He also said they'd done a good job of hiding not only the money, but also a lot of the transactions. One of the reasons, Rodriguez told Morris, why Pederale is involved.

The lieutenant's rough sketch, his working theory for the moment, was that Barrett had access to, control perhaps, of the offshore money. Barrett and Katherine conspired to kill Steve and escape the country. Picked me as the fall guy, everything hinged on getting me into the apartment. Somewhere along the line Katherine changed her mind and decided to go it alone. Pretty simple, I said. Yes, Morris said, Rodriguez likes simple. Except there are still a lot of unanswered questions, a lot of holes. Like if Katherine killed Barrett as well as Steve then she must have had access to the accounts also.

This was true, I realized. I hadn't thought about that.

"What did he say about the girls and tapes and the whole sex scheme Steve and Barrett had going on?" I asked.

Morris looked at me slightly puzzled. "That's another one of the holes," he said.

"What do you mean?"

"There is no evidence any of that ever happened," Morris had said last night. He looked at me as if he'd been misinformed. I was stunned and felt as if the wind had been knocked out of me. "It's one of the things that puzzles Rodriguez about you. He wonders why you would make something like that up."

"I don't believe it," I had said. "What do you mean no evidence? I didn't make it up. What about the tapes?"

"There are no tapes. They only tapes are the ones of you and Katherine. Katherine, according to her statement and what Rodriguez told me, claims she has no idea about any tapes. Never heard of such a thing."

I couldn't believe it. No sex scheme? Katherine had spent hours, days, outlining the whole thing to me. There had to be some kind of evidence somewhere.

"What about Barrett?" I asked, trying to regain my equilibrium. "Why did Katherine shoot him if it was their conspiracy?"

"That's another inconsistency," he said. "He doesn't know." Morris also said he felt too that there seemed to be something missing in that part of the theory. "If Katherine wanted to get Barrett out of the picture she had to have access to the money also and apparently she claims she doesn't. Rodriguez said he'd eventually find out. It'll just take time. Also the forensics on the guns, the apartment, the DNA, all that stuff will take some time."

That worried me. "What about me?" I said. "Where does he think I am in all of this?"

"He thinks you were some kind of fall guy, but," Morris said last night, "he doesn't know what kind."

"What do you mean?"

"He doesn't know if you were Katherine's fall guy or Barrett's. And part of the reason he thinks he doesn't know is because you are not telling him everything you know. I'm beginning to wonder about that too."

I let that last sentence drop. Where I thought only three days ago I knew exactly what was going on, now I had absolutely no idea. Certainly I knew more than I was letting on, granted not a whole lot more, but enough to make me feel more confused than I would be if I knew nothing. This was the strangest part.

And I wondered what Mickey Thompson would have to say. As I lay in my bed on West Tenth Street watching the soft September sun stream through my bedroom window, grateful to be here rather than some dingy jail cell in the Tombs or on Rikers Island, listening to the morning sounds of the Village filter in, I recalled only moments ago Mickey's words, "heavy stuff." What did that mean?

And then the phone rang again. I looked at my watch. 7.15. Mickey would be on his way by now, riding the Metro-liner to Penn Station. I picked up the phone.

"Jed?" It was Morris.

"Yes, Morris," I said. "Good morning."

"Listen," he said quickly. He sounded as if he'd been awake for hours.

"Where are you?" I asked

"Listen," he said again, "you need to be here, in my office, this morning. We've got a meeting set for 11.00. Downtown. Rodriguez will be there. Also Pederale. And some others. Come to my office early so we can talk first, we'll go downtown together. And don't be late. There seems to be some new developments."

"Oh? Who else is coming?"

"Some people from Washington," he said.

"Washington? Why?"

"Just get over here," Morris said. "We've got things to talk about, things to decide. This thing is changing. Rodriguez is expecting you. Oh, and bring your passport and whatever you do, Jed, don't be late. They don't like that with guys out on their own recognizance." Then he hung up.

FORTY-SEVEN

THE WAVERLY DINER IS OPEN twenty-four hours and is always packed. It is by far the most stereotypical Greek diner I know of and serves stereotypical Greek diner food: eggs and bacon, cheeseburgers and fries, soups and sandwiches, moussaka and spinach pie and a couple dozen other dishes. The clientele are mostly NYU students, tourists, and elderly people who live in the neighborhood. I normally eat at another place on West 4th Street, a much smaller and therefore quieter place, strictly local. The Waverly is always noisy, no matter what time of day, loud in fact, and I thought it a good place for Mickey and me to meet. We wouldn't be noticed and no one would hear us. I walked in, found a booth, and ordered a cup of coffee.

Who might these people from Washington be? I wondered. FBI agents from the Joint Counter-Terrorism Task Force? What the hell did terrorism have to do with the murder of Steve Cahill and Arthur Barrett? When Morris mentioned Pederale and who he was last night it kind of went over my head, I didn't really think about it beyond the initial question of why. But now Morris said some people from DC were coming to see me, this morning, that quick, and the question became more serious. Why would the FBI's terrorism task force be involved in a New

York City homicide? Was Katherine some kind of underground terrorist? Were they coming to see her too?

It was 10.15 when Mickey walked through the door. I needed to be in Morris' office by 11.00 at the latest, and by cab or subway, I'd have to leave no later than 10.40. Don't be late, Morris had said. If I got there by 11.00, I figured, we could talk on the subway going downtown.

"Jed, Christ, how are you doing?" Mickey slid into the booth. He held a thick leather briefcase which contained too many bulging papers and multiple notebooks to close all the way. He shoved it in the corner between himself and the wall and leaned against it. In his other hand he had an old gym bag, like a carry-on bag, and he dropped that on the floor under the table. He shook my hand.

"Good, Mickey," I said. "Considering."

"So, tell me, what the hell happened?"

"Cops think Katherine killed Cahill and Barrett. Shot them. In an apartment on Eighty-Second Street. Tuesday. They've arrested her. Took me in for questioning too. Yesterday. I can't believe it. Everything has happened so fast it's still something of a blur." I finished my coffee.

"Why? Why'd she shoot them?"

"Why do you think?" I asked. "Money."

Mickey looked at his briefcase and said, "Yeah... certainly seems to be a common thread around here."

A waitress came over and Mickey ordered a glass of orange juice and a bacon and egg sandwich. I took another coffee.

"So?" I said. "What did you do in Washington?"

"Tracked down an old friend used to cover Treasury and budget matters on the Hill. He has some contacts over at the SEC. His brother-in-law is head of compliance over there. Sees every piece of paper that goes through the SEC. Wanted to find out what the 'classified' thing with regard to Cahill and Company was all about, like I told you. Took a little pushing and shoving, a little arm twisting here and there, but I got some interesting stuff. Funny thing is I started at the SEC and ended up at the State Department, Department of Defense, and the CIA, believe it or not. Fortunately the *Times* has a great bureau down there, extensive sources and a lot of resources. But it's crazy, Jed. Some wild stuff with these guys. Definitely a story here. Possibly a very major one." He pointed his thumb at his briefcase. The waitress came with my coffee and Mickey's juice. I looked at my watch. 10.25.

"Sorry, Mick, but you gotta be quick. I've got to be in my lawyer's office by 11.00. In midtown. More questions."

Mickey nodded and downed the orange juice in one gulp. He slapped his glass down and the waitress came back with his sandwich and slid it in front of him. Mickey ordered another orange juice and a cup of coffee and reached over to his briefcase. He pulled out one of the notebooks and took some papers from it.

"Seems Cahill and Company has some kind of relationship with the US government. Haven't been able to pin it down precisely but it begins with Arthur Barrett." Mickey flipped through some papers. "All right, here... back in the late sixties, early seventies Barrett was in the Marine Corps. Served in Vietnam. Was involved in a program called 'Phoenix.' It was a CIA operation. Top Secret. Basically they were tasked to locate primary political and military targets and 'neutralize' them in North Vietnam, Laos, and Cambodia. Barrett didn't neutralize anyone, he was logistics, mostly in funneling money from MACV, the Military Assistance Command in Saigon, to pay for stuff, equipment, covert transportation, but mostly bribes to Vietnamese, Laotian, and Cambodian officials and informants. In other words he was in charge of funding and dispersing the Phoenix program in Vietnam. Highly classified. And because it was a Top Secret operation the funding had to be secret, no one could know about it, not the Army, not Congress, no one. He got a green light from his superiors to develop a covert money laundering scheme and oversaw it in Saigon. All government money. Millions. Tens of millions. Could have been hundreds of millions, no one really knows. It was what they call a 'black operation.' He took his orders from Washington, from CIA. His contact was a guy called Coldwell." Mickey took a quick bite from his sandwich and held up his hand. A bright yellow line of egg yolk ran down his chin. "I know you're thinking 'what the hell does this have to do with the price of tea in China' but stay with me. It gets interesting." Mickey wiped his mouth with his sleeve and took a sip of his juice. "Okay, Barrett gets out of the service after the war and starts his career on Wall Street. Rookie trader and all that and it seems to me he was put there, if you get my drift. Very interesting thing, though. He doesn't quite quit the CIA. He becomes a contractor, a contract agent, in other words, he does freelance work for the CIA in specific cases when they need a cover like a Wall Street executive. Not only that, he is a recruiter for them. He spots potential talent and introduces them to the CIA, brings them in." Mickey leaned across the table and got close to my face. "Your buddy Cahill was one of his recruits."

"What?"

"Yeah. Steve Cahill. Worked for the CIA."

"I don't believe it."

"Well, you better, pal. It's all right here." Again the thumb pointed at his briefcase. "Those three years in B-school? Oh yeah, he studied some at Wharton, took some classes, specialized stuff, forensic accounting, investigative auditing, subjects like that, but he spent most of his post-graduate work at Langley. When he was done they let him and Barrett loose on Wall Street to create exactly what they did. A financial services company that did investment banking, venture capital, taking companies public or private, private equity, you name it. A sort of one stop shop. Except their clientele was pretty specific. In fact they essentially had only one customer. The CIA."

"I don't get it," I said.

"It was how the CIA, particularly the clandestine departments, the classified areas, paid for a lot of their covert operations. The CIA, under the guise of some pseudo defense or intelligence sub-contractor, would 'invest' money in Cahill and Company in some way. Say a small fictitious company in Podunk, Iowa that supposedly manufactured invisible widgets or something or a fictitious company in Backwater, Idaho that made stainless steel screws for tanks. The money ended up in an untraceable account offshore and then dispersed to whoever or whatever operation was supposed to get the funds. Bogus companies like Indo Asia Air Charter, Ltd. Or the East-West Trading Company. Completely hidden, untraceable, practically invisible. Funded covert, 'black ops' all over the world."

"Jesus Christ, Mick. How the hell..." I looked at my watch again. 10.45. "Damn," I said. "I've got to go, but Mickey, you've gotta tell me more. Is this what the accounts in London and Jersey are all about? What were Barrett and Steve doing with the money? Did Katherine have a role? Did she know Steve was in the CIA? What kind of operations were they funding?"

"Jed," Mickey said as he polished off the sandwich. "This is just the tip of the iceberg."

I stood up and threw a few bills on the table. "If I don't show at my lawyer's the cops will come after me. I'm a 'person of interest' in this whole thing. Mickey, I need to know more. What are you doing this afternoon?"

"I'm heading back to the office. I need to start organizing my work for this story and I've got some digging to do. My editor thinks maybe a two or three part series, maybe even a Sunday magazine cover story or something. It goes beyond the business section obviously. But it is still a story in progress. And I want to talk to you about Katherine. Do you think she'll let me speak to her in jail?"

"Can we meet later?"

"Call me when you get done at your lawyer's."

It was 10.50. I quickly left the Waverly Diner and got the first cab I could find. I was going to be late but there was nothing I could do about it. This information Mickey had about Barrett and Steve was mind boggling. I now realized why 'some people from Washington' wanted to meet with me in my lawyer's office. If I knew Katherine, if I had had a relationship with her, and she was the one accused of killing two of their employees, or contract agents, or whatever you call them, then obviously they wanted to talk to me. What did Katherine know that they, perhaps, didn't?

FORTY-EIGHT

I WAS STUCK IN TRAFFIC in Herald Square. The clock by Macy's said 11.05 but I didn't know if it was right. My watch said 11.00. Either way I was going to be late. What would Rodriguez do, send a couple of patrol cars out to look for me? I didn't know. The cabbie should never have gone up Sixth Avenue to begin with. It was too late now. That's the problem when a city becomes a tourist destination. You get traffic. You get crowds. The waves of people streaming across Thirty-Fourth Street and Broadway to Macy's or Toys-R-Us, or the Gap, or the hundreds of other stores around here were holding up every car in a half mile radius. It was a logjam. And the traffic cops seemed to be simply standing by and watching. This is the price you pay to have a crime-free, tourist friendly city, I thought. Wait till the theme parks and mega-malls arrive. And for the first time in my life I entertained the thought of moving somewhere else. The driver looked in his rear view mirror at me and shrugged.

But the truth is my anxiety over being late to my lawyer's office paled against the fact that Steve Cahill was a CIA agent. I simply couldn't get my head around it. It was unbelievable. Inconceivable. A complete and total shock. Is that what he did in London every August? Meet with his spymasters? He frequently took trips during the year, of course. I knew that, Katherine knew that. Was he a secret agent on those trips? In fact, I couldn't remember Katherine ever going with him on those three or five day trips to Europe. She only went in August. And was it Europe? That's what he'd say. But who knew where he went? Steve Cahill. CIA agent. Un-fucking-believable.

And Barrett, too. Although that didn't shock me as much. I didn't know him. But that stuff about Vietnam was pretty crazy. Did Katherine know all this stuff? Did she know she was hanging around CIA agents?

It was 11.20 when the cab pulled up to Morris' office building in midtown. The sun was high and bright and hurt my eyes when I got out and on the sidewalk. I saw two large men in dark suits approach as I walked toward the entrance of Morris' building.

"Mr. Chase..." one of them said and suddenly they both grabbed my arms from either side and turned me around and marched me back to the curb. Their grip was firm and there was no doubt as to who would win in a struggle. A black Ford Crown Victoria with tinted windows slid up to us and the rear door opened. The two men pushed my head down and put me in the car.

"What are you doing?" I asked, somewhat meekly. "Who are you?"

Nobody said anything. There was a driver and someone in the passenger seat. They wore dark suits too and all of them kind of looked the same, as though they were related or something. The two men slid in on either side of me. I could see a red light, the kind the police use in unmarked cars, on the dashboard. The driver gunned the engine, swung the wheel, and pulled out into traffic. The guy in the passenger seat pushed a button on the dashboard and the red light started flashing. Then he took a small radio out of his inside pocket, pushed a button, and said, "We have Mr. Chase." Then the siren started to wail. If these guys were bad guys, I thought, they did a pretty good job of disguising it.

With the siren and light the car sliced through traffic easily. In minutes we sped into Broadway and where I was stuck only minutes ago these guys flew. I could see the towers of the World Trade Center rising above lower Manhattan gleaming in the noon sun and growing larger and larger as we drove down-town. Downtown is where Police Headquarters is, I thought. It's also where all the Federal buildings are. And all the courthouses. We flew out of midtown and charged through the Garment district, Madison Square, Flatiron, the edge of Chelsea and then the Village, then Soho and Tribeca, and finally, just before City Hall we entered the underground parking lot of the Federal building. These guys are Federal agents, I thought. Or Pederale's people bringing me to Federal agents. One thing was for certain, I realized. These guys were serious.

We got out of the car and the two guys who grabbed me at Morris' office slid out with me and grabbed me again and escorted me toward the elevator. The underground lot was full of black Crown Victoria's and SUV's with tinted windows. There didn't seem to be too many civilian looking cars here. In the elevator one of the guys pushed the top floor button and within minutes we were walking down a long corridor, offices on either side, mostly secretarial types sitting at computers, with the occasional beefy looking guy standing in a doorway – a shoulder holster with a fat pistol bulging under his armpit, a paper cup of coffee firm in his hand.

We entered what I thought would be an office but when we went through the door it led into another short hallway and then to the left another door with a keypad on it. One of the men punched in a series of numbers and the door swung open into another short hallway to yet another door on the left with a keypad. Wherever we were going it was like going through a maze. We entered into a sort of an office that doubled as a reception area. There were oak bookshelves filled with leather volumes on two walls and behind the polished oak desk along the adjoining wall were wooden file cabinets, the kind that used to be in old office buildings. It was a very woody office. A pretty woman sat behind the desk and when she saw us she said, "Oh, hi. They're inside waiting. Go on in." There was a heavy oak door beside her desk and we went through it. It felt like we were entering the inner sanctum of some sort of secret fraternity or something.

FORTY-NINE

WE ENTERED INTO A LARGE office with dark mahogany paneled walls, a nice thick burgundy carpet, a lot of ornate mouldings, a large mahogany desk with a computer, a few neatly stacked papers, an ink blotter, and a bunch of telephones. There was a sofa against one wall, three armchairs around a coffee table, and two walls of windows that looked out onto lower Manhattan. The view was stunning. The Woolworth Building, the World Trade Center, City Hall, the Brooklyn and Manhattan bridges, New York Harbor, the Verrazano-Narrows bridge, Staten Island, New Jersey; the rest of the world could be seen from out these windows. My two escorts let go of my elbows, turned, and left the office, closing the door softly behind them.

"Hello, Jed. You're late," Morris said sternly. "I told you not to be late."

"I'm sorry," I said. "I got stuck in traffic."

Morris was standing by the desk. Behind the desk stood someone I didn't recognize, a tall, thin man with white hair, and a large head. He was impeccably dressed in a dark blue pin striped suit. He looked like a high priced lawyer or an investment banker. Standing beside him was another man I didn't recognize who was shorter, thicker, with salt and pepper hair and a thick moustache. He looked foreign. He wore khaki pants and a brown tweed jacket, no tie. To his right stood Rodriguez and Pederale. It seemed my entrance interrupted a conversation they were having.

"I told you not to be late," Morris said again. "You got these guys nervous." Morris stepped toward me. "Did you bring your passport?"

"Yes," I said and I took it out of my pocket. I handed it to Morris who handed it to the tall thin man standing behind the desk. It was obviously his office we were in.

The tall thin man studied my passport, leafed through it, and placed it on his desk. There was not much to look at. A few stamps from the Caribbean, one, I think, from Mexico. I felt the eyes of the others on me and Morris, sensing my unease, said, "Jed, this is David Coldwell," Morris gestured to the tall thin one and then to the other, shorter one, "and this is Bill Dimon. They represent the United States government. The government has an interest in this case. You know Lieutenants Rodriguez and Pederale."

I nodded at everyone.

"Why don't we all sit down," Coldwell said. He had an old school New England accent. He waved his hand at the sofa and chairs as he sat behind his desk. Morris led me to the sofa where he and I sat. Dimon, Rodriguez, and Pederale each took an armchair. The coffee table before us was barren except for today's issue of the *Times* and *Journal*.

"Not that it matters," Morris said. "But we are being recorded both audio and visual. The reason we are here, well," Morris looked at Rodriguez first and then to Coldwell. "Why don't one of you start?"

Coldwell cleared his throat. "Yes," he paused, "right. Lieutenant Rodriguez, jump in at any time." Rodriguez nodded. Coldwell turned to me. "Mr. Chase, I've read your statement and the transcripts of your interview last night. I have been briefed by Lieutenant Rodriguez with regard to the existing evidence in the murders of Mr. Cahill and Mr. Barrett. We should be getting the preliminaries from the forensic people this afternoon. I understand your involvement, to some extent, with Katherine Cahill, and to a lesser extent with Steve Cahill. It appears you haven't any involvement at all with Mr. Barrett save for a brief introduction by Ms. Cahill three or four weeks ago at a chance encounter in a restaurant. Are you with me?"

"Yes, sir."

"The government of United States has an interest in this case because Mr. Cahill and Mr. Barrett were employees of the government, specifically, they were my employees." Coldwell began to tap his fingers on his desk. He glanced at the man called Dimon for a split second and then back at me. "There are a couple of issues here, aside from the murders, which are quite sensitive and could be harmful to the United States. Information that is considered classified at the highest levels. Do you understand me?"

I didn't but I nodded anyway.

"In addition to the classified nature and the sensitivity that surrounds this incident there is a large amount of money that seems to be missing. A very large amount." Coldwell stopped tapping his fingers. "Because of your relationship with Ms. Cahill and her husband, or ex-husband I should say, we are interested in you. This is why you are here and not in jail." Coldwell leaned forward and folded his hands together in front of him. "If you were in jail there would be a public record of your arrest. There would be an interest on the part of your lawyer to prove your innocence which would cause him to launch his own investigation. In the case of murder, in New York State, there is the possibility you would face the death penalty. This would bring a lot of attention to things that perhaps are best left alone. Are you with me?"

I had no idea where this was going but I nodded as if I did.

"You have known Mr. Cahill for quite some time, haven't you?"

"Since college. Almost twenty years."

"Did you ever know that he worked for the United States government?"

"No."

"You've known his wife, Ms. Cahill, for quite some time as well, correct?"

"Yes. Maybe ten years."

"Did she ever indicate her husband may have worked for the United States government?"

"No. Never," I said.

Coldwell's demeanor was cold, unemotional, unlike a lawyer who may be trying to lead or draw out information. He was simply sending and receiving, like a radio. Or a robot.

"Has Ms. Cahill ever mentioned the word 'Dakota' to you?"

I looked at Morris.

"Don't look at your lawyer, answer me please. Did Katherine Cahill ever mention the word 'Dakota?'"

"No. Katherine never mentioned that word." I paused. I looked at Morris again, quickly, and then said, "But Steve mentioned it."

Dimon uncrossed his legs and sat up in his chair.

"Cahill mentioned it?" Coldwell asked calmly. "When?"

I looked at Morris again. I couldn't help myself. I was lost. I had lost any sense of center in this. It seemed to me the murders of Steve Cahill and Arthur Barrett had been put on the back burner, were almost ancillary to why we were here.

"I asked you not to look at your lawyer, Mr. Chase. Simply answer my questions. I told you, I have no interest in putting you in jail. Lieutenants Rodriguez and Pederale are with me on this. When we are done with this project we are willing to begin the process of protecting you from any legalities that may arise from this case. Immunities, witness protection, what ever the case may be. But in order for us to move forward with these arrangements we must have your complete co-operation, even further involvement on your part if necessary. Do you understand me?"

"Jed," Morris interjected. "Listen to Mr. Coldwell. He is not misleading you. We didn't get a chance to talk this morning. You were late. We were to go over all this in my office. You were to sign some papers. Time is an issue here. Please answer Mr. Coldwell's questions openly and candidly. I am advising you as your lawyer to do so. I will explain later."

I nodded. Immunity? Witness protection? What were they talking about? "Okay, Morris. Sure. Whatever you say."

"So, Mr. Chase," Coldwell continued. "When did Steve Cahill tell you about 'Dakota?'"

"Well, as I've said, I went up to the Eighty-Second Street apartment after Katherine came down. This is when she told me she shot Steve. She said she had left the gun up there. It's in my statement. I told Lieutenant Rodriguez this last night. What I didn't say was when I went into the bedroom to look for the gun Steve was still alive. Barely. But still alive. I went over to him. I asked him what happened. I hadn't known Katherine had gone there to shoot him. He looked at me, surprised I was there. He said Barrett and Katherine had shot him, one or the other, I don't know exactly who or what he meant, Barrett was dead too. Steve said something about how Barrett had control of the accounts. Then he said the word 'Dakota' and that was it. Something about 'the Dakota accounts' is what he said. Something like that. That was it."

Coldwell and Dimon looked at each other. Rodriguez looked at me and his words from last night came back and echoed in my ears, '...makes me wonder what other information you are withholding.'

"That's it? 'The Dakota accounts?' Did he say what the Dakota accounts were?"

"No. That was it. Then he just stopped, he stopped breathing."

"I see." Coldwell turned to Dimon but Dimon simply sat there without saying a word. Then suddenly he looked at me.

"What about Barrett?" Dimon said. He had a New York accent. "Did he say anything?"

"He was lying on the floor. He'd been shot. I assumed he was dead." I paused, remembering the moment I shot him, his gun aimed at me and about to shoot. "No," I said, "he didn't say anything."

"Does 'Dakota' mean anything to you?" Dimon asked.

"No," I said. "At first I thought he meant the Dakota apartment building, over on the west side, like maybe he had an apartment there or something. In fact I went there Wednesday to see, I asked the doorman, but no, he doesn't, they hadn't heard of him. I was curious though, what he meant by it."

Nobody said anything. I could tell the room was soundproof, I couldn't hear a thing. Nothing from the office next door where the pretty woman sat or any street sounds from outside, no sirens, no horns, nothing. Very rare in New York.

Coldwell broke the silence. "Do you know why Katherine Cahill would go to London after murdering Steve Cahill?"

"London?" I was surprised. Is that where she went after the coffee shop? Did she go to the airport? "Is she there now?"

"Just answer the question, Mr. Chase."

"I have no idea. I know Steve went every year in August, everyone knew that. Katherine would join him. This year, of course, she didn't. She shot him the day after he came back. But no," I said. "I didn't know she went to London."

More silence. Dimon went over to Coldwell and whispered something in his ear, then returned to the armchair.

Rodriguez spoke. "Let me go through the timeline one more time," he looked at Coldwell and then Pederale, "then you can have him. I'm done."

"Sure," Coldwell said.

"Mr. Chase," Rodriguez said. "You said that Ms. Cahill approached you to help her with her divorce settlement, right? About three weeks ago?"

"Yes, she…"

"Cut the shit, Chase," Pederale said. "She came to you with a plan. She knew Cahill and Barrett had hidden a lot of money somewhere, maybe she knew where, and she came to you with a plan to kill Cahill and you two would take off with the money and live happily ever after. Isn't that more like what she came to you with?"

I simply sat there. I didn't know what to say. I felt the eyes of everyone on me.

"That's enough for me," Rodriguez finally said as he stood up. "I'm done."

Pederale remained seated. Morris tapped my arm. I turned and he said in a low voice, "You and I need to speak." I nodded. Morris looked at Pederale and Coldwell.

"Can my client and I have a few words, alone?"

"Certainly," Coldwell said. He turned to Pederale. "Any objections?" Pederale was reading through some notes. He looked up. "No, go right ahead."

Coldwell pushed a button on one of his phones and the door immediately opened.

"Take these gentlemen to room four," Coldwell said. "When they are done bring them back, please."

The same two men who had escorted me from Morris' office building waited at the door for us. We followed them through the reception area, back through the maze, and at the second door with the keypad we went left rather than right. There was another door with a keypad and one of the men punched some numbers and we went through. He opened the first door on the right and led us in to a small office.

"We'll be outside the door," he said. "When you are done just knock and we'll take you back." He closed the door.

"Morris," I said. "What the fuck is going on?"

Morris looked at me with his sad, basset hound eyes. "I was going to ask you the same thing," he said. The room had a small metal desk and chair, a small sofa against the wall, and two chairs. It was a mini version of Coldwell's office without the mahogany paneled walls or burgundy carpet, done in a more standard government style. It did have, though, the same view out the windows. Morris and I drifted to the windows. We both stood there looking out at the city. This room wasn't as soundproof as Coldwell's and I could hear the traffic below. It was bright but I could see dark clouds miles away over New Jersey. A storm brewing perhaps.

"Here's the deal," Morris said as he stared out the window. "As I said last night about Rodriguez, the feeling is you are on the periphery of this thing, more innocent than any of the others, Katherine included, but not completely. There's a deal on the table. Fortunately NYPD and the Feds aren't fighting over this one. As Coldwell said, they're willing to let you out of any charges, and right now they think there are a few serious ones, if you not only co-operate but perhaps continue to actively help."

"What do you mean? With Katherine?"

"Yes."

"How?"

"I'm not sure. That's up to Coldwell. But this is the deal. NYPD is willing to let you go, give you to the government so to speak, in exchange for two high profile drug cases the government is pursuing that Rodriguez wants. Pederale and Coldwell made it happen this morning and so Rodriguez has backed out. This thing is now strictly federal, under their jurisdiction. The Feds want to keep this quiet until they know exactly what's going on and then put it to bed. The case apparently touches on some highly classified stuff. If that means Katherine going to prison for the rest of her life, so be it, but what they really want is to find out where this missing money is."

"What missing money?"

"They haven't told me everything but apparently Barrett, and to an as-yet-unknown extent, Cahill, have somehow squirreled away close to a hundred million dollars of Coldwell's, well, the government's money. Hidden it somewhere. How, where, and when, I have no idea. Coldwell runs a counter-terrorism program for the Defense Department and apparently Barrett and Cahill, through Cahill and Company, were working for him in a financial way, handling the program's money I guess, I'm not sure exactly. When Barrett and Cahill were found dead Pederale knew right away who they were and thought at first it might have been linked to some kind of terrorist thing, an assassination or something. When that didn't pan out Coldwell and this guy Dimon began to focus on you. So tell me, Jed. What is really going on with you and Katherine? Did you know about all this? That she wanted to kill Cahill, or Barrett did? Or you? Did she ask you to? Did you? If you want me to represent you, you've got to level with me. Seriously, Jed. Or I'll walk out of here now."

"Morris..." I said. And then I told him everything I hadn't told him before. About Katherine's plan to kill Steve from nearly the very beginning and about me shooting Barrett with Katherine's gun in the apartment. I also told him that at no time did she ever mention Steve or Barrett working for the govern-ment or anything about stolen government money. Simply that Steve had more money than he told her and she wanted it, as I said originally. I could tell, though, that my confession of me shooting Barrett surprised him.

"He had a gun, Morris. He was going to shoot me," I said.

Morris looked at me. "You should have told me," he said.

"I'm sorry. I couldn't. I was scared."

Then I told him everything Mickey Thompson told me. About Barrett, the CIA, everything.

"Jesus H. Christ," Morris said. "No wonder they want to keep this quiet. Where is Mickey now?"

"In his office. At the *Times*. I told him I'd call him when I was done with you."

We stood at the window for a few minutes. Morris was thinking. I could see the storm clouds approaching out over New Jersey. Another hour or two, I thought, and it will be raining. Morris looked at his watch. "All right," he said. "Let's go back. Don't say anything until I get your deal all sewn up. Got it?"

"Sure, Morris," I said. "I'm in your hands."

FIFTY

IN COLDWELL'S OFFICE MORRIS WORKED out my deal. In exchange for my complete co-operation and active involvement, if necessary, I would be granted complete immunity from any prosecution on matters relating to the murders of Steve Cahill and Arthur Barrett. I signed papers, they signed papers, Morris signed off on everything, and then Coldwell told Morris about one last thing.

"Most of where this is going is classified, Counselor," Coldwell said in a mildly grave tone. "Most of it is Top Secret. You and Mr. Chase are going to hear things, come across things, from the past as well as present that are considered at the highest levels to be very sensitive to the security of the United States. In view of that both of you are going to have sign clearance forms, specific only to this investigation. What that means is that from now on your involvement with me, with Mr. Dimon, with Lieutenant Pederale, is classified. You can tell no one, you can reveal no information to anyone other than us, under penalty of the law, which in Mr. Chase's case could be very severe. The penalty, by the way, for revealing classified information is a term in prison. In Mr. Chase's case, he'd violate the terms of his immunity agreement as well so he'd be facing further prosecution. The combined time for conviction of conspiracy to murder, accessory to murder, revealing classified information, probably a few other crimes as well, would amount to multiple decades in a federal prison. Do you both understand me?"

"Yes," Morris said. "I'm familiar with classified status."

"Mr. Chase?"

"Yes, of course."

Further forms were signed and Pederale gathered all the papers up and went out the door. Then Morris told Coldwell and Dimon about me shooting Barrett. "Barrett was about to shoot him," he said. "It was self-defense."

"It would have probably come out in the forensic report," Coldwell said. "But still. It adds a new wrinkle. For the case as well as for Mr. Chase."

"What do you mean?" I asked.

"If you violate any of our agreements we can add murder to the list of charges."

Morris looked at me.

"I can assure all of you," I said. "I am acting in good faith and have no intention of not living up to any of the agreements I have just signed."

"Good," Coldwell said. "I wouldn't expect otherwise."

"What's the next step?" Morris asked.

"Ms. Cahill returns from London tomorrow. We have her in custody there. When she does, Mr. Chase, you and Mr. Dimon will continue our investigation."

"How did you find her in London?" I asked.

"Mr. Dimon will fill you in on everything you need to know." Coldwell stood. "Just so we're all clear on this, Mr. Dimon is my representative; he has the authority to make decisions and rescind them. If he feels you are not living up to your agreements with us he can and will cancel them and have you arrested. Do yourself a favor, Mr. Chase, please keep that in mind at all times."

"Believe me Mr. Coldwell, I have no reason not to live up to my agreement." I paused a moment and looked right into his eyes. They were cold opals, as if they'd been carved out of arctic ice. They frightened me. "Please don't doubt that."

"Good," he said. He turned to Dimon. "All right, William, it's all yours now." Coldwell bent over and picked up a black leather briefcase from under his desk, he nodded at Morris and me, and strolled out of the office. I watched him close the door softly and then turned to Morris.

"Now what?" I asked.

Dimon stepped up to me and Morris. "I've rented a suite of rooms at the Waldorf," he said and reached into his pocket and pulled out a business card and a room key. Morris put them in his pocket.

"Now," he said. "When Katherine Cahill gets here..." And for the next three hours we talked about Steve Cahill and Arthur Barrett. Pretty much what Mickey Thompson had told me but in more detail. The scheme was fairly simple, Cahill and Company acted as a front for this unnamed government agency to disperse money to undercover operations throughout the world. Certain accounting activities had become suspicious over the last year and Coldwell assigned Dimon to follow the money. "Barrett is the key," Dimon said. "But the girl, Katherine, is a big part of it." Then the murders happened followed by Katherine's flight. We talked about tomorrow and what kind of role Dimon thought Morris and I should take, what our goals were with Katherine, and where Dimon would be in all this. He detailed various interrogation techniques, evasive maneuvers, the art of deception, drops, all kinds of stuff. Just in case, he said, others beside Katherine were involved. He called it 'tradecraft' but to me this was simply stuff spies did, the work of secret agents. I began to draw an image of this guy Dimon and I became fascinated by him. He spoke of things I'd only read of in books or seen in movies. He was very serious, very professional, and I could tell he'd been in this business for quite some time. He was not at all what I imagined a secret agent to look or be like. He spoke with a slight New York accent and I just knew somehow he'd been raised in Manhattan. We were about the same age and I felt like asking him where he went to school. For some reason, though, I didn't think he'd answer truthfully. Anyway, I decided I liked this guy Dimon and looked forward to working with him in this, my new, albeit temporary, job.

When he was done I asked him about Katherine, how they found her.

"She had a good jump, she had time, she must have had a plan," Dimon said. "The bodies weren't found until that evening. Cahill hadn't returned to his office and his secretary got worried. He was only going to lunch, she said, and it was his first day back, he had a lot of work to do. She knew about the Eighty-Second Street apartment because she paid all the bills. By the time someone got over there Katherine Cahill was some-where over the Atlantic. Our people met her at Heathrow. That's where you guys begin tomorrow. Why she went to London." Dimon went over to Coldwell's desk and opened a drawer. He reached in and withdrew a brick of bills and peeled some off.

"Here," he said. "Just in case you have some expenses." He handed me a thousand dollars in fifties. "We'll meet at the Waldorf tomorrow morning at 9.00. If for any reason you need to reach me beforehand, call the number on the card I gave you. Tell the person who answers your name and a phone number. I will call you within five minutes. Until then try and have a quiet night and get a good night's sleep. I will see you both tomorrow morning."

We shook hands and Dimon escorted us down to the lobby of the building. It was almost 5.00.

FIFTY-ONE

WE STOOD ON BROADWAY IN the rain. There was a slight chill in the air and a cold north wind was slapping rain into the sides of buildings, people, and cars. Neither Morris nor I had an umbrella. We stood in the doorway of the Federal building watching the traffic back up and saw no empty cabs.

"We need to talk to Mickey Thompson," Morris said, staring down at his expensive shoes and watching the rain splatter them. "Just to cross-reference what Dimon said. I worked in government long enough to know that sometimes they only tell you what they want you to know, not what you need to know."

"But we signed agreements," I said. "We can't talk to Mickey Thompson. This is classified stuff. You heard Coldwell. We'd be breaking the law, Morris. You're a lawyer, for chrissakes."

Morris looked at me. "Yes, I'm a lawyer and you're not," he said. "Of course we can't tell Mickey Thompson anything, what we know, you are correct about that. But no one says we can't listen to him."

Broadway was at a standstill now and my shoes and the bottom of my pants were getting wet. "Come on," I said. "We might as well take the train." Morris and I puddle-jumped over to Chambers Street and took the 2 train to Forty-Second Street. When we got out the rain had let up some but Times Square was tied up in knots. Rain will do that to New York City traffic, I don't know why, but whenever it rains or snows traffic comes to a grinding halt, as if the weather robs everyone of their ability to drive. We cut through the pre-theatre crowds and stepped into the *Times* building. I flashed my ID. The man at the desk recognized me and let us through to the elevators.

"We'll go to my office," I said. When we got to my floor it was empty. I suddenly remembered I was supposed to go back to work this week, on the Tuesday after Labor Day, the day Katherine shot Steve and I shot Barrett. The events of the last 72 hours had completely blanked that out of my mind. And now, walking back onto my floor, my life before Tuesday seemed so far away and I felt no attachment to it, or to the *Times* anymore. Fifteen years disappeared, just like that, and I remembered Joe Lieberman had resigned a few weeks ago. All that seemed now to be another lifetime. Maybe someone else's life. I saw one of the staffers pass through the hallway.

"Where is everyone?" I asked.

"Big meeting in the auditorium, didn't you get the notice?"

"No," I said. "I've been on vacation."

"Oh," she said. "You're one of the lucky ones. The rumor is those that were given vacation time are coming back. Most of those in the meeting, at least from what I've heard, are among the new round of layoffs. It's part of the new reorganization."

"Oh," I said. "I didn't know."

"Yeah," she said. She looked at me. "You're in sales, right? Print Ads?"

"Yes."

"Well, that's part of it too, became official this week, you guys are merging with the web people, everyone's moving down to the fifth floor. That's partly why it's so empty around here, people have already started to move."

"Wow," I said. "Go on vacation and look what happens."

She smiled and went down the hall.

"Looks like you're still gainfully employed," Morris said.

"Not unless we succeed with Katherine," I said "And then I think I'm going to need another vacation. This one hasn't exactly been the rest and relaxation kind."

In my office we called Mickey Thompson's extension. He answered on the first ring.

"Thompson."

"Mick, it's Jed."

"Where are you, pal? Some serious shit going on here."

"Downstairs. In my office. What's going on?"

"My managing editor is getting huge pressure to kill my story. It's coming from the publisher. I have a meeting with them tonight. How'd it go with your lawyer?"

"He's with me now."

"Can we talk?"

"Sure."

"Your office or mine?"

"Mine."

"I'll be there in a minute."

I hung up and pulled another chair over to my desk. Morris stood by the window. I didn't have an exciting view or anything, just the street below, which, by the sound of it, was nothing but standstill traffic. The rain began again and I could see gray sheets of it falling outside my darkening window.

"He'll be here in a few minutes," I said.

"Let me do the talking," Morris said. "I don't want any slips of the tongue, if you get my drift." I could see his reflection in the window, the white light of my office illuminating his face in the gray-black glass like a mirror. And then I thought of the two way mirror in the Eighty-Second Street apartment and the camera set-up and I wondered what the video tape that was in it showed. Rodriguez hadn't told me when I asked him.

"I think Mickey is going to want to ask a bunch of questions," I said. "About Katherine, at least that's what he started to ask me when I left him at the diner. He wants to try and see her. He thinks she's in jail."

"We can tell him what you did with her before the murders, but about the murders themselves and anything afterward you can't say a thing."

"You do the talking, Morris. I don't want to go to jail."

Morris walked over to my desk. "You won't go to jail, Jed. Just don't say or do anything stupid." Morris stepped behind my desk. "Let me sit here, do you mind?"

"Sure," I said. "Go right ahead."

"What kind of guy is this Mickey Thompson?"

"A good guy. I've known him for years. A great reporter. He lives for the story. He's tenacious, hard working, loyal. A good guy to have on your side."

A good twenty minutes went by and no Mickey Thompson.

"I thought you said he was in his office," Morris said.

"He was, that's where I called him. He's only two floors away."

"Call him again."

I was about to pick up the phone when Mickey pushed through my door.

"They're pulling my story," Mickey said, his face twisted and red. He stood in the middle of the room seemingly out of breath. I imagined he'd been yelling for the last fifteen minutes.

"What do you mean?" I asked.

"I just got off the phone with my managing editor and the publisher, conference call. No meeting. Just a fucking conference call. Hold the story. That's it."

"Why?"

"Washington. Massive pressure from Washington. Publisher said the White House is involved but I don't believe him. Claims national security is at stake or something. Somebody heavy got to him, that's for certain."

"Jesus, Mickey. I'm sorry," I said. But actually I was glad. The last thing I wanted right now was publicity and the way I knew Mickey he'd have played the Katherine connection for everything it was worth. I could tell Morris was a little relieved also.

"Tell me about the story," Morris said.

"Who are you?"

"I'm sorry," I said. "Mickey, this is Morris Bergman. He's my lawyer."

"I don't know if I can," Mickey said. "Under the circumstances."

"Attorney-client privilege," Morris said. "You can tell me anything you want."

Mickey looked at Morris, then me.

"Mick," I said. "You owe me."

FIFTY-TWO

MICKEY OUTLINED FOR MORRIS EVERYTHING he told me in the Waverly Diner earlier. Beginning with Arthur Barrett, Vietnam and the Phoenix program, the CIA, his recruitment of Steve Cahill, the creation of Cahill and Company, and the existence of secret offshore bank accounts that Mickey said he was able to trace to Cahill and Company.

"How were you able to do that?" Morris asked.

"It wasn't easy," Mickey said. "I simply got lucky. My eyeballs were burning from reading all this financial mumbo-jumbo down at the SEC; I'd been doing it for a couple of days and not really getting anywhere. I was about to call it a day when I saw something strange. I had noticed in all the filings I was looking at that whenever Cahill and Company took 'investment' funds from what I learned later to be one of the CIA's dummy companies, Steve Cahill would create a subsidiary of the company and offer stock to the public. It was a way for Cahill to raise up additional money for the CIA, later I learned he was trained to do this. The subsidiary actually did something, at least on paper, and paid dividends, filed financial reports, etc. After the purpose was served, i.e. dispersing now untraceable money somewhere, Cahill fabricated a takeover, a buyout of the subsidiary, in other words, take it private. It had served its purpose, now it was time for it to disappear. It was the perfect method of cleaning up, leaving no trace. Always it was Cahill and Company who bought the dummy company. Again, that's how it appeared on paper. The stockholders would get paid out and everything was on the up and up. A couple, three million dollars, whatever it is, goes to some secret operation in Timbuktu and there isn't a soul who can prove where it came from. Anyway, whenever a deal was done and funds went offshore Cahill would sign off on the transfer using one of his account numbers. It was a way to mask the dummy companies as the source of the funds as well as hide where the money ended up. There would be no names, just a series of account numbers. Always. That is, until last August. Cahill was in London but a transfer was made from New York. By Barrett. It was the first time, as far as I could see, Barrett had done this. It had always been Cahill. Barrett made the transfer and he named the account the money was to go into 'Dakota Holdings, PLC.' In other words, instead of transferring money from account #1234 into account #5678 as Cahill would have done, Barrett transferred the money from Cahill and Company, New York, into the account of Dakota Holdings PLC, Jersey, United Kingdom, care of Kasper & Benson Ltd. Kasper & Benson is the oldest bank in the Channel Islands. Jersey and Guernsey. It's where Cahill and Barrett set up their offshore accounts when they started Cahill and Company. Until then I had no idea where the money was going, all I saw were numbers and the name of the bank. Privacy laws protected Kasper & Bensen from having to reveal any information. There was never any connection to a recipient and Cahill and Company until I saw that."

So that's what Steve meant when he said, 'Dakota,' I thought. It has to be. Maybe it has something to do with Barrett gaining control of the accounts. That was something he also said. I wondered whether this Dakota Holdings PLC had something to do with Katherine and the murders. And Barrett.

"Jeez, Mickey," I said. "I never knew you could really hide money, especially large sums, anymore. I figured there were laws and regulations these days. What about taxes?"

"Well, there are laws and regulations but it's really a gray area if you want to know the truth. And Cahill and Company had the CIA watching its back. I'm sure if the IRS or anyone was looking CIA got them to back off quick." Mickey leaned back in his chair and rubbed his eyes. It had gotten darker outside and thickening rain began pelting the windows. I could hear the static whine of an ambulance siren stuck in the traffic outside. Gridlock, I thought. The city is all tied up, not even ambulances can get through.

"What would happen to the money once it went to Kasper & Benson?" Morris asked.

"Haven't got that far," Mickey said. "I was about to go to London where Kasper has offices and see if I could dig around looking, even go to Jersey if I had to. My assumption, and I'm pretty confidant about it based on the bits and pieces I've uncovered at the State Department and CIA, is that further transfers were made from Kasper & Benson, to banks in countries where Barrett and Cahill's bosses were running operations. Some super-secret agency, run by a guy by the name of Coldwell. Remember, Cahill had bosses; he was doing a job he had been trained to do. But instead of a company on Wall Street it was for *the* Company in Langley."

"Coldwell?"

"Yeah," Mickey said. "Some DC guy layered up deep in the folds within the Federal government. Been around since late sixties. He supervised Barrett during Phoenix, that's the initial connection to all this. Haven't gotten too much but he seems to bounce between Defense, State, and CIA. This is his baby. Cahill and Company that is. He masterminded the whole program as a way to covertly pay for his operations. Totally illegal. Remember

Iran-Contra? This is basically the same model, just a variation on the theme."

"Why?"

"Congress authorizes a budget, they want to know what the money is doing, where it's going. It's called oversight. What this guy Coldwell is doing is completely off the books, off the radar screen. No one knows, no one is accountable." Mickey paused. "Since Watergate it is completely illegal. That's why Iran-Contra was such a big deal. This is a totally covert operation, what's known as a 'black' operation." This, I realized, is why Coldwell and Dimon are involved. This whole thing is theirs.

"So if money is sent from New York, Cahill and Company, to Jersey, to this bank, and then can't be found, where is it?"

"Could be anywhere. That's the whole point. Kasper & Benson get a transfer order from Cahill, or whoever controls the account, to send 'x' amount to such and such account number in a bank in Khartoum, say. Guy shows up in Khartoum, gives the right ID, codes, whatever, and withdraws the money. Simple."

"So," Morris said, "once the money leaves Jersey, leaves this Kasper outfit, it basically disappears."

"Basically. None of these banks or companies outside of the US are accountable to the US. Theoretically we could get subpoenas and try and get records but unless there is a strong motivation to do that, it won't happen. And this money is essentially for stuff that nobody knows about. So what you have is no beginning, no middle, and no end. Nothing to look at."

"Who is he?" Morris asked. "This Coldwell?"

"Good question. Not exactly sure but he's deep in the Intelligence community, I don't think he's simply CIA, something way beyond. All I could learn was that he came in as a protégé of William Casey back in the Nixon administration, went to CIA eventually landing as director of clandestine services when Casey became director during the Reagan administration, but he's since moved on. Currently heads an agency called the 'Office of Special Plans.' Never heard of it before and not sure what they do but whatever it is, it's highly clandestine, highly secretive. I'd call it stealth operations, frankly. Can't get a thing on him or his office which is officially listed as an independent agency created by executive order during the Reagan administration. Casey was director of Central Intelligence at the time and apparently it was his idea. One thing I did pick up from CIA is that all the operations of this Office of Special Plans are overseas and centered on counter-terrorism and national security issues. The pitch is basically good guys who operate behind closed doors in bad places."

Mickey seemed anxious and I could tell he desperately wanted to talk. He'd been working on this story nearly two weeks and obviously hadn't told anyone other than his editor. Since the lid was clamped down he seemed to want to tell it to somebody. We were as good as anyone, I suppose. And Morris being a lawyer obviously gave him good cover. Me? Supposedly I knew it all already. I was one of Mickey's sources. He could certainly prove it if he hadn't named me in his piece to begin with.

"What role did Katherine Cahill have in all of this?" Morris asked. He clearly wanted to keep Mickey on his roll.

"I'm not sure," Mickey said. "She's a whole story herself. She's known Barrett longer than Cahill, that's for starters."

"What?" I didn't believe it. "Barrett? Arthur Barrett? How do you know that?"

"Never reveal my sources, Jed. Not even to you, but I can tell you, since I name her, that Cahill's secretary has been with him a long time. She knows a lot."

"How did Katherine meet Barrett?"

"I don't know. When she was around sixteen or seventeen she ran away to Hollywood. Not sure where she came from, but Barrett met her out there and brought her to New York. He introduced her to Cahill, I learned. He set them up and Cahill apparently fell head over heels for her."

"That's true," I said. "I was there."

"Anyway, for me the meat of the story, as far as I'm concerned, begins with what I told you about Barrett and the transfer. The money Barrett transferred came out of thin air. No transfer into Cahill, no sale of a subsidiary, no investment money, nothing. It had to come into Cahill somehow in order to be transferred; I just haven't been able to find it. And Steve Cahill was in London at the time. Another oddity. He historically handled this part of the business, handled all the transfers, the accounting and bookkeeping, Barrett just sort of oversaw things. He was Coldwell's guy. So why is he suddenly transfer-ring money from Cahill to Dakota?"

"How much was it?"

"Twenty-five million."

"Twenty-five million?" Morris whistled. "And you can't find where it came from?"

"That was last year, in August. There was another the first week of August this year, and another a week later. A total of seventy-five million dollars as of last week. And every transfer was done the same as the first, from Cahill and Company to Dakota Holdings PLC, signed off by Arthur Barrett. A lot of clams for Steve Cahill not to be involved."

And, I thought, each transfer occurred in August. When Steve Cahill was in London. Away from New York.

"He had to know about it," Morris said. "It'd show on the bank statements."

"Of course," Mickey replied. "The question is what did he do about it?"

"Or what didn't he do about it."

Morris had his chin resting in his hand. He looked at Mickey with a quizzical gaze. "But back to Katherine," he said. "Do you think she knew any of this?"

"Yes," Mickey said without hesitation. "I think she knew everything Barrett was doing. I think they were in it together. My theory? I think Katherine and Barrett had something going on behind Cahill's back. I think Barrett somehow had a lot of money he wanted to hide, get it out of the country, or out of wherever it was, and into someplace where it wouldn't stand out, at least until he could get to it. I think Steve Cahill found out something was going on, perhaps when he was in London, perhaps before, the bank statements, something, and either tried to stop it or was in Barrett's way. And I think in the end Katherine decided she wanted the money for herself and killed both of them to get it. Something like that. At least that's what I think. When I first saw the stories in the newspaper down in Washington that was the first thing I thought of. And my instinct is pretty good." Mickey put his finger to his nose. "I have a notebook full of questions for you, Jed. You and Katherine."

"Don't know that I should answer anything right now, Mickey. Under advice of counsel. I'm a 'person of interest', don't forget. Don't think the police would like it very much if I started mouthing off to the press. What do you think, Morris?"

"He's right, Mickey. My advice is not talk to the press right now."

"What about background, off the record type thing?"

"Give me a day or two, Mickey, please. You can't print anything right now anyway. From the sounds of it possibly never. Hearing all this, Christ, no wonder Washington doesn't want you to publish this story. But listen, I'm out on my own recognizance. I don't want anyone to yank that right now."

Mickey looked at me and I could tell he was trying to decide whether to press me or not.

Morris scratched his head. "What do you think, Jed? About what Mickey says about Cahill and Company and Barrett?"

"I don't know what I think, Morris. I have absolutely no idea. This is all so wild, like a movie or something." I paused for a moment. My head was trying to put some order into everything Mickey had said. It was disconcerting in an odd way.

"I guess one of the big questions I have is where did all that money Barrett had come from?" I asked.

"That's exactly what I want to know," Mickey said.

"Just because you can't publish right now doesn't mean you have to stop investigating, does it?" Morris asked.

"No," Mickey said. "It doesn't."

FIFTY-THREE

THE NEXT MORNING MORRIS AND I met Dimon in the lobby of the Waldorf-Astoria hotel. He had someone with him, a guy called Delbarton, and he was big and beefy, like he'd spent most of his life in the Army weight lifting or something. He didn't say much. When Dimon introduced us he simply stuck out a hand that resembled a baseball mitt and shook ours. He was strong and it felt like he had muscles in his fingers. He gave a nod, no smile, and mumbled something about meeting us. We went up to one of the rooms Dimon had booked, a suite actually, with a living room, a bedroom, and a small kitchenette with a little dining area. When we walked in I saw a fresh pot of coffee by the tiny stove and a plate of rolls and pastries on the kitchen table. Morris and I helped ourselves to coffee. Delbarton took a pastry and went to the refrigerator, reached in, and pulled out a can of Coke.

"The preliminary forensics came back," Dimon said as we stepped away from the kitchen. Delbarton sat off in the dining area while Morris, Dimon, and I sat on chairs in the living room. Delbarton was too big for the chair he was on and as he tried to get comfortable, draping his arm over the chair next to him, his jacket fell open and I saw a pistol snug in a shoulder holster hanging below his armpit. It was not a .38; it was bigger, and black.

"And?" Morris asked as he leaned forward and sipped his coffee. "What'd they look like?"

"The bullet that killed Cahill came from Barrett's gun. The bullet that killed Barrett came from the other gun, the one Jed used. That means if Katherine shot Steve Cahill it was with the gun Barrett was holding," Dimon said.

"Or," Morris said, "Barrett shot Cahill."

"Right."

"What about prints?"

"This is the mystery. The fingerprints on Barrett's gun were Jed's; the bullets had Jed's prints as well. The prints on the other gun were Barrett's." Dimon looked at me.

"I had a handkerchief," I said. "I wrapped the gun in a hand-kerchief."

"That's why your prints were not on that gun," Dimon said. "But Barrett's prints were on that gun. He probably put it on the kitchen counter." He stood up and went into the kitchen, poured himself a cup of coffee, and said, "In Barrett's pockets were two strips of scotch tape, tape that had Jed's prints on them. In other words, Jed's prints were lifted from something, a glass perhaps, and Barrett intended to plant them somewhere. Obviously in the apartment. He didn't get the chance, of course."

"Interesting," said Morris. "What was the point of sending Jed up there? I mean, if they were going to plant all that stuff anyway?"

"Insurance, I think, or to kill him. I'm not sure yet," Dimon said. "The original plan, it seems, called for him to be set up for the fall. The prints, the gun. But something happened. The plan changed."

"Jed shot him."

"Yeah, but something else was going on. I don't know what yet. It seems to me something changed before Jed got there."

"What was on the videotape that was still in the camera?" I asked.

"Didn't Rodriguez tell you?"

"No."

"It shows Cahill standing with his back to the camera holding his hands up, you know, like he was under arrest or something. You can hear Katherine saying, 'I can't, I can't...' and then a shot. Cahill is hit and falls to the floor. Katherine screams and says, 'No, no.' She isn't crying but simply saying, 'No, no, poor Steve...' You can't see anything else. Then the camera is shut off."

"Do you think she knows she was being filmed?" Morris asked.

"No," Dimon said. "I don't think so. And I don't think she shot him either. And," Dimon sipped his coffee and reached into his pocket. He took out a pack of cigarettes and lit one. "I don't think that tape was supposed to be left in the camera, either."

"You can smoke in here?" Delbarton asked. It was the first thing he'd said.

Dimon looked over at him. "$900 a night," he said, "you better be able to."

Delbarton took out a cigarette and then I did too.

"All right," Dimon said. "Let's go over this one more time." Dimon walked over to the window and pulled the drapes back. Outside the sky was bright, clean, and cloudless. Dimon cracked the window and pushed it out as far as it could go. Muffled street sounds filtered up and I felt cool September air enter the room. Dimon took a long drag on his cigarette and blew the smoke out the window. Then he turned to Morris and me. "Katherine lands at 1.30. Delbarton and I will escort her from JFK to here, ostensibly releasing her into the custody of her lawyer, you. You'll advise her of what she's facing, her arraignment tomorrow, ask her what happened, etc. Jed, you'll be next door with me and Delbarton. When Morris gives the word we take it from there, right?"

I remembered what Dimon said yesterday when we were downtown at the Federal building. 'Why'd she go to London? And where is the money?' That's all Coldwell wanted to know. I thought of everything Mickey told Morris and me and every-thing Dimon and Coldwell said. The money, Barrett's money, seemed to be the most important thing here, where is *that* money? The money Mickey said Barrett had been sending to Kasper & Benson, for the Dakota account. That was what Coldwell and Dimon wanted. But even Mickey said he had no idea where it had come from. 'Barrett' was all he said. It came from him.

It was almost noon. Dimon and Delbarton said they had to make some calls and left the room. Morris and I sat there, poured more cups of coffee, and waited.

FIFTY·FOUR

BEFORE DIMON AND DELBARTON LEFT for the airport they took me into the room next door. It was similar to the one we had been in, in fact, exactly the same except the color of the drapes and carpet and furniture was different. Dimon led me into the bedroom. On a table next to the wall sat what looked liked a ham radio. It was a black boxy thing and had dials and some switches and a thick black antenna that rose about three feet. There were three sets of headphones, a note pad, a couple of pencils. Next to the radio and clearly wired into it was a cassette tape recorder, the kind that used those tiny, mini cassettes. There was a chair beside the table. Away from the table but pushed up against the same wall were two small black leather bags, they looked like doctors bags, and each one had a white tag with a red cross on it.

"What's this?" I asked, pointing at the radio.

"A receiver," Dimon said. "Delbarton will explain it."

Delbarton sat in the chair and flipped a switch. A small red light suddenly glowed.

"Okay," Delbarton said. "This is a wireless receiver. We have some well hidden transmitters placed in the room next door that can pick up nearly every sound in there. The idea here is to filter out what you don't want to hear and listen only to what you want to. That's what this dial is for. You want to hear them talking, right? There'll be a lot of background noise, the microphones are pretty powerful and you'll hear the ventilation system, the air conditioning, the toilet flush, whatever, shit you don't want. So you turn this dial until it focuses on what you want, the voices you want to hear. It's called a selective sound system, pretty high-tech; we got a parabolic installed in the cabinet in the living room so you'll have no problem."

Dimon stepped over and picked up one of the headphones and put it on my head. I could hear static noise and Dimon pointed at the dial. I turned it and different sounds grew louder and some grew faint. I played with it for a minute until I could clearly hear Morris tapping his fingers against the arm of his chair. Then I heard him sigh. It was as if he were right next to me.

"Wow," I said. "That's incredible."

"When we put Katherine in there I want you to listen to what she and Morris talk about," Dimon said. "You'll hear what she has to say. It'll help you decide how to approach her."

"What if you find out what you want before I have to go in?" I was anxious and the truth is this is exactly what I wanted to happen. The thought of seeing Katherine again made me uneasy.

"If that happens then we're done."

"Where will you guys be?" I asked.

"Right here," Dimon said. "I'll be listening too, so will Delbarton."

"Man, you guys don't fool around." I had to admit, it was pretty impressive spy stuff. These guys probably did this kind of thing all the time. "Is this legal?"

"This is a classified operation, Jed. You are not permitted to discuss it, remember?" Dimon said this as calmly as if he were ordering a ham sandwich.

"Yes, of course," I said.

Dimon looked at his watch.

"Okay, Gary," he said to Delbarton. "We gotta go. Remember, Jed. We'll be back around 3.00. Be sure you're in here and at the radio by then, right?"

"Yes, of course," I said and I watched them leave. I walked into the other room and went to the window. It was beautiful day, the kind that can only come after a terrible storm, and I looked down below and saw Park Avenue. Bright yellow taxis, black limousines, people packing the sidewalks going to lunch. I looked uptown and thought I could see Katherine's old building, the one where I first had sex with her. Or rather, where she first had sex with me. I realized now I never had sex with Katherine. I never had anything with her. I was simply someone she had pushed along and walked over to get somewhere else.

The thought of seeing Katherine again bothered me. A lot. I'd been putting it off, the thought of it that is, since yesterday when Coldwell first mentioned it. It bothered me because of what happened of course, but also because as much as I thought I knew her, I know now I was simply fooling myself, I had no idea who she was. I only knew what I wanted to know, what *she* wanted me to know. And if something existed that I didn't want to know I conveniently ignored it. Yes, you could say she used me. But the truth is I let her. I willingly let her use me. *Willingly,* there's that word again. It seems that word has almost become my middle name. I gave myself up to her on a silver platter. *Willingly.* She must have thought I was the biggest fool in New York City. Hell, I *was* the biggest fool in New York City. Maybe I still am.

But Katherine was coming back, not to me particularly, but back into my life. Would this be the last time? To be frank, I hadn't asked for this, hadn't asked to see Katherine again, but given the circumstances I had no choice. I had to see her again in order to save my own neck. That was as good a reason as any the way I saw it. But still. Knowing I was to see her again made me queasy and I felt my stomach tremble in a bad way. Seeing her again could only mean one thing. And it was not good.

Did she know she would see me again? Probably not. Dimon said the plan was for them to pick her up at JFK and bring her here to meet her lawyer. She knew Morris, knew him from when his firm handled her divorce, knew him through me. So it would make sense for him to step up to the plate and offer his services, at least upon her arrival. Dimon said that she would be told she was being given the opportunity to meet with her lawyer before being arraigned for murder which was to take place tomorrow morning. Morris would tell her he had arranged for her to stay here at the Waldorf until then, under guard of course.

My role in this episode, as instructed by Dimon, was that unless Katherine easily confessed all to Morris, specifically where the missing money was, I was to be the bad cop to Morris' good cop. I would walk into their room, claim I'd heard she was back, and confront her about everything I'd learned since she betrayed me. I'd make her betrayal the cornerstone of my attacks; emphasizing that I was willing to testify against her at trial. Between Morris and me we'd needle her about the scam she and Barrett had going and try and pin down the missing money. Once she gave up the money I was free. But now, as I stared out the window at the rest of the world, all I could do was wait. And the more I thought about it the more I did not want to see Katherine again. The thought alone made me nauseous.

At ten minutes to three o'clock there was a knock on the door. Delbarton stuck his head in and said, "She's here."

FIFTY-FIVE

I WENT TO THE TABLE and put the headphones on. I could hear Dimon talking. Delbarton stayed by the door, standing half in and half out.

"...you understand now what the program is? You will be brought to the courthouse downtown tomorrow morning at 9.00 to be arraigned. I and my partner will wake you at 7.30, you will be ready to leave here by 8.30, and we will proceed downtown. Your lawyer, Mr. Bergman, knows the procedure. My advice would be to listen to him."

"Yes," she said. "I understand." Her voice was weary, tired. I heard some rustling of clothes, perhaps she was taking a jacket off or something, then I heard Dimon again.

"Oh, in case Mr. Bergman forgets to mention it, there are eight police officers between the lobby and this floor, plus two outside the elevators and by the stairwell and two beside your door. If you try and leave without me or my partner you will be restrained by force. You understand this, yes?"

"Yes."

"Okay then, Ms. Cahill," Dimon said. "Have a nice evening."

I heard the door close and then Dimon and Delbarton walked into the room. Without saying a word they pulled up chairs and put on headphones and Dimon grabbed the notepad and pencil. Delbarton cocked back in his chair and closed his eyes. Then we listened.

"You remember me?'

"Yes," Katherine said. "Of course. Morris Bergman. Your firm, one of your associates, handled my divorce. You're Jed Chase's friend."

"That's right."

I heard some chairs being pushed around and then the rattling of a coffee cup in a saucer.

"How was the flight?" Morris asked.

"Terrible. I'd just flown over there. They were waiting for me on the other end. They put me in a cell at the airport, then took me somewhere in the city where they put me into a room with a couple of thugs who kept asking me questions I wouldn't answer without a lawyer, then they took me back to the airport, back into the same cell, and then the flight back here. I haven't slept in three days."

"You know why you're here?"

"Of course. I'm not stupid."

"Do you want me to represent you? Would you rather someone else?" Morris sounded a little too nonchalant. What if she said she wanted another lawyer, then what?

"Do I have a choice? Am I allowed that?"

"Certainly. This is the United States. You have a right to a lawyer. Any lawyer."

I heard footsteps and then what sounded like a cabinet door opening, or the refrigerator. Cans or bottles were being pushed around. "I'm starving," Katherine said. "Anything decent to eat beside potato chips or nuts?" she asked.

"What would you like?"

"A nice salad and a tuna sandwich. And a pot of fresh coffee. Could I have that?"

I heard Morris pick up the phone and then I heard him push a button on it and ask for room service. I don't mean I heard him like I heard them talking, I heard him *on* the phone. The phone was tapped into the radio somehow. I looked at Dimon. He was busy writing notes. I heard someone say "room service" and I looked over to Delbarton. He glanced at me and winked. I could tell he liked the gadgetry and the fact I was impressed by it.

"Would you please send up a salad, a tuna sandwich..." I heard Morris cup the phone and say, "What kind of bread?"

"Whole wheat."

"...on whole wheat and a pot of coffee?"

"Certainly, Mr. Dimon. Will that be all?"

"Yes." Morris hung up the phone.

"Katherine, I need to ask you again. Would you like another lawyer? You are going to be charged with some serious crimes, capital crimes. I am capable of defending you, probably the most capable in this kind of law, but I need to know from you if you want my services. Before we begin."

Why is Morris doing this? Why is he giving her an out? He's compromising our role in this, my whole arrangement. Doesn't he realize this?

"Oh, I suppose so," Katherine said. "I don't know anyone else. Jed always said you were the best criminal lawyer in the city. That's what I need, right? A criminal lawyer?"

"Yes."

And then I realized Morris was simply covering himself. As a lawyer, he needed to be engaged by the client before he could officially evaluate and advise. In this case there was a dual track, me and Katherine. Me because of my immunity deal with Coldwell and Katherine because she was facing homicide charges. Morris, I suddenly realized, was treading a very fine ethical line here. Perhaps he's crossed it. His only possible out, I realized, was the fact that my role was classified. In fact this whole situation was classified. Probably took care of any ethical issues on Morris' part.

"Do I need to sign anything, or something?"

"No," Morris said. "We can take care of all that later. What we need to do now is for you to tell me why you have been arrested by the United States government. I mean, I know the charges, but I need you to tell me what happened. Did you shoot Steve Cahill and Arthur Barrett?"

"No."

"Neither one of them?"

"No."

"But you were there, correct?"

"Yes. I was there, but I didn't shoot anyone. Arthur shot Steve. I have no idea who shot Arthur. In fact I don't even know if he was shot. He was very much alive when I left him in the apartment."

"Barrett was shot. He's dead. The authorities are going to charge you with his murder. His and Steve Cahill's."

"I didn't shoot them."

"You say Barrett shot Steve. Can we prove that?"

"I don't know," Katherine said. Her voice dropped a little and I heard a slight tremor in it. "They're really dead, aren't they?"

"Yes," Morris said softly. "They are."

There was a knock on the door and I heard a chair push back, some footsteps. "I'll get it," Morris said. I heard the door open and the room service cart being rolled in, then a voice, "Where would you like it?" "Over here," Morris said. And then the clattering of silverware, china, footsteps, and the door closed.

"God," Katherine said. "I'm so hungry."

"Do you know why the U.S. Attorney's office is charging you with these crimes rather than the NYPD?" Morris asked.

"I don't know," Katherine said between bites. "Because I left the country?"

"No. If that was all, they'd turn you over to the local author-ities at the airport. Jurisdiction is important in these things, especially capital crimes. No, it wasn't because you fled the country."

I heard coffee being poured. Two cups.

"I haven't had a decent cup of coffee in days," Katherine said, as if she wanted to change the subject. I could hear her blowing in her cup. Christ, I thought. This bugging equipment is unbelievable. If I wanted to I could probably hear flies buzzing around a lamp.

"So why?" Katherine finally asked. "Why is the government after me instead of the New York City Police?"

"Don't get me wrong," Morris said. "The NYPD wanted you too but they made a deal with the Feds."

"Why?"

"It seems, apparently, there is a fairly significant amount of money missing. To the tune of seventy-five million dollars, maybe more. Money that belongs to the United States government. Money that the government thinks you and Steve and Arthur had something to do with the taking. The fact that your ex-husband and Barrett were employees of the government heightens, or rather, solidifies I should say, their suspicions. I'll be perfectly blunt Katherine. The interest here is the money. If I can establish some kind of reasonable doubt about the killings, and you can help them locate the money, I'm confidant we can make some kind of deal. At least a strong possibility of no jail time."

"It's always about the money, isn't it?"

"Yes," I heard Morris say wistfully. "It is."

What was interesting here, I thought, was that Katherine didn't protest Morris' statement that Steve and Barrett were employees of the government. I made a mental note of this. I saw Dimon scribbling in a steady scrawl.

"Well, I have no idea what you are talking about," Katherine said. "I don't know anything about any missing money and I don't need to make a deal because I didn't kill anyone. If you're as good as you say you are you will get me off based simply on the facts. And the fact is I didn't kill anyone."

I looked at Dimon. "I don't like where this is going," he said. "Morris has to toughen up a bit here."

"You want to switch gears, Bill?" Delbarton said.

"No, not yet. We'll send Jed in first. Maybe that'll get her going in the right direction."

"Now?" I asked nervously. My anxiety sent a shiver up my spine.

"No, give it a little more time. She's establishing her parameters, that's all. Drawing lines. Let her do that a bit and we'll see where we are, where she thinks she is."

I heard someone pour more coffee. Then Morris said, "Why did you go to London?"

"I have a friend there." Katherine paused. "When the whole thing happened with Steve I freaked. I didn't know where to go, all I knew was I wanted to get as far away as I could. I have a friend in London. So I went there."

"It could be seen as fleeing the scene of the crime."

"So what?" Katherine said. "I didn't do it. I didn't do anything. I went to London for a few days."

"Why didn't you go to the police?"

"Are you crazy?"

"You could have gone anywhere, Katherine. Why London? Why out of the country? London, by the way, is a focus in this investigation. They don't see it as a coincidence."

Katherine didn't say anything.

"You were in the apartment at the time of the killings."

"I didn't kill anyone."

"All right," Morris said. "If I'm going to defend you I need to know everything from the beginning. Everything leading up to the killings."

"Have you talked to Jed?"

"No," Morris lied. "The police have him. They haven't charged him with anything yet, but they think he was your accomplice in some kind of conspiracy. He's been talking, I know that."

"What's he saying?"

"That you conspired to kill Steve and Barrett for money. For the money that's missing."

"What? He said that? He doesn't know about any money."

"What money?" Morris pressed.

"He's crazy," Katherine said. "Absolutely nuts. There is no money. Never was."

"Tell me what happened. Why were you in the apartment? Why was Jed there?"

"Nothing happened. I got divorced. You know that, you handled it..."

"My firm did."

"Your firm did. The divorce came through first week or so of August. Steve was already in London. I was happy with it, the settlement, that is, ask your associate, he put it together. I got two mil and an apartment. Who's complaining? I started seeing Jed a little. We're friends, we've been friends a long time. He went to school with Steve, did you know that?"

So did you, Morris, I thought, you went to school with Steve too. I thought I had told Katherine that. Maybe she forgot.

"Yes," Morris said. "I know that. I went to the same college. I knew him too."

"Really? Oh yeah, I think I recall Jed mentioning that. Yes, come to think of it he did. When he introduced us, when I was looking for a divorce lawyer. That's right. So you knew him too. Turned out to be a real dick, excuse my French."

"So you started seeing Jed Chase."

"Right. Jed and I go way back. I always liked him, I mean he's a nice guy, you know? Always there, trustworthy, loyal. He's safe. When you need someone to be with, he's perfect." Katherine paused. I heard her sip her coffee. "Yes, Jed's all right. I don't know why he'd say such things. I mean to the police."

"Why? Why would he say such things?"

"I don't know. Panic maybe? He's in trouble. Maybe he killed Arthur. Maybe that's why."

"Why were you in the apartment?"

"Steve was in London. The divorce had come through. I moved out of our apartment, the one on Park Avenue, that was part of our agreement, and Jed helped me. I rented a place over on Seventy-Second, near Lex." Katherine paused and I heard her light a cigarette. "Steve always kept this apartment on Eighty-Second Street, for business, for when clients came to town. He put them up there, you know, instead of a hotel. It was a perk, they could bring their wives, families, have a New York vacation on Cahill and Company while he tried to screw them in an IPO or a merger or something. Frankly, I never really understood what Steve did. Steve and Arthur. It was always hush-hush. Secrets. Always secrets. Secret deals, secret trips. Steve flying off unannounced for three days here, two days there. You could never keep track of him. Arthur was always nonchalant, you know, 'It's business, Katherine.' After a while what did I care? Anyway, I helped Steve furnish the place on Eighty-Second and after the divorce I was supposed to get some furniture and stuff from there. I had a new place and I needed some things, so when Steve came back from London I asked Jed to help me move some of the stuff. Like I told you, that's what Jed was good at, you know, always being there to help. Anyway, Steve had the keys so I met him there. We were still friends, I mean, we were civil. Jed went to pick up some sandwiches at a Deli and I went up to the apartment first. Jed said he didn't want to see Steve right away, you know, seeing his ex-wife and all, I understood that. Anyway, when I went up Steve was there waiting. We said hello, I asked how London was, and suddenly Arthur Barrett walks into the room."

"Which room?"

"The bedroom. We were standing in the bedroom."

"Why was a camera and a two-way mirror set up?"

I heard Katherine take an extra long drag on her cigarette. Then I heard her slowly exhale. In my mind I could clearly see her face, the smoke easing out of her nostrils, her perfect mouth, her moist lips curled back slightly, her head tilted slightly back and to one side with her silky blonde hair tucked in behind her ear. That was one thing about Katherine. Watching her smoke was like a seduction. I imagined Morris looking at her at that moment. I wonder what he's thinking right now, I thought.

"Yeah," she said slowly. "I guess the cops are flipping out about that one. Weird, huh?"

"Let's just say it's odd. Leaves a lot to the imagination."

"Yeah, well, let me tell you something Morris. Those two guys were fucking weird. Strange birds. Steve and Arthur. What do *you* think? They liked to watch, you know what I'm saying? That's why that was there. The shit they were into. Christ almighty. They'd hire whores and get some shmoe off the street, a cab driver, say, and get them up there. They'd watch through the window and film it. Just for kicks. You believe that shit? That's how Steve got off. He and Arthur tried to talk me into doing it too. Why the hell do you think I divorced the son of a bitch?"

Katherine's voice was hard, angry, edgy. Even her intonation seemed different. I never heard her like this before. It was yet another side of her I hadn't ever seen. In fact, I wasn't seeing it, I was hearing it and hearing her without seeing her made it all the more striking. Just hearing her swear was strange. She never used those words around me. In fact, I can't remember her ever swearing. This was not the Katherine I knew. I looked at Dimon. He was writing away. I looked at Delbarton. He grinned at me and rolled his eyes back.

"The police say you denied there was any sex being filmed, any kind of scheme with Steve and Arthur."

"Yeah, well, I denied it, sure. Wouldn't you? I wasn't involved in that. Let the cops figure it out."

"I thought you said Steve gave the apartment as a perk for clients to use. Wouldn't they wonder about the mirror? Wasn't Steve afraid they'd ask about it?"

"Nah, Steve had another mirror for it, he had it made to fit over the window side of the wall. When guests were there each bedroom had a matching mirror on that wall. When Steve and Arthur wanted to play they removed the mirror in the one bedroom. Believe me, Steve was into all this covert type of stuff. Secret recordings, the video thing, mirrors and walls, all of it. He knew what he was doing. He was like a magician with this stuff."

"Why did Barrett shoot Steve?"

"I don't know. I don't even know why he was there. Everything happened so fast. Arthur shot him, I went over to Steve, he was bleeding badly, he looked up at me, and died. Just like that. I lost it. I ran out of the apartment. I went down to the deli, the coffee shop, whatever it was, and Jed was gone. I couldn't find him. That's when I really flipped out. I thought something terribly awful was going on, I panicked and I left. All I wanted to do was get the hell out of there, out of New York. Jed was the best and last friend I had and I thought if he ditched me I'm alone. Totally alone. So I went to JFK, bought a ticket to London, got on the plane, and got the hell out of Gotham."

Dimon looked up from his notepad and shook his head. "He's got to get into the money thing, he's got to keep it flowing. We can't have her leading him like this. I thought he was a fucking lawyer, for chrissakes."

"He'll get there," I said hopefully. "He's good, you'll see."

Delbarton nodded at Dimon, tilting his head toward the other room. Dimon shook his head. "Wait," he said.

Then we all heard Morris clear his throat and say, "What does 'Dakota' mean?"

Katherine didn't miss a beat. "I don't know," she said. "North or South?"

"Neither," Morris said. "Just the word. Dakota. Does that mean anything to you?"

"There's an apartment building on the West side..."

"No. Not that."

"All right," Dimon said. "That's enough." He motioned for me to take my headphones off. I took them off. "Okay," he said. "It's your turn. You know the drill."

"What do you want me to do?" I said, sounding a little too helpless for my own good.

"What do you mean what do I want you to do?" Dimon said, his voice rising. "What we talked about, for chrissakes. Go in there swinging. Slam her. Get to the money."

I looked at Dimon. I didn't know what to say. I didn't know what to do. I didn't want to go in there. I didn't want to see Katherine. I don't know why. Actually, I did know why. I was afraid.

"I don't know..."

"Oh Christ, what do you mean, Chase? We have a deal, you've got to go in there. We talked about this. You and I and Bergman. And Coldwell. We made a deal. You made a deal, remember? You can't back out now, or I'll arrest your ass."

Dimon was visibly angry. Delbarton took his headphones off. "Bill," he said. Dimon turned.

"What?"

"Fuck him, let's go in there. We're wasting time. She's still on the high ground. We got to change it. Now."

Dimon looked at Delbarton, didn't say anything.

"Bill," Delbarton said. "This weenie ain't gonna do anything. He's afraid of her. Don't you see that?"

Dimon turned to me. I felt my face turning red. I was helpless. As helpless as I've ever felt in my life. Delbarton was right. It was obvious. I was afraid of her. I knew what she had done to me and I was afraid of what she could do to me again.

"Listen," I said. "I'm sorry, I'm just not cut out..."

"Forget it," Dimon said in disgust. He turned to Delbarton. "Come on. Let's go get her."

Delbarton grabbed the two black bags against the wall and followed Dimon out the door. I put on the headphones again and listened to Dimon and Delbarton go into the room next door.

FIFTY-SIX

I HEARD THE DOOR SWING open. It banged loudly as it slammed against the wall. Katherine gasped loudly and said, "What's wrong?" Then I heard heavy steps and struggling, Katherine said, "No, no, what are you doing? What are you doing? No! No! Don't!" Then I heard her muffled voice, just muted sounds really, and Morris said, "What the hell?"

Dimon said, "Back off, Bergman. It's our turn now."

"What do you want to do?" Delbarton said.

"Just give it a minute or two," Dimon said.

"How much?"

"Just one dose for now."

"What did you guys shoot her with?" Morris asked, trying to mask the surprise in his voice. He was clearly disconcerted and confused.

Neither Dimon nor Delbarton said anything. I could hear Katherine's breathing. It was heavy and fast. But then I heard her say, "But, but, wait…"

"Ain't like the usual customer, eh, Bill?" Delbarton said.

"No," Dimon said. "Let's put her in the armchair."

I heard some lifting, a grunt, and dragging across the carpet. Then I heard Katherine giggle. "What are you guys doing?" she asked.

"Don't..." I heard Dimon say. Then I heard a heavy thump on the floor. Then Katherine laughing. "I can't walk," she said.

"Don't try," Dimon said. "You'll fall. Please sit down. You'll feel more comfortable."

"I'm feeling pretty damn comfortable right now," Katherine said, her voice odd, giddy.

"Come on," Dimon said. "Here."

I heard them lifting her up again and Katherine said, "Whoa," and Delbarton said, "Should we tie her?"

"No, I don't think so. Not yet, anyway."

"What are you guys doing?" Morris asked again. "I don't know if..."

"Listen," Dimon said. "This is classified, remember? Let us do our work."

I heard someone walk across the room and sit down in a chair. I figured it to be Morris. I heard Katherine's breathing, too, but she seemed content where she was. Then I heard a chair scrape across the kitchen floor and then onto the carpet, right up near to where I figured Katherine to be sitting.

"Okay, Ms. Cahill," Dimon said. "I'm going to speak in simple terms, terms you will have no problem understanding. Does that make sense to you right now?'

"Yes." Her voice seemed quieter now, not as giddy.

"You can make this fast and easy, or slow and hard. It's up to you. Do you understand me?"

"Yes."

"Where is the money Arthur Barrett wired to England? To the Isle of Jersey? To Kasper & Benson for the account of Dakota Holdings, PLC?"

Katherine was silent, like she was confused. "I don't know," she said. "I don't know what you are talking about." She spoke slowly, methodically, as if she had rehearsed the scene a thousand times and this was simply another labored performance. A performance she wasn't quite up to. A performance she would rather do another day. A day when she was feeling a little better, a little more herself.

"Where did Barrett get the money from?"

"I don't know."

Then I heard a loud slap and then another and Katherine cried out, "No, please, you're hurting me."

"You don't feel that."

"Gary, don't," Dimon said. I heard Morris move in his chair.

"She's still playing," Delbarton said. "Maybe she needs another shot."

"Maybe," Dimon said. I heard him step around near where Katherine was sitting.

"Why are you hitting me?" she asked. "Please don't, I didn't do anything. Please."

It was completely silent for a few minutes and I was debating whether or not to go into the room. Then I heard Katherine grunt and some struggling and she gasped, "Oh," and then more silence until I heard her start to cry softly. For some reason I thought it was an act. But then I realized they had given her some kind of drug. Another shot. Maybe it was the drug making her cry, I thought. I wondered what they gave her.

"Katherine?"

"Yes?" she whimpered. "What do you want?"

"Did Barrett or Steve ever talk about something called 'Phoenix?'" Dimon asked.

Katherine didn't say anything.

"Katherine?"

"Yes?"

"Did you hear me?"

"Yes."

"Did you ever hear them talking about this, about 'Phoenix?'"

"I don't know," she said as her voice trembled a little. Then she heaved a weary sigh, gasped, and, her voice quivering, said, "I don't know, maybe." Then she started to cry again. And even though she was crying softly I sensed a lot of pain; hidden pain, buried perhaps, but clearly pain.

"What do you mean, maybe?"

"I don't know," she said sniffling. "I'm a little confused. What did you do to me? I'm thirsty. I need something to drink."

"Gary, get her something."

I heard Delbarton's heavy steps as he walked over to the kitchen and opened the refrigerator. I heard the pop and hiss of a carbonated can open as his footsteps crossed back over the floor.

"Here," he said. Katherine gulped as she drank and then her breathing evened out. She took a few deep breaths and I heard her put the can down.

"Wow," she said slowly. "What *is* this stuff?"

"What do you mean, maybe?" Dimon said.

"Maybe? What do *you* mean? This stuff is making me feel strange."

"Phoenix. Barrett and Cahill. What do you mean 'maybe' you heard them talking about it?"

"Maybe they did, I don't know. Yes, they talked about it sometimes," she said angrily, like she was talking to someone else. "It made Steve angry. They didn't want me to know about it; that is, Steve didn't. Arthur told me. But Arthur had told me and swore me not to tell Steve. It was something Arthur did a long time ago, when he was in the Marines. He was in the Marines. In Vietnam. Arthur was in Vietnam, you know. It had to do with that."

"What did it have to do with?"

"I don't know, I'm not sure. Something Arthur did when he was in Vietnam."

"Where did the money go, Katherine?"

"I don't know about any money, I have no idea what you are talking about."

She said this blatantly, almost as a challenge, as if accepting the fact everyone else knew it was a bald faced lie. And then I knew Katherine was completely involved in something with Arthur Barrett. That's what this was all about. It was all true. This whole thing was about Barrett and Katherine. Everything Mickey Thompson had said began to make some kind of sense. Especially now, hearing Katherine say these things, her evasiveness, her anger, it all began to make sense to me. There was a long silence and then I heard a crack, a painful smack on flesh, like a whip, and Katherine let out a scream.

"Gary, for chrissakes," Dimon said. "We're in a fucking hotel. In New York City. What are you going to do? Shoot her?"

"We got guards. The cops will stop anyone coming in."

"Jesus, Gary, cool it, huh? Let me work her a bit, *please*. Then you can do what you want."

Katherine was crying. "Don't," she said. "Please."

I felt I should go into the room, but something was holding me back. I don't know what it was, something about Katherine's betrayal. Her betrayal made me think I didn't care what happened to her, and something about my realizations of her made me afraid, but then something in her voice, my memory of her, of us, of how things suddenly started to make some kind of sense, it all made me want to go in there and do something.

I heard some movement back and forth, like someone pacing the floor. Then I heard someone open a window and sounds from outside entered the room. I could clearly hear the street below. Then I heard Delbarton, it sounded like his head was outside the window, say, "Fuck her, Dimon. She ain't worth it."

"Katherine," Morris suddenly said. "These guys can help you, do you understand? What I was saying before about some kind of deal is true, they can do it. All you have to do is tell them what they are asking about. About the money, about where it went. That's all they care about. Can you do that?"

"I don't know..." She was still whimpering a little and sounded fearful. "How do I know I can trust anyone anymore after all that has happened? Even you?" Her lack of confidence was something I was not used to hearing in her voice. Then I heard her breathe deeply and clear her throat.

"I don't know what you guys are doing to me. I don't feel so good, I don't know what I'm thinking. You all look funny to me, strange… it's all so strange… everything now." Her voice trailed off and then she cried. Openly wailed, uncontrollably, as if she had just been told the worst possible news in her life and the pain was nearly breaking her. I heard Delbarton whisper, "How much did you give her?" I did not hear Dimon answer. I heard someone walk up to Katherine. Whoever it was kneeled down beside her, I could hear his knee crack and the movement next to her sobbing sounds.

"Katherine," Dimon whispered. "Listen to me."

Katherine sobbed softly now, sniffling. She blew her nose and I decided I had to go into the room. The drugs, or whatever they had given her, were screwing her up. She was clearly confused. She needed help, she needed me. I was afraid, but not *that* afraid. It was hearing her voice that did it. I had to go in there and get her to give them what they wanted even if it meant facing her, even if it meant ignoring the fact that she had betrayed me, ignoring the fact she probably couldn't care less about me. All that didn't matter to me now. I didn't care anymore. I took the headphones off and got up from the table. I took a deep breath, ran my fingers through my hair, and went into the other room.

FIFTY-SEVEN

WHEN I ENTERED EVERYONE LOOKED UP but it was Katherine who said, "Jed? What are you doing here?"

She looked terrible and the first thing I noticed was her hair. It was black. Black as night. It made her look strange, like one of those punk rock heavy metal kids down in the East Village. Her eyebrows were black too. But her teary eyes were still green. Her face was streaked red and wet with tears, her eyes and lips swollen, and I could see the mark of a hand on her cheek. Her nose was running and her black hair made her face look pale, ghostly.

"Chase, don't..." Dimon stood up from his kneeling position.

"Katherine," I said, ignoring Dimon. "It doesn't matter anymore. Tell them about the money, tell them about Barrett. That's all they want to know. Tell them everything, tell them about me, your mother, you and Barrett, the set up with Steve, the stolen Phoenix money, the plot against Steve, tell them all of it, how Barrett made you pull me into it, everything. That's all they want to hear. Morris is right. It's all about the money. Nothing else. They just want the money back. You tell them all that and I know things are going to be all right. I promise. Don't worry about me and what you did. It's going to be okay. I forgive you. Trust me. I will never betray you. No matter what."

That last sentence was to let her know I knew everything about why she betrayed me, there was nothing left to hide, nothing to hide from anyone. I understood her now. I knew her story, knew why she'd done what she did, and I forgave her for it. I forgave her for it because I now knew how life, her life, the life she had been brought into, had betrayed *her*. Betrayed her cruelly. She'd been robbed of everything any normal human being was created for. Love and affection. A family and a family's love. Simply that. Love for Katherine had become a currency, not an emotion.

Katherine looked at me, her face filling, swelling up, her eyes now cascading tears, her lips trembling uncontrollably, her hands shaking against the arms of the chair. She looked a mess, as if everything she had aimed for, everything she had hoped and dreamed of had vanished right before her eyes. Forever. Never to be seen again. I could tell she had touched it, this dream, had held it in her hands, like a precious jewel, a reward, for all that she'd been put through in her life. She was *that* close. And now it was gone. That's how she saw it. All of it, the sorrow, the loss, the pain of her life, a vast sum of money, all of it was running down her cheeks in streams of tears, in the contortions her face was making as she cried. I could see the drugs had control of her now. She had been fighting against them but they seemed to have won. She's giving in, giving up, I thought. She leaned forward, as if to stand, but then stopped, her hands now gripping the arms of the chair. She looked at me, a painful look, as if I conjured up some kind of past, an emotion of some kind, and she said, "Oh, Jed... I am so sorry. I am so, so sorry. You have no idea... I didn't mean..." And as Katherine cried we all simply stood there and watched. Then Dimon glanced at me and gave me a quizzical look.

"Wait," I said. "She'll tell you. She'll tell you what you want to know."

Delbarton sat at the window, Morris in a chair across the

room, Dimon stood next to Katherine, and as I stepped toward Katherine Dimon eased away. I grabbed hold of a chair and pulled it over next to her. I sat down and looked at her and said, "Its okay, Katherine. Really. You can tell them what happened. It's all right. It's over now." I reached over and put my hand next to her arm and stroked it softly.

She looked at me as Dimon went over toward Delbarton and sat in the other armchair. He crossed his legs and sat back and took a pen and a small black notebook out of his shirt pocket. I took out my pack of cigarettes and offered one to Katherine. She took it and I lit it and then I lit one for myself. Then I took her hand and held it. She felt stiff but then, slowly, her hand relaxed in mine. I sensed relief, a weight lifting. She looked at me, her eyes full of hurt and sorrow. "You did love me, didn't you?" she asked. "You truly did."

"Yes," I said slowly.

"You're probably the only one who ever has..." And then she broke down again, quietly and shaking uncontrollably, her panting breaths almost like hiccups. After a while she calmed and was silent for a few moments, her eyes closed.

"Go ahead, Katherine," I said gently. "If you ever do anything for me, do this."

Then she opened her eyes, looked at Morris and then me, took in a breath, and slowly began to speak.

"I met Arthur Barrett in Hollywood. California. About ten, twelve years ago. I was just seventeen. I had run away from home. It wasn't really a home. I had no home. I lost my family when I was a child. My father and my two brothers. My mother survived but has been in a coma for twenty five years. She's a vegetable. Can't move, can't speak. She's in a nursing home type of place in upstate New York. When I met Arthur I was struggling in the worst way. You can't imagine. I went days without food, slept in shelters, on people's couches, once in a while on the beach. I looked for work in film but all men wanted to do was have sex, put me in porn flicks, whatever. It was tempting; that is, the money was. Then I met Arthur at a party. I had a friend and we used to crash parties, mainly to eat, but also in the hopes of meeting someone who might give us that so-called 'break.' Arthur was kind." Katherine paused and got her breath. She let go of my hand. She took a tissue and wiped her face and looked at me. I nodded at her. "Go ahead," I said. "It's okay." She took a drag off her cigarette and slowly, calmly, exhaled. She looked at me again and reached for my hand.

"Arthur took me to New York. I trusted him. He wasn't like others in that he didn't want to fuck me. I felt like he knew me, like a kindred spirit, you know? He didn't seem to have an agenda. He took care of me and didn't ask for anything back. He helped me. He got me a place to stay, some clothes, a decent job; he got me on my feet. I knew he was a powerful and successful man. Like I said, I trusted him. We'd have dinner once a week and at those dinners he told me stories about himself. Eventually the stories had a common thread. He had a lot of money he had gotten while he was in the Marines over in Vietnam. A lot of money. The Phoenix thing you were talking about. It had to do with that. Stolen, obviously, but I didn't ask. I don't know how he got it, I didn't care really, but he had it hidden away and wanted to get it somewhere where he could collect it legitimately and leave New York, leave his wife, his career, everything. He had dreams of another kind of life. He'd seen stuff in his life, he said, and he was involved in things he said he couldn't talk about but what he wanted was to go and live away somewhere, some place he could live anonymously and not be bothered by anyone or anything and not have to worry about money. I understood that. I wanted the same thing. Believe me, I understood that better than even Arthur did. It was my mission in life. Eventually he asked me if I would help him. I said yes, of course I would. I said I'd do anything for him. You have to understand that. He saved me. Do you understand? Do you understand what I mean? Where I was? Where I came from? Arthur Barrett was an angel to me. Of course I would help him. Arthur promised me ten million dollars if I did everything he asked of me. *Everything.* I said yes, I would. Ten million dollars! Can you imagine? Arthur was taking care of me. It was like hitting the lottery, a dream come true. I would do anything for him and Arthur knew it. Anything he wanted. This is when he introduced me to his partner, Steve Cahill."

The sun had begun to go down and the sky was pink and blue and yellow, dark silhouettes of buildings scraped against the horizon, sharp squares, needle points, slants. Delbarton closed the window and moved over to the couch. Morris stood and suddenly said, "Would anyone like anything? Coffee, soda?"

"I'll take a beer," Delbarton said.

"Coffee," Dimon said.

"Me too. Why not another pot of coffee and some sandwiches?" I said.

"That sounds like a good idea," Dimon said. He stood and went to the phone and ordered. Katherine seemed a little woozy. She was leaning over to one side of the chair and seemed to be falling over.

"Katherine," I said. "Do you want to use the bathroom or anything?"

"I'd like to wash up a little."

"Sure," I said. "I'll help you to the bathroom."

I walked her to the bathroom. She held onto me tight but was unsteady, like a drunk on the downside. I ran the sink and she placed her hands before her on the counter and leaned forward. "Whew," she said. "I don't know what they gave me but I'm fucked up."

"The coffee will help," I said. "And something to eat. Are you all right?"

"No, not really," she said. "I have some toiletries in my bag, by the door. Would you get them for me?"

"Sure," I said.

When I returned she went through her things and took out some facial wipes and creams and washed her face. Then she took out her makeup and began try to do her face. She struggled, her hands shaking. Then she turned to me and said softly, "I really blew it, didn't I?" Her eyes welled up again and she let her head drop down so her chin rested on her chest.

I didn't know what to say. We just looked at each for a few minutes.

"You dyed your hair," I finally said.

"I know. I was afraid."

"You're better blonde than brunette."

"You think so?"

"Yes," I said. "Definitely."

When we went back into the living room the room service cart was there with two pots of coffee, Delbarton's beer, and a platter of assorted sandwiches. We all went back into the same seats we were in before and I helped Katherine into hers. She held a cup of black coffee in both hands and looked at Dimon.

"Arthur and Steve worked for the government. I knew that. Arthur told me. I'm not sure what they did exactly, some sort of secret agency having to do with financial stuff. They said it was part of the Treasury Department but I never really believed that. It wasn't normal government stuff. It had to do with moving money around and stuff like that. Anyway, Arthur encouraged Steve and me to become a couple. It was part of the plan, you see. Arthur's plan. Ultimately he said he wanted us to get married. There were other things, all part of the plan, Arthur said. I didn't understand some of these things but I trusted Arthur. Part of the plan was to create the appearance of a sex scheme he and Steve ran. That was why the apartment on Eighty-Second Street was set up. It was for show, part of the plan, part of Arthur's idea. He told Steve it was for him, that he liked to film himself having sex with girls. I knew Arthur fooled around, Steve knew too and he never questioned Arthur's antics. But what it was really for was as part of his plan to frame Steve. He wanted to tie the monkey business of the money, wrapped up in sex and drugs, and throw it like a bomb at Steve. Set it up like Steve had something to do with it. We needed to get someone else, though, Arthur said. Then things took a wrong turn. Steve wanted a divorce. It changed things. I held off as long as I could before it finally happened. That was when we learned Steve had found out about Arthur's money, about me and Arthur, everything. That's why he wanted a divorce. He didn't want any involvement in what he said was fraud against the government and he saw me as part of it. He didn't know our entire plan, though. The one thing we didn't know, though, was how he found out. Steve eventually confronted us. Arthur thought someone in the government told Steve, someone in the department they worked for. Arthur was paranoid that way, always thinking someone else knew. That's why he waited so long. We never really knew who it was but Steve and Arthur fought. This is right before Steve went to London. Then Steve left. The plan, Arthur said, had changed. We needed a new plan and we had run out of time. Cahill and Company, Arthur said, was his only chance of getting the money out to a place he could get at it."

"How much did he have?" Dimon asked.

"He told me fifty million. I always thought it was more."

"Where did it go?"

"To a bank in England, the Channel Islands."

"How was he going to get it?"

"Arthur had me set up an account there a few years ago. Dakota Holdings, PLC. He picked the name. He had started to trickle in the money last year, just to see how it worked, if Steve would pick up on it, or anyone else. At first he didn't but, of course, eventually he did. You can't hide that amount of money. Arthur knew that too but also wanted to see Steve's reaction. It would help Arthur figure out how to do the rest. When Steve finally confronted Arthur he said he knew it was stolen money, knew Arthur had stolen it from the government. He found out about that. That's what got him so angry at Arthur. He was angry because by association Steve was being dragged into Arthur's plan."

"When did Steve find this out? Find out this was stolen money?"

"Sometime before he left for London. Last spring, maybe."

"How?" Dimon asked.

"You people. Arthur was convinced of it."

"And that's why they fought?"

'Yes."

"Steve knew Arthur had stolen it from the government? From the military?"

"Yes."

"And Steve didn't want anything to do with it, didn't want it to affect Cahill and Company, their cover?"

"Yes."

"How did Barrett get the money into Cahill and Company?"

"Russians. Some Russians he knew in Brooklyn. They handled it. They handled everything. The money was still in Vietnam, you see. In Saigon. Arthur said there was a Vietnamese guy, an old partner of his from the war; they used to work together in the Phoenix program. They split whatever they had taken from the government and this guy had held Arthur's half for all these years but Arthur couldn't move it himself without getting caught. He knew that. These Russians did it for a fee. I remember Arthur complaining about how much they charged to wash it."

"Wash it? You mean launder it?"

"Yeah, right, launder it. Money laundering. That's what the Russians did."

"Did Barrett tell you how he got this money?"

"No. It was when he was in Vietnam is all I know. I remem-ber once he said the government had been throwing so much money around over there it was virtually impossible to keep track of it. What he had done was twenty-five years ago, he said, and they still didn't know about it. That was his plan, you see. He waited twenty-five years. He believed by now no one was looking for it. He could take it now."

Katherine was exhausted. Her eye lids were half closed, the empty coffee cup lay in her lap, and her head started to drop. I looked up at Dimon.

"She needs to rest," I said.

"A few more things," he said. "Then she can sleep."

Katherine was already dozing off. I nudged her.

"Katherine," I said. "A few more minutes, okay?"

She looked at me, her tired eyes soft, swollen, but not wet anymore. "Sure," she said.

"How was he going to get the money from Dakota Holdings?" Dimon asked.

"Me," Katherine said. "That's why I went to London. I was the only one who could withdraw the money. I was the only one he trusted. I was to put it into a numbered account in Geneva. Arthur's account. He was planning to meet me there."

"But he was dead."

"I didn't know that."

"You didn't kill him."

"No. I told you that."

"You could have kept all the money."

"Yes. I could have."

"Why was Jed in the apartment?"

"Jed became part of the new plan."

"Which was?"

"Steve had to go, Arthur said. He would kill him. And some-one had to take the blame for it. That was Jed."

"How?"

Katherine had begun to speak in a monotone, as if she were in a deep trance, as if she were on autopilot. As if no one was in the room. Her face went blank and it seemed like she was under hypnosis or something.

"The gun. We had the gun with Jed's prints on it. His prints were on the gun and on the bullets. We had another gun too, just like Jed's. The .38. I told Jed I left the gun in the apartment, you see, but Jed wasn't supposed to find it. Arthur was supposed to kill him. Leave the one with Jed's prints there. The whole thing, you see, was Jed thought I was going to kill Steve so I could inherit his estate. He went back up there for me, you see, he thought he was going to save me. That was the new plan."

Dimon looked at me. I held my hand up. Dimon said, "And then what?"

"Arthur was to shoot Jed with his gun, the gun with Jed's prints on it, and put the gun in Jed's hand. Make it look like Jed shot Steve, then shot himself. Make it look like they fought over me, a murder suicide thing. We had tapes of us, of me and Jed, the idea was for it to look like Steve found out about us, that kind of thing."

"Where is the money now?"

Katherine didn't say anything.

"Katherine," Dimon said, louder. "Where is the money now?"

"In Geneva."

Katherine was beaten. Down to the bone. Her head dropped to her chest. Dimon walked over to her and lifted her head by her chin.

"Katherine," he yelled. "Where is the money?"

Katherine opened her eyes and began to cry. "In Geneva," she said. "In an account. In my account. It's my money, for God's sake! Don't you see? It's mine. It belongs to me now. Arthur's dead."

"How did you get it into Geneva?"

"Oh my God, what's happened? What has happened to me?"

Katherine cried now, hysterically. I looked at her and wondered what she had been thinking these last few days. That she was almost there? Almost to the point she dreamed of back in Windham? Almost at the end of this long road she'd been on for all these years? Suddenly she stopped crying. She wiped her nose and dabbed at her tears, took a deep breath, and said, "I had set up an automatic wire transfer from Dakota Holdings to another account I had set up in Geneva. It was my account, in my name only. If I didn't withdraw the money from Kasper & Benson within forty-eight hours of the transfer from New York they were instructed to wire it into the Geneva account. If Arthur hadn't shown up in London by the next day I was to go straight to Geneva. That was it. That was the plan."

"Why wouldn't Arthur show up in London?"

"If something happened to him. Anything. Got arrested, got run over by a car, whatever. Arthur cared for me in a certain sort of way, don't you see? He knew me. He knew the kind of life I had come from, he came from it too. Did you know that? He was an orphan too; he lived on the streets, in shelters, in homes. In Brooklyn somewhere. An area called East New York. It wasn't until the Marines that he ate three meals a day. He told me that. He went into the Marines when he was seventeen years old, the same age I was when he met me. It's where he learned everything, he said. In the Marines, in boot camp, in the jungle, in Vietnam. He took care of me, you see, that's all. He was only looking out for me. He never wanted anything *from* me; he only wanted to help me. I was him, you see. If something happened to him he wanted me to have the money. I've never had anyone do that for me before. No one ever looked out for me. No one. That's why I'd have done anything for him. He was like a father to me. But now he's dead. And the only person who could have killed him was Jed and I'm the one who sent Jed up there. Don't you see? Don't you see what's happened? Don't you see what I've done? It's like I've killed myself." Katherine sobbed uncontrollably.

I reached for her hand and she let me take it. I squeezed it and said softly, "He was going to shoot me."

"I know..." Katherine put her head into my shoulder and stifled her sobs. She said something, but I couldn't quite hear her. I leaned over and felt her lips come to my ear. "I'm so sorry, Jed." I put my arms around her and held her, smelling her familiar scent. After a few minutes she stopped and sat back pulling her legs up and folding them under her. She leaned her head against the back of the chair and closed her eyes.

"What about the tape of Steve's father?" I asked "And all those other men?"

Katherine kept her eyes closed. "I made it all up, Jed. That wasn't Steve's father, it was someone Arthur knew. We staged it. The guy looked like Steve's father, we made the light dim, remember? We made it as part of the plan, to bring you in. We wanted you to hate Steve, don't you see? It was all part of Arthur's plan." She opened her eyes and looked at me. "The camera, the set up, all of it was for appearance, throw the police, make Steve look bad, you know. That's all. It was Arthur's idea."

FIFTY-EIGHT

WE PUT KATHERINE TO BED and left two Federal agents posted in front of her door. Dimon went to make some phone calls and then met Morris, Delbarton, and me downstairs in the bar. It was nearly midnight. I ordered a double martini. So did Morris and Delbarton. When Dimon came down he had a whisky. I was exhausted.

"So what happens now?" Morris asked. "Are we going to court tomorrow?"

"We're drawing up warrants now," Dimon said. "If the money is in the account in Geneva and we seize it, then tomorrow the government is going to charge her with conspiracy to murder and harboring stolen government money. Because of her co-operation we will recommend a suspended sentence, probation, community service, stuff like that. We can make this happen, Morris. I believe you know that."

"Yes," Morris said as he sipped his drink. "I know, but these are some pretty heavy crimes here, not sure a judge will completely look the other way. Having said that, what if the money isn't there?"

"We prosecute. Gary and I will continue to look for the money. I think we've narrowed it down some. Don't you?"

"Damn right we did," Delbarton said.

"We'll get it," Dimon said. "Just a matter of time now."

I was curious about a few things though and wanted to ask about the money, about how they knew about Barrett.

"Can I ask a few questions?"

"Remember our deal, Jed," Dimon said. "We're still classified."

"Sure, of course," I said. "I know. But listen, how did you guys find out Barrett had all this stolen money to begin with?"

"We always knew," Dimon said. "Coldwell ran Barrett in Vietnam, ran his program, ran Phoenix. Knew him well, recruited him for chrissakes. Granted, the accounting was a little loose over there, but when the war was over Coldwell knew a significant amount had gone missing. Something north of a hundred and fifty million. All monies dispersed into the program went through Barrett's hands. He was Coldwell's man in the field. Barrett had good cover, said the money was spent in Laos and Cambodia, places where he knew we had little to no accounting. Hmong tribesmen, local politicians, double agents, military officers and, obviously, Barrett's Vietnamese partner. But a hundred and fifty million? Remember, this was 1971-72. When a hundred and fifty million really meant something. Coldwell stayed suspicious and kept Barrett employed after the war. Set him up in business. And watched. Kept his eye on him for twenty-five years. We know Cahill and Company. It's ours, we own it. We know everything that moves there. When we saw money with no source, no origin, we knew it was coming from either Cahill or Barrett. Coldwell knew it was Barrett. Knew he was finally making his move. We were ready for him except we didn't know about the plan with Katherine and you. We simply thought he was running behind Cahill's back, wiring the funds, and was ready to jump. That's why we told Cahill about it, to put pressure on Barrett, to smoke him out. The murders surprised us."

"What about me?" I asked. "Where am I now?"

"We're done, Jed," Dimon said downing his scotch. "We got

what we wanted. It wasn't exactly how we planned it but then, it never is, is it? You did good, my friend. You opened her up. We made a deal and we're sticking to it, right Morris?"

"Yes, we did," Morris said, smiling at me.

"You mean that's it? I can go?"

"That's it, pal," Dimon said. "Have a nice life. Stay out of trouble. Be a little more careful about your girlfriends, that's all." Dimon took a long pull on his drink. Then he put his hand on my shoulder and said, "And listen, don't take this the wrong way, ok? Don't be such a wimp. Take charge of yourself. Otherwise you'll be pushed around and used forever. This world is a tough, unforgiving place. Full of bad guys, both men *and* women. Don't forget that."

"Women, bad guys, and wimps..." Delbarton said, chuckling loudly and shaking his head. "Jesus Christ..."

We held up our glasses and toasted. Then we downed them, had one more, and went home. I never saw Dimon or Coldwell or Delbarton again.

FIFTY-NINE

THE NEXT MORNING MORRIS CALLED me. I was in my new office. On the fifth floor. It was my first day back. Marie was all excited about the new department. I was still in advertising sales although I had a new title, or at least I was told by Marie they were going to give me a new title. Vice President of Print Ad Sales. And I had a partner. She was Vice President of Internet Ad Sales. We still had a boss; he was President of All Advertising Sales. Marie told me Joe Lieberman would have had my job if he hadn't resigned. I didn't know if I should have felt bad about that or not, it was all water under the bridge as far as I was concerned. The events of the last month were enough to last a lifetime for me and all I wanted to do, I had decided when I woke up that morning, was to look forward to my future, whatever it was, and get past this rough patch. Work hard, keep my head down, and keep things simple. That's what I needed. To stay focused by maintaining a simple, routine oriented, healthy lifestyle. Know my limits and stay within them. The world of Dimon and Coldwell, even Morris for that matter, was a little too much for me. I needed a chair at the beach and a good book, a living room with a big fat leather recliner and a stool to put my feet on, and a nine to five with the weekends off. That was the life I wanted now. Nothing else.

Marie said Morris was on line three and I picked up the phone wondering what he thought of my antics over the last month. Probably thought I was crazy, missing a few screws, the way I was with Katherine, and he wouldn't have been wrong to think that.

"Jed," Morris said. His voice was soft, quiet but firm, and I knew right away something was wrong. Were they reneging on my deal? Had something happened? Were they coming to arrest me?

"Hi, Morris."

"Jed," he said again. "Listen..."

"What's wrong?" I said quickly. "Am I in trouble again? Did I do something wrong?"

"No," he said. "It's Katherine."

"What? What is it?"

He paused. A little too long, I thought, and I heard him take in his breath. "She's dead," he said, letting out a soft, sad sigh.

"What?"

"They found her this morning. At the Waldorf."

"No," I said, my throat collapsing. "It can't be." I felt a stab in my chest and my eyes began to fill up.

"They found her in the bathtub. Slit her wrists with a razor. Also ate a bottle of valium. When Dimon went to wake her at 7.30 she didn't answer the door. They went in and found her. Said she'd been dead about three hours. There was nothing they could do."

"Where is she?"

"Downtown in the morgue. Dimon is there now. He doesn't know what to do with the body. Who to contact."

"No one," I said. "There is no one to contact. Her mother is in a nursing home, she's been in a coma forever. She can't do anything."

"If no one claims the body they'll Jane Doe her, put her in a potter's field somewhere."

"No," I said. "They can't do that. Where's Dimon now?"

"Still downtown. He needs to sign the body over to someone. I thought maybe you'd want to make that decision."

My God, I thought. Katherine's dead. I felt my throat tighten up again. I choked a little and said, "Wait a minute Morris, will you?"

"Sure."

I didn't know what to think. Oh, Katherine, why? Jesus Christ, why? We had a deal, she had a deal. Didn't they tell her? Didn't Morris tell her all they wanted was the money? Why did she do that? I sucked in some air, swallowed, and said, "Morris, we can't let them take her to a potter's field, you know that."

"I know."

"What do I do?"

"I'll have Dimon sign the body over to you; you'll have to go down there."

"I don't want to go down there. I don't want to see her like that. I don't want to see Dimon either."

The line was silent for a moment.

"I can have him sign her over to me," Morris reluctantly said. "But you have to tell me where to send her."

"I need to make arrangements," I said, as much to myself as to Morris.

"Can you be here at my office by lunchtime?"

"Yes, sure," I said.

"We'll make the arrangements from here and then I'll go down and sign the necessary papers. It's probably easier, me being her lawyer and everything."

"Yeah, sure," I said. "You're her lawyer, you can do these things."

I hung up the phone. I felt terrible and all I could do was sit there staring out my window feeling rotten, like my insides had been carved out or something. After a while Marie came in and said, "Jed, is something wrong?"

I looked up and without saying anything just shook my head.

"Jed?" she said again.

I took in a deep breath and said, "I just heard some bad news, that's all. I have to run out. I'll be back after lunch."

"Can I do anything?" she said.

"No," I said. "Nothing can be done."

SIXTY

THERE'S A CEMETERY OVER IN Queens, it's huge, the biggest cemetery I've ever seen. Not that I've seen a lot of cemeteries, but still, this is impressive. In fact, it is the largest cemetery in the United States with over three million bodies buried there. Calvary Cemetery it's called. It's a Roman Catholic cemetery so a lot of Italians and Irish, but also others too. A lot of mobsters buried there. Thomas "Three Finger Brown" Lucchese for one. So is Alfred E. Smith, former Governor and presidential candidate. And a whole bunch of other famous and infamous people. When I read the little pamphlet in the office it said the first person buried there, in 1848, was Esther Ennis who died of "a broken heart." That killed me when I read that. It's also the cemetery where the burial scene in 'The Godfather' was filmed. You know, the one where Don Vito Corleone is buried and everybody comes up and kisses his son Michael's hand. Morris and I took Katherine there. It was the only one I could think of when the morgue wanted to know where to send the body.

Morris and I made arrangements for a fast burial. It was just the two of us, Morris and me. Katherine stayed in the morgue for two days, that's how long it took, paper work having to be properly done and all, and having Morris with me was a tremendous help. He seemed to know what to do.

335

It was a gray day but it didn't rain. I'm not religious or anything, I don't have much use for that kind of thing, but I felt she needed a priest or someone like a priest to be there, just to say a few words, you know, sort of seal the deal with the here-after. There's a church near where I live, Our Lady of Pompeii, a Catholic church, over on Carmine Street. I didn't think Katherine would have minded. Hell, for all I know she might have even been Catholic. But the Catholic's always seemed pretty good when it came to rituals like death and so I went over there and spoke to a priest who said for a small fee he'd go over to the cemetery the next day and perform the burial rite. Traveling expenses he called it. I didn't care.

So under a gray sky Morris and me and a middle aged priest black as coal stood by Katherine's gravesite. The priest spoke some words and mispronounced Katherine's name. He called her 'Kathleen' and that kind of depressed me but I didn't want to interrupt him. Morris, thank God, had no qualms and correct-ed him and I was grateful he did.

I stood there with the jagged skyline of Manhattan before me, and the East river between us, and thought of Katherine. It kind of bothered me that she was being buried with her hair still dyed black, there was something phony about that and I knew I would always remember her blonde hair. I knew I would think of her often and for the rest of my life and I wondered if there was any good in that, if it was worth all I'd done and been through with her. The truth is I had loved her, or at least the image I had of her, or maybe I was simply in love with being in love with her, which for me was enough at the time. It isn't enough now. And so now I will think of her as a person who drew out the deepest feelings of love in me but that at the same time I had allowed myself to be used by those feelings all for the sake of feeling loved by this beautiful woman. This beautiful woman who allowed me, *wanted* me to believe she loved me, at least for a short time, so that she could finally put her restless life at ease, and although it ended badly it was all I had of her and I knew I would remember everything about her for the rest of my life. One thing I knew, though. At the end she knew I loved her, more than anyone had perhaps. It made me happy to think at least she died knowing someone in her life had truly loved her.

The priest finished, made the sign of the cross, and the grave diggers began to throw dirt on top of her. I watched for a while and Morris handed me a flower, a red rose, and I threw it on top of her casket. Then I watched as shovels of dirt piled up on top of the flower until I could no longer see any sign of it. Then I lifted my head, saw the buildings of Manhattan before me, the tall ones, the twin towers of the World Trade Center, the Empire State building, and the Chrysler building, all pointing defiantly skyward toward the heavens, and I looked up above them, as if I might see Katherine's body rising up to heaven, not that she necessarily belonged there, but she didn't belong in hell either, I was convinced of that, and I looked up and thought I could see something, a shadow maybe, rising high above New York and then disappear. Then it started to rain and the priest opened up an umbrella he had thoughtfully brought with him and the three of us huddled under it as we walked out of the cemetery, leaving the gravediggers shoveling the remainder of the dirt pile into Katherine's grave.

JACK SUSSEK lives in New York City.

11783879R00217

Made in the USA
Charleston, SC
20 March 2012